PARTICULAR PASSAGES 4

SOUTH WING

Dedication

Welcome, intrepid
reader.

This book is for you.

We are grateful you have
chosen to brave these
unknown passages with us.

May your bravery bring
you that for which
you search.

May your search be that
which brings you
the most pleasure.

And may your search be
never ending.

Table of Contents

The Green Room

by
Alex Zalben

The Green Room

*T*he Man sat in the Green Room staring at the Blue Door and, for the fourth time that day, willed himself not to turn the knob and step through.

The Green Room had everything The Man needed, and there was no reason to open the door. Inside the room was a bed with comfy pillows and luxurious sheets, a small kitchenette with an array of spices, foodstuff and cooking implements, and, to the side, a nook with private facilities for bathing and using the toilet. Not that he needed privacy, because there was no one else in the room. But still, it was courteous to excuse oneself when taking advantage of the facilities.

Beyond the bare basics of living, the Green Room also provided plenty of entertainment. One wall of the room was entirely taken up with a bookshelf filled with books on nearly every subject, and games one could play by oneself. There was a standard deck of cards for solitaire, but in addition to a game of chess—The Man had become adept at playing both sides against himself and there were several books of puzzles of varying difficulty.

The one thing the room lacked, other than company of course, was a window. The sconces on the walls exuded a fair approximation of sunlight during what The Man assumed were daylight hours, and they could fade to a wisp reminiscent of candles as the night waned on. But there was no portal to see outside, and there had never been that option; not in the Green Room, nor any of the previous rooms The Man had inhabited.

That was part of the reason the Blue Door called to him. It was a plain, wooden door, without any particular markings on it or indication of what existed behind. Only a rectangular plank of wood that had either been painted blue, or always existed that way. And in the exact middle of the door, height wise, to the left-most side, there was a round knob, also colored blue.

The Man knew that if he moved close enough to the door, he would be able to see his own reflection in the knob; his skin the color of the sky, face somewhat distended by the curve. But he also knew that if he moved too close to see said reflection, the urge to turn the knob would be too strong, and he would be compelled to step through.

This was, after all, the sixth such room The Man had lived in, and he knew from past experience that once you passed through a door, the room before it was gone for good.

Instead, he pulled one of the books of puzzles from the shelf, and idly nibbled on a pencil while staring at a grid of numbers. It was hard to concentrate on the puzzle, though, because as the numbers floated in the foreground of his vision, the Blue Door was always in the back of his mind, as well as in his line of sight.

Frustrated, The Man put down the book of puzzles and walked to the kitchenette, intending to make himself some tea and buttered toast for breakfast. The cupboards in the kitchenette were always full, no matter how much he ate, yet the options never varied. Toast with butter and tea for breakfast. Ham and cheese with a side salad for lunch. And for dinner, grilled chicken, broccoli in garlic sauce, and a small slice of chocolate cake for dessert. It was perfectly serviceable, and The Man considered himself a fair enough cook that the food was prepared with ease. Previous rooms had provided other options, some stranger and more difficult to tackle than others. But the Green Room provided a level of simplicity that made cooking relaxing, and less of a chore.

As the bread toasted, the man once again found his thoughts turning to the Blue Door and what might be behind it. What if there were new books? Different food? Perhaps another person, someone to talk to or while away the hours with? As adept as he was at playing chess on his own, would another person make the game more exciting? The risk was that the room was the opposite, perhaps even more bare bones, than his current furnishings; the food inedible, the books non-existent. The Red Room, where he had been previously, had been a nightmare, albeit a brief one, as he had scurried from the unlivable surroundings to his current domicile.

But what if the next room had no door, no exit, no way of escape? The Green Room was fine. He was, if not happy here, at least pleased. It was a perfectly adequate way to live the rest of his days; eating buttered toast and playing solitaire.

The smell of the bread burning broke The Man from his reverie, and delicately he plucked the charred slices from the stove. He would skip breakfast today, it seemed, and instead wait for lunch. His stomach grumbled slightly, but at least the ache would give him something new to look forward to, a different sensation to while away the hours.

The Man did not know how he had gotten to these Rooms. He only knew that he had been here as long as he could remember, moving from room to room with no seeming end. Sometimes, when the lights were low and he lay in bed, he wondered if this was a prison, and he had done something wrong. It certainly seemed like he was suffering from some sort of punishment that had cursed him to start each day the same as the last. On those same nights, he wondered what the point of this would be, and what he could have done that might have wiped his memory of his life prior to the Rooms. Perhaps there had been nothing prior, and he had always lived here. Or maybe he was someone else entirely…

A criminal? A king, deposed and sentenced to live out his days? Or the victim of some sort of mistaken identity, a regular man resigned to eternity despite having committed no great crime.

When the lights changed to morning, though, once sleep had passed and he was thinking more clearly, he would rationalize that it didn't matter why he was here, just that he needed to push forward and keep on surviving. It wasn't a bad life, anyway, and if he wanted to change his circumstances he could always pass through a door. He had options. It was up to him to take them.

But whenever he felt that urge to walk through the Blue Door, he thought back to his time in the Purple Room, with its array of paints and canvases. He had been happy there; inspired, even. Yet over time the Red Door had called to him as inspiration waned. One day he had put down his brushes, walked to the door, and—he thought—bravely turned the knob and walked through.

The heat from the Red Room had immediately singed his skin. Panicked, he turned back to where the door had been mere seconds earlier, only to find that as with previous rooms, the way back was no longer there. He had lost the Purple Room, and could only choose to be in this hot, bare chamber or proceed to the next. Ahead was the Green Door, and he briskly walked to it and through the entryway into the Green Room.

The smell of burnt toast still in the air, The Man stared at the Blue Door, willing himself to figure out what lay behind. He had never exhibited any psychic abilities, or truly any special abilities of any kind beyond the normal ken of man. Yet the circumstances he found himself in, on examination, seemed so strange that occasionally it did not seem out of the realm of possibility that if he thought about it hard enough, he might be able to see through walls, or fly.

The Blue Door remained opaque, and The Man reminded himself of what he had in the Green Room: food, shelter, entertainment. What more did one need in one's life than that?

Deep down, past the grumbling of his stomach, The Man knew he needed more. Or at least, he wanted more than what was provided to him. On those nights when he wondered how he had ended up in The Rooms, usually moments before sleep took him, he would realize that he desperately, achingly needed something else. The trick was, he did not know what that something else was, or if he would ever find it behind one of these doors. Was it companionship? Some artistic stimulation? Or maybe just the simple knowledge that there were no more doors to pass through, no more options to choose. That the room he was in at the moment was the room he would be in until the end of his days.

It was the choice that weighed on The Man, more than anything else... The knowledge that there was something "other" out there; some other person he could be, some other way of living that focused all his attention on the door in front of him, instead of the room he was in.

Without realizing it, he had already started to walk towards the Blue Door and was close enough now to see the reflection of his hand, reaching out to grab the knob. Looking down, he saw himself in it, distorted and colored blue like the door itself.

Mentally, he tried to tell his hand to pull back, that behind him was all he needed: books, food, a bed. He was, if not happy in the Green Room, at least surviving.

But his body didn't listen. The urge was too strong, and he watched as his hand grasped the knob and turned it slowly. The door opened with a click.

The Man stepped through into the next room and saw what lay before him.

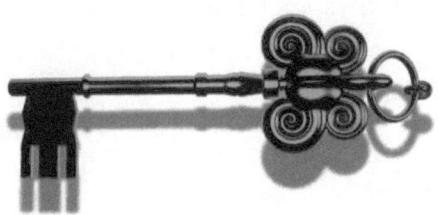

From the Author

Though "The Green Room" is by no means a pandemic story, it's hard to argue that it wasn't inspired, in part, by sitting in the same room day after day, doing the same things time and again, feeling trapped in the place you live, no matter how much you love living there. That was the spark, but ultimately it isn't about the place and time we're (as of this writing) still in, it's about that universal feeling of fear of the unknown, and the courage it takes to try something new.

About the Author

Alex Zalben is the author of an all-ages comic book series for Marvel, Thor and the Warriors Four. His short fiction has recently been featured in *Splickety Magazine*, Gypsum Sound Tales' *Thuggish Itch* anthology, Third Flatiron's *Galileo's Theme Park* anthology, and an issue of Enchanted Conversation Magazine. For the past decade he's hosted the live show and podcast *Comic Book Club*, which has been profiled in the *New York Times*.

He currently works as Managing Editor at Decider.com, with previous bylines on *TV Guide*, *MTV News* and more.

The Measure of My Portion

by
Thea Hutcheson

The Measure of My Portion

*T*he moon hung huge in the sky, highlighting the fen in silver light. I knelt at the pool's edge a few nights after spring's turning, holding my bleeding cloth—proof of my entry, late or not, into womanhood. Victorious, I lifted my arms up so that the moon shone through the cloth, red and full, a blood moon of my own making. Exhilarated, I smiled.

"Thank you, my Lady, for giving me my womanhood," I prayed. My parents had feared that I would never ripen, and, though they loved me, would bear the burden of keeping me the rest of their days.

I could smell the thick odors of my menses, the rotting marsh water and the cold mud as the breeze freshened. In the shifting waves and light and shadow on the water's surface, the vision of a woman appeared—the Goddess Seldona, surely—wearing an ermine cape against the cold of the departed winter. She opened it a little to show me the blood red sliver of a moon in her belly, her womb, waxing.

The folds fell together and, gesturing with her right hand, I saw Derryth, strong and pleased with his success at sucking the earth's bosom. He hadn't asked yet, but it was widely known that he'd held out for me as his wife, much to Fionn's chagrin.

My Lady gestured with her left hand and a brilliant ruddy spark illuminated a man. He was a stranger and very finely made, unlike we Sarmatae, who are short and stocky with brown hair and pale skin. His skin was the color of marsh mud, and his hair was pale silver like an old man's, yet his hammer stroke upon the anvil spoke of much younger, vigorous man. He looked up, smiling a crooked smile as if he saw me, and I blushed at the spark between us.

Seldona held both men in her palms, offering them to me, "Yours to *choose*, Nia, for the potency of your blood moon offering, the clay of my Son's earthly jar. Yours too, when the time comes; your portion to measure either way."

The wind ruffled the surface of the water and Seldona was gone. I sat back. Behind me I could hear the villagers driving the goat to the causeway for the sacrifice in honor of the newest section. When it was finished, the solid trail that wound its way back around to the marsh to the east would be several miles closer.

The Grey Dame put a hand to my shoulder, and I turned to look up into her ancient face. Thirty-five winters in the marsh were etched into her face. Her milky white eye reflected the moon.

"I saw a great vision, Nia. Our holy Mother Seldona has blessed you with a choice that will set change upon the world."

Breathing deeply, I flushed again thinking of the stranger's gaze on me. He was exotic and graceful next to Derryth's placid strength and capable hands. *A choice.* I had been given *a choice.* What a heady thing, I thought, full of my impending womanhood.

Eager to complete the ritual and be away from her heavy gaze, I rose. She removed my cloak and robe, and I made my way gingerly into the pool. It was cold, and I broke a rime of ice as I splashed into it. Quickly, I washed off my girlhood and offered the first blood of my womanhood to Seldona. Rinsing the cloth, I rose up shivering, and the Grey Dame met me, toweled me off with a rough cloth, and handed me my cloak.

She kissed me on both cheeks. "I will honor you, Nia, when the time comes to measure your portion, do not fear."

I hugged her and made my way to my family's hut and opened the press to find the fine woolen shift I had labored over in anticipation of this moment. Letting it to fall over my head, I wound the braided leather belt I had made around my waist, sliding the strings of my bag onto it before fixing it with a precious copper pin.

I took my hair down and combed it, winding it in a woman's knot against my head and weaving a piece of carved bone through it. Opening the door, I saw the moon had silvered the path, lighting my new way as a *woman*. The knot of people was breaking up at causeway—Seldona had accepted our sacrifice, the causeway was sanctified, and our labor endorsed. I breathed a prayer of thanks for all our blessings and went to join my people making their way back to celebrate Seldona's generosity and the causeway's progress.

Two moons shy of four years later I hear my neighbors bringing my dinner. I'm of a mind to refuse it, though I can still feel the sting of the Grey Dame's hand on my face two days ago. A fool she had called me then. Would Derryth call me so now? I know what Fionn would do. She'd wanted Ansharat if she couldn't have Derryth, and it grated that she ended up with my leftovers at every turn.

I wasn't surprised last spring when Derryth spoke out against Ansharat after riders brought news of raids on our neighbors, the Sarmes.

"We are Sarmatae," Derryth had said. "Far away from their troubles. We have our own mouths to feed and our own lands to tend. Hydd must stand up on his own land."

Ansharat had shaken his head. "And where will the invaders go after they have slain Hydd? They'll look to here and see you Sarmatae, fat from sucking Seldona's breast, and my smithy. Or they'll decide we're a threat they cannot abide at their backs. Ask yourself, Derryth, whose coin would you rather pay with, theirs and ours together or yours alone?"

My heart had turned cold. Ansharat meant to go, as much to sell his work as stand with the Sarmes.

They brought him home on a litter at the beginning of last fall.

"I have loved you as much as Adonai loved Cybele, Nia. I couldn't bear to die away from you," he whispered. "Kiss me, Wife." I could barely hear him and searched his pale face for the man that had always met my eyes so slyly over fences and walls, and our child's head.

I realized this is what I'd set in motion by *choosing* Ansharat, the exotic stranger, over Derryth. I pressed the full lips that had loved me so well with mine and he kissed his last breath into me. I held it as long as I could, keeping his spirit with me until I could hold it no more. Then I laid my head down on his chest.

The smell of him—copper, smoke, sunshine, and his foreign spice lingered. Would I have chosen differently those three and a half years ago knowing this moment awaited me?

It was dark before I washed him, dressed him in his finest clothes, combed his pale silver hair smooth, laid him out on the trestle, and brushed his cheek lightly as was my wont every day we'd shared.

The Grey Dame came, painted his face, and folded his body, tying it tightly so that he would fit back into Seldona's cauldron. The men came and carried the trestle out. When they laid him in the hole, I stared at his face, pale under the red ochre that marked his passage into Her cauldron. I pressed lumps of copper, tin, and a piece of the sky metal with his hammer into the crook of his arm where he could find it.

Using our son's first knife, I cut off a hank of my hair and our son's hair and laid them next to his heart.

"I would not have chosen otherwise, Husband, than our son, Eirlys, and the love we shared," I whispered.

I didn't stay after they threw in the first shovel of dirt.

Ansharat had been a skilled smith and men had come from far and wide to acquire his handiwork. I could not, however, work the metal, nor could we eat it. I struggled to keep myself and Eirlys fed during the fall, knowing that winter was coming.

When the fodder was gone, I asked Derryth to slaughter my cow and pigs for the winter. He stared at me, then at Eirlys playing in the dirt. I knew he considered the years since I'd turned him down and all the babies Fionn had lost. He'd given me up with gentle words and looked to Fionn almost immediately after I told him that I'd said yes to Ansharat.

Finally, he nodded and came back the next day.

Now, in the dead of winter, the causeway work is complete and, on the chill air that slips in through chinks in the mud, I can smell the gruel they bring. A stick in the fire snaps and I flinch, remembering the crack of the Grey Dame's hand on my cheek two days ago.

"Fool," she'd said. "Your choice was made. There is no going back, no choosing again, no regrets."

I'd rubbed my cheek, staring at her wizened face and eyes, now both milky. I moved to where Eirlys lay. His birth day was the same as the night I had offered my womanhood to Seldona. He was almost three year now, a little boy sleeping, thumb in his mouth.

Not a likely vessel for a god, I thought. Just a child born of a fiery love.

"You've not forgotten the henge brothers came to you at the solstice and told you they'd return," the Grey Dame said flatly.

"I thought they coming to live here."

The Grey Dame shook her head. "You lie to yourself, woman. They're returning to take him to the henge house. They will raise him there, train him so that he's ready to be the hand of Seldona's holy son."

Her gaze softened. "Ah, Nia, great things are afoot. Ansharat, he caught the smell of them and followed his path. You must follow the course you chose."

"But he's mine, my only son." I remembered Eirlys' beautiful dark eyes looking out of that olive-rose face as he suckled. He'd followed Ansharat around the smithy as soon as he could walk. He made the boy a tiny hammer and Eirlys beat it in hard imitation of his father. *My only link left to Ansharat,* I thought.

"I should go with him, to care for him. Tell me the way and I'll take him myself."

She rose and touched my shoulder. "Eirlys is born of Sarmatae blood and Ansharat's fire by *your* choice, the one She gave you at your blood offering. Mitrea is coming, and all the fighting and talk of uniting is Seldona laboring to bring Him into the world. Eirlys will make a fine vessel for Her Son on Earth. Your path is here."

My lips made a tight line as I brushed pale hair from his sweet sleeping face, adding this loss to that of Ansharat.

I can hear them coming. They pass the smithy. What will happen to it? The day I saw Ansharat walking about the village, he noticed me noticing his pale silver hair, his exotic fine features.

"I'm deciding to stay and build a forge," he announced cheerfully, looking at me over the top of a stock wall. "Where do you think I should put it, Nia?" which is how I knew he'd asked after me and why my face grew warm while my heart recognized the smoldering heat of the spark from that night at the pool a few ten days before.

"I know a place that would suit you."

"Then show me," he said. As we walked up the path, he sang a song about a man named Adonai who offered to take his goddess

17

Cybele to his orchard. From his sly smile, I knew he was asking me to go with him into *his* orchard where he would make the little man in the boat rise up and sail away on a river of milk and honey.

Blushing in ways that Derryth never inspired, I led him past the causeway to a large flat area that was protected from the storms and wind by the three low, lazy hillocks in a U behind it.

"You see, the path and the causeway are still close, and you have space for your smithy here and the house here with the livestock sheds there," I said, running breathlessly to each spot. "A fine place to build on, a place to put down roots and live your life."

"You've thought much upon it, then, have you? Perhaps you think you should be its mistress too, Nia?" I could smell him—soot and the sharp smell of copper, and some foreign essence of his far away home, I thought. He laid his arm on the limb of the tree and watched me over it. I couldn't see his mouth but what he spoke with his eyes was sly and hopeful in a language that was exotic and far away from anything Derryth ever said to me. That same spark from the night at the pool ran from his eye to mine and white hot down my body, and I *chose*.

Derryth knocks upon the door. He'll open it if I don't, and I realize that I'd rather have my dignity. I open it and gesture him in, but he shakes his head, only holding out the tray covered with a rag. What will he do if I refuse to take it? Would he come into the fine house that Ansharat built me out of sod and thatch? Would he see the difference between what he would have given me?

But this is my choice too, and I take the tray from him. He meets my eyes for a long moment, then nods and turns. The moon is rising behind him.

I lift the cloth on the tray. Wisps of steam rise from a bowl of thin gruel. It's accompanied by a hunk of bread and a cup of wine. I smell the Grey Dame's handiwork in the wine and go to grasp it, hesitate and lift the bowl instead. As I drink, I realize the moon has fully risen now. In another hour and a half, it will bleed and so will I.

The Grey Dame came last night, after the lottery, and said, "It's time. They're waiting for the boy."

I held the door tightly and didn't move aside. "I should go.

He's a small boy, and he will be alone with strangers."

"You've done your part, Nia. He must be on his path as you are on yours. They'll care for him and raise him to be Mitrea's vessel."

"I can't do this. He's just a baby."

She tried to move past me into the house. I shifted again.

"What did you think you were choosing, Nia?" she asked. "None of the other girls I brought to the pool to offer their womanhood had a vision, not to mention one of such power."

I said nothing, knowing that I had offered my own blood moon that night.

"Don't keep him from his path, Nia," she said. "Don't waste the choice you made, the gift that's come of it."

I closed the door, turning to lean upon it, and slid down to sit on the floor. Did the gods measure Eirlys so fair that it was worth this pain for them to have him for their own?

I could hear the Grey Dame waiting on the porch and knew she wouldn't leave. She was right. What kind of life would there be for him in the coming days? I finally stood. Eirlys seemed so tiny when I wrapped the fur-lined wool snugly against the bite of the cold night.

I followed her down to the causeway. The still air was thick with cooking smells, the animals, the midden, the marsh. The moon would be full the next night and everything was brightly lit. The newly finished causeway rose black against the silver water.

The moonlight shown upon Eirlys' sweet face, slack except for his full mouth sucking the tiny thumb. I squeezed him tightly, realizing the darker spot in the water beside the walkway was a small, flat-bottomed boat. He moaned a little, complaining in his sleep, and tears tightened my throat.

Would I have chosen differently had I known my son would wake among strangers, alone, set on his path by my hand?

"You are the fruit of our love, my son, a jewel beyond measure," I whispered and kissed his cheek gently. I reluctantly allowed the dark-robed man in the boat to take him from me.

Mitrea, use him gently. Seldona, look upon him lightly, I prayed as they pushed off and began to row away. Their oars' splashing carried for long time across the quiet marsh.

The people I grew up with gather in the village square, talking and joking. I wonder if Fionn would be here now if I'd chosen Derryth. Would she have pulled the white stone from the bag yesterday in her turn and seen the looks of pity and relief and pleasure in the eyes of her kith and kin as she held it out for all to witness? Would she be in here, sopping gruel with hard, coarse bread and drinking drugged wine?

I finish the dregs of the cup to make sure I get the whole of the Grey Dame's hand. They strike up a hymn to Seldona. I wonder if it is the drugs that make their voices seem slow and ponderous, like wind upon the marsh. My belly roils, whether from the broth or the wine, I don't know.

The moon's edge is red, a wound my people believe reflects the sins of the village, the world. Tonight, my people will offer them up to Seldona, praying for the causeway to be blessed and themselves and the moon to be healed. Tonight, I will measure their sins and the full portion of my choice as Seldona births what had been the tiny sliver of the blood moon in her belly the night at the pool.

I smell pitch from the torches and hear their footsteps. Sweat breaks out on my body and my hands clench. I recognize Derryth's heavy knock at the door. Is that a blessing, some small mercy? Fear rises despite the thick blanket the drug wraps me in.

The fire pops, outlining the fireplace for a moment and the pin Ansharat made me for my wedding gift sparkles. I make my way unsteadily to the mantle. It's his most beautiful piece of work I think—precious sky metal woven around a red carbuncle, a blood moon he called it, fitting, I think. I fasten it over my heart and take a last look, wondering what will happen to my home.

Derryth stands at the door when I open it. He stares at me, but I don't know what it means.

Someone reaches from behind Derryth and pulls me out to the stoop. The people line the path to my house. Their eyes and their teeth glint crimson in the light of the moon's enlarging wound.

"Well, then, get on with it," someone shouts.

Derryth reaches into his cloak and pulls out a thong, his eyes never leaving mine. I swallow hard against bile and tears as he turns me, pulls my hands behind me. He's gentle, though the windings are tight and tied in Seldona's triple knot. He steps off the porch.

Someone throws a rock, and it begins. I stumble when someone kicks me as I walk the path to the causeway. All along the way, my fellow villagers rain dung, sins, and blows upon me. It takes forever to reach the causeway. Derryth steadies me after a potsherd hits my forehead.

Blood trickles down my face and, through it, I see the Grey Dame stands at the causeway entrance, against the Grandfather Post. She's looking at me, her milky eyes reflecting the moon. She nods and her hands work in a blessing or maybe a spell.

The moon reflects bloody spots across the water. I smell me—dung, blood, hatred, and shame in equal measures.

Was my choice worth the loss of Ansharat, my love, Eirlys, my son, and, finally, my life?

Derryth stands beside me. The torches gutter and reflect pain warring with the purpose in his eyes. And I know, after all this time, he still loves me.

He searches my eyes and nods decisively. I trust his sure and gentle hands will do what they must, and I'm grateful that his heart is big enough to stand by his portion even though I have thought my choice must have made it small and sour. I smile at him and nod, but when he pulls a braided thong from beneath his cloak, I feel fear deep beneath the blanket the wine has wrapped me in. He sees and reaches a hand to steady me. Looking past him, I see the Grey Dame's milky red eyes on me, her hands busy.

Derryth catches my chin in his hand, forcing my head down. The thong goes around my neck, and he snugs it up under my jaw.

"See her," cries the Grey Dame. "See the sacrifice to the moon, come freely to the holy place. See the blood on both their faces. As it is in Heaven, so it is on Earth. Honor this woman who takes your sins upon herself, offers her own blood to cleanse up and sanctify our holy labor on the causeway. Regard her gift and accept her grace."

Fionn stands next to the Grey Dame. Does she know that Derryth still loves me? Ansharat was a virile husband, and we shared a fiery love that made a beautiful son. Together they brought joy to my life. It *was* a generous portion. I see, though, it wasn't so sweet a measure for others; Fionn's lost babies, Derryth's broken dreams, flown upon the days he whispered them to me. That knowledge makes it seem a small thing to carry their sins when I pass into Seldona's cauldron.

The thong grows tighter and I'm glad my hands are behind me so that I can't reach up to it. My face is hot and feels huge as it bites into my throat, making my breath rasp.

The Grey Dame approaches holding a knife of the sky metal. She lifts it so that people can see it. The bloody moon is captured in the dark silver of its blade. Her milky eyes lock onto mine as Derryth pulls my hair to bare my neck. I understand now what she meant when she said she would be there when I measured my portion.

The blade seems to caress my taut skin and hot blood sprays outward, covering her face and chest before showering the planks behind her.

"Behold the sins of the people are shed, and blood offered to heal the people and cleanse the causeway. Look, the moon heals!"

As I fall, I see silver edging its face. Her labor is over then. My eyes dim and Derryth lifts me and carries me to the causeway, lowering me gently, slowly over the side into the water.

Seldona holds Her swaddled Son in one arm as she wipes the blood from my face with Her other hand. The slate of the world clears, opening the way for the Child to slip in through my choice. She gathers me gently into Her cauldron, accepting the Sarmatae's offering as I accept the measure of my portion. I sense Ansharat's exotic thread and dive deep to find him.

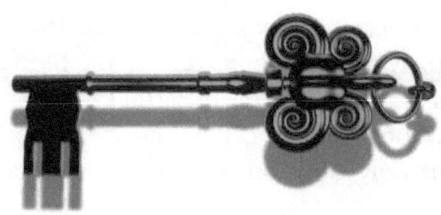

From the Author

I love anthropology. I love ancient history. I am happiest reading about ancient cultures and how they lived their lives. But living their lives doesn't speak to what's happening in their hearts, the things that happen that drive them to do things. This story is a way for me to think about what life might have been like for ancient peoples and why they willingly give up their lives in the ultimate sacrifice for their community. I also got to play with structure a bit and I had a fun time with that.

About the Author

Thea Hutcheson explores far away lands full of magic and science with one hand holding hope and the other full of wonder. Lois Tilton of Locus said her work "is sensual, fertile, with seed quickening on every page. Well done..."

She lives in an economically depressed, unscenic, nearly historic small city in Colorado with four semi-feral cats, 1000 books, and an understanding partner. She is a factotum when she is filling the time between bouts at the computer.

www.theahutcheson.com

Astrym Horizons
by
H.Y. Gregor

Astrym Horizons

*L*uther Hale surveyed the sweeping vista of red stone and scrub brush below with a critical eye. A grin split his lips at the sight of the slot canyon snaking away from the cliffside. It was perfect.

"Couldn't have found a better spot if we tried, huh?" Syvannah Klein, Luther's prentice going on two years, echoed his own thoughts. Her dark brown eyes glittered with anticipation from beneath her wide-brimmed hat. She wore tan breeches and worn leather boots, a revolver on one hip and a shiny, astrym-fueled cannon on the other. At seventeen, what she lacked for in tact she made up for in enthusiasm.

"I guess everyone gets lucky at least once in their lives," Luther said. They both knew astrym—the finest raw energy source on Cassus—fell wherever it damn well pleased.

"Better make it count." Syv rolled her eyes. "Too easy."

"I'm glad one of us is confident." At the newcomer's voice, Luther and Syv turned away from the ridge. Reid gave Luther a mock-salute as he drew level with them. "Bad news, Luth."

"You forget how to count?" Luther asked.

Reid hesitated, then scowled. "Good guess."

"I figured it would be more than three. The smugglers have taken too much astrym over the cycle for it to be such a small crew." Luther and Syv were guards at the Citadel, home of the largest city on the planet—and the most dependent on the astrym reserves that men like Reid helped collect and ship to the city for refining.

Luther had been sent to assist Reid and Meridian Venture Corps, a private guard company. The private company didn't have the resources—or the authority—to take any drastic action against the smugglers.

If they could nab even one crew, Luther had a suspicion they'd sing like canaries. The most recent astrym storm had left a large deposit of the glittering, crystalline resource within the slot canyon. Syv was right; they couldn't have set up a better ambush point if they'd tried. Everything was in place.

"Well, there's a storm forecast out, so they'll be here soon." Reid looped his thumbs over his belt and frowned at the steep-sided crevasse carved into the desert floor.

Only fools and amateurs got caught without shelter in the deadly astrym storms that ravaged the planet. These smugglers weren't amateurs, and Luther couldn't count on them being fools. They'd have to nab the crew before the storm hit that night. Luther glanced up at the late afternoon sun. They'd been waiting for their mark since dawn.

"We just have to hold 'em 'til backup comes. 'Cause here comes the trouble." Syv pointed toward the sandy washout near the mouth of the canyon, where a handful of figures had just rounded a pinnacle sandstone formation. Reid's hunch had paid off—the smugglers were here. "Came from the east, though. Didn't expect that."

"Give the others the signal. They'll probably try to escape back the way they came." Luther had been certain that the smugglers would come in from the west; they'd been operating long enough to have a semi-permanent hideout to weather the worst of the astrym storms, and the vast desert waste was riddled with unmapped caves ideal for it.

If they were coming from the east, it meant they'd just transferred a load of goods to their contacts in the city—almost certainly too late for Luther to intercept it. *Damn.*

"Better late than never. Everyone in position?" Luther asked Reid. His old friend nodded. "Then let's play."

Luther and Syv slipped and skidded down a narrow ravine that dropped beneath the ridge where they'd been hiding out. They crawled on their bellies to another drop off, just above the steep canyon walls. Reid's men with Meridian Venture Corps were already positioned farther north, guarding the astrym load, and the Citadel men would close in on the mouth of the canyon as soon as the smuggling crew was inside.

Like smoking foxes out of a den.

"I only counted five." Syv chewed on her tongue as she peered over the edge of the canyon. Luther grabbed her sleeve and pulled her back from the drop.

"Wagon's coming. Count on at least four more."

"Want me to take the wagon?"

Luther cocked an eyebrow at her.

She burned red. "I can take four."

"Maybe. If they were unarmed—which they won't be. We'll wait for Reid."

Syv scowled. "I ain't been training all this time to sit on my hands and whistle."

"Not enough training, apparently. Whistling would give away your position."

Syv opened her mouth to protest, but Luther put a finger over his lips. Crunching footsteps sounded from below. The first of the smugglers had entered the narrow canyon.

Luther pulled a palm-sized slate of gray metal from a holster clipped to his belt. Shimmering blue lines of text appeared on the astrym tablet—Reid confirming that he and his men were in position, ready to nab the smuggler's wagon. Luther nodded, scrawled a reply with a nail-sized stylus, and slipped it back into its leather pouch. "All five are inside. Citadel'll take their lookout crew. Let's go."

Syv pushed herself up on her elbows with a grin. "*Let's?*"

"Don't make me regret it," Luther said.

They mirrored the smuggler's path from the rocks above, careful to keep their footfalls quiet and their shadows away from the split in the rock. The astrym drop point was less than a mile north.

Luther saw the astrym's tell-tale viridian glitter before catching sight of any of Reid's men. The light from the astrym below shifted and danced up the canyon walls, broadcasting its location to fortune-seekers. The stuff would sear flesh and muscle alike if you touched it without the right protective gear, but Luther had to admit the effect was dazzling.

Clusters of astrym crystals dotted the earth, embedded in the canyon walls where the crevasse widened. The glimmering blue-green element stood out starkly against the reddish cliffside.

"Luther, where—" Syv had barely spoken the words before a man's shout echoed from below. A scuttling, crashing sound of rocks clattering down a slope reached them.

Luther drew his revolver—using his astrym-powered ignis cannon here might bring the whole canyon down—and ran toward the copse of low trees that was supposed to shelter Reid's men, Syv hot on his heels.

"What in the hell?" Luther skidded to a halt when he reached the hideout. Another warning call joined the first, then another, their words washing over each other in a panicked barrage.

"Bad news." One of the Meridian Venture Corps men, Kit, scrambled out from beneath the scrub next to Luther and Syv. His face was ashen. "We got a reaper."

"*Shit*," Syv swore.

Shit was right, Luther thought. The armored desert scorpions could grow to almost eight feet long, their curling tails barbed with razor-like stings. "How did we not find it when we checked the area?"

"It's a damned maze down there, Luther. More cave than canyon, I swear. We couldn't check every nook." Kit's voice was shaky.

A barrage of gunfire broke out from the canyon below. Luther glanced over to the rig of ropes and rappelling gear they'd prepared the night before. Reapers loved astrym deposits, but their territory was farther west—nobody had thought to check.

"We—If we just leave 'em... Maybe they'll handle it themselves." Kit's eyes darted over to the crevasse as a piercing scream filled the air. It was cut off just as abruptly as it started.

Luther exchanged a glance with Syv. Reapers were damn hard to kill under the best of circumstances.

"Leave 'em to get *eaten*?" Syv demanded. "You gotta be joking."

"It *would* solve the problem. Sort of." But Luther didn't need Syv's glower to know they had to act. He lifted his hands in surrender. "Fallen hell, Syv, I'm kidding. Get the gear."

A reaper complicated the job ten times over. Luther could only hope that the smugglers were up to carrying their weight in a fight—he certainly couldn't take a reaper on his own.

Syv kicked the coil of rope over the rim and pulled on a pair of heavy leather gloves. She was fussing over the harness buckles when Luther took up the rope.

"Kit, go tell Reid. Nobody enters that canyon until he gets a comm ring, you hear me?" The idea of asking Reid to send in backup was sorely tempting, but cramming more bodies into the narrow nooks and crannies of the slot canyon would only increase the chaos and chance of injury. Friendly fire was just as deadly as enemy fire, and twice as tragic. Luther would just have to be quick.

He holstered his gun and pulled on leather gloves, then accepted the rope from Syv. He waved away the harness. "And *you're* staying up here. No arguments."

"Luther, I—"

"*No.*" Luther looped the rope between his legs, brought it around his waist, then crossed it over one shoulder. He gripped the slack end with his left hand and held fast to the upper portion with his right. "You stand guard here until I say so."

Syv's eyes blazed, hard and defiant. Luther met her gaze for a weighted moment before lowering himself over the lip of the crevasse.

The long drop, while sheer, was far from smooth. The canyon walls were riddled with outcroppings of stone. Luther's boots scuffed against the red stone wall as he dropped, moving as fast as he dared. He glanced down over his shoulder when he was almost halfway down, just in time to see a man in a bloodstained shirt running toward the opening of the canyon.

Luther wasn't a betting man, but he'd put good money that the man wouldn't survive—not unless all that blood wasn't his.

He quickened his pace, feeling the heat of the friction burn through the gloves, then dropped the final few feet to the ground.

An earsplitting scraping sound rent the air. Luther scrabbled to disentangle himself from the rope, swearing as he tried to draw his gun at the same time.

It was a pitiful weapon against a reaper—but leaving the smugglers to the mercy of a reaper was no option at all. It was no mercy that the venom in their barbed tails didn't kill. Reapers ate their prey alive.

A wide-eyed man came skidding around the narrow switchback, pursued by an insect-like clicking noise. It echoed off the walls of the tight space. An enormous pincer slashed into an outcropping over the man's head, narrowly missing him. The smuggler cried out and threw himself to the ground with his hands over his head.

Idiot. Luther dragged the man to his feet. The reaper's pincer scrabbled against the canyon wall. One long, clawed appendage curled around the switchback, but the space was too narrow for the reaper to fit through—a mercy.

"Get outta here, go!" Luther threw the man toward the canyon's exit. He saw a fleeting glimpse of the whites of the man's eyes before the smuggler took off.

An inhuman screech tore through the air as the reaper's appendages clawed at the stone. The creature bashed its head against the opening in the rock. Luther caught sight of the two smaller, claw-like pincers protruding from its mouth.

He let off two shots in quick succession, aiming for the probing maw. The reaper recoiled from the gap with an anguished hiss.

Luther crept forward. Dark, sticky blood had splattered against the stone. He peered around the corner, gun at the ready. The canyon widened beyond the switchback. The passage might comfortably hold three or four wagons and their teams, but the reaper's menacing form managed to make the opening feel claustrophobic.

Crystalline astrym glowed in the shadows at the far end, jutting out of the stones like dagger points. Three people cowered behind a cluster of small boulders at the far side.

Why weren't they running? Luther's gaze swept the space, and his heart sunk. A second, smaller reaper crouched at the other edge of the passage. It stood at the ready, lobster-like tail raised high and poised to strike. Its carapace was still gray and soft-looking—a juvenile.

The clicking noise redoubled as the larger reaper's eight legs carried it toward the remaining smugglers.

Luther fired. He didn't have to kill it, he just needed to distract it long enough for the smugglers to escape. If Kit had done his job, Reid and the Citadel men would be waiting at the mouth of the canyon to apprehend them on their exit.

The reaper screeched and raised its tail as it whirled toward Luther. Heart pounding, he unloaded the revolver into the creature. The last round bounced off the shiny black carapace with all the impact of a pebble.

Luther ducked back behind the switchback. He twisted the revolver's cylinder, jammed his palm down on the ejector rod, and inserted a new speed loader.

Several more gunshots rang out as he turned back. "Shoot the joints!" He shouted, hoping the smugglers could hear him. Taking off one or two of the thing's legs should do the trick.

"Luther!"

Bewildered, Luther looked around for the source of Syv's voice. The reaper scuttled in a circle. One of its front legs was curled in on itself, oozing black blood. In the confusion, the smaller reaper had shuffled sideways—toward the smugglers.

Luther edged away from the safety of the switchback, keeping his back to the wall as he tried to get a clear shot on the smaller reaper. The smugglers were throwing rocks; they'd come unequipped for a fight.

Syv yelled from up above again, but Luther couldn't spare a thought for her. The huge black reaper had caught sight of him. It charged.

The thorn-like stinger struck the wall just above Luther's shoulder. He stumbled away and drew his belt-knife with his free hand. It had never been made for combat like this, but it would have to do.

Gambling, Luther ran at the monstrous scorpion—too close for the stinger to strike him. A pincer snapped at him, but Luther anticipated the move. He dropped to his knees and fired upward into the thing's great triangular head, once, twice.

The reaper reared up, and Luther darted beneath it, away from the pincers.

The reaper's belly rippled with interlocking scales, like armor. Luther struck his belt knife into a gap between two segments. Thick beads of hot blood rained down on him. He twisted the blade, grateful for the leather gloves protecting his palms. The reaper's legs curled around the injury. Luther wrenched the blade free and darted out between two of its legs.

His heart dropped into his stomach as he ran toward the smugglers huddled in the rocks. Syv was hanging on a rope halfway down the canyon wall. He watched as she drew her weapon, dangling precariously and supporting her weight on the rope with one hand.

"Get down!" she shouted.

Too late, Luther realized she'd drawn her ignis cannon. "Syv, don't—"

The astrym round barreled into the gray reaper with an earthshaking boom. Luther blinked against the whitish-blue light that streaked across his vision. The ground trembled. A wide crack split the base of the canyon wall.

Luther reached the rocks where the smugglers were hiding just as the canyon wall collapsed. He threw himself to the ground. Sand and rubble scattered across the canyon floor with a deafening roar. When he finally looked up, Syv was nowhere in sight.

"Syvannah!" he shouted, clambering to his feet and looking around wildly. The rope she'd used to rappel into the canyon dangled to the ground, loose and empty. "Syv!"

"Yep." Syv's hoarse response came from somewhere near the now-collapsed far passage. Luther vaulted over the rocks sheltering the smugglers and ran to his prentice.

The blast from Syv's ignis cannon had thrown Syv from her rope. She crouched near the wall, the weapon still clutched in one hand. Her other wrapped protectively around one knee. Looking around, she caught Luther's eye and gave him a shaky grin.

"I got him."

She had. The collapse had buried the gray reaper, and a boulder the size of a wagon had crushed the other's curving tail. The black reaper thrashed and hissed. All eight legs scuttled against the ground, but it was stuck fast.

"Damnit, Syv." Luther wiped a hand over his face and knelt beside the girl "You damn near got *us*."

Syv grimaced and looked down at her leg. "I think it's okay."

Luther grunted. "Let's see it."

Syv took her hand away from her leg and winced. "Sprained, maybe."

Luther palpated the injury, careful not to apply too much pressure. Her knee was already noticeably swollen.

"Can you walk?" he asked. Sensitive about her age and inexperience, Syv had downplayed injuries before.

"We'll find out." Syv accepted Luther's proffered hand and let him draw her to her feet. She hissed and immediately put most of her weight on her uninjured leg. "Mostly."

"What the hell were you thinking?" Luther asked.

Syv pointed at the cliff face. "Saw the fault line. Knew she was comin' down."

"Who the hell are you?" a woman's voice interrupted.

"I'll yell at you later," Luther told Syv. She'd acted brazenly, but it had been effective. Hopefully the injury would be enough to teach her a bit more caution; it would be hard for Luther to lecture her when she'd managed to bring down two reapers singlehandedly.

Satisfied Syv wasn't badly hurt, Luther turned to the small smuggling crew. The two men still crouched against the wall, but a woman with a long, dark braid and wide-brimmed straw hat stood with her arms crossed. She stared Luther down with narrowed eyes.

"We're doing just fine after saving your sorry asses," Luther said wryly. "Thanks for asking."

"What do you want?" the woman demanded.

Syv scoffed. "Whatcha think? Astrym, same as you." Syv gestured at the glittering crystals—half of them had been buried in the crush of rock. "'Cept you've gone and made me ruin the haul."

Luther had to applaud her quick thinking. He glanced between Syv, standing haughtily with one hand on her hip, and the smuggler's glower. The two could have been sisters. He almost laughed, but the reaper behind them knocked over several small boulders. The fresh wave of rubble scattered across the canyon floor.

Syv glanced over her shoulder, wide-eyed. "We gotta get gone."

"Don't have to tell me twice," one of the men said.

"You ain't going nowhere!" the woman said sharply.

"Going *anywhere*." Syv corrected the smuggler with a huge grin, but the woman ignored her.

"We're getting that haul, what's left of it."

"Suit yourself. I ain't reaper food," said one of the smugglers. He exchanged a nervous glance with his companion. The two seemed to reach an unspoken agreement. Together they edged around the reaper toward the narrow passage that led back to their wagons, stumbling in their haste to escape.

Luther holstered his revolver and held his hand out to the woman. "Name's Luther," he said. "You can thank Syv for saving your life, now."

"Hollie," the woman snapped. "And don't pretend it wasn't self-interest."

"Lot easier to take the haul ourselves after those things ate you." Syv narrowed her eyes. "Might say you owe us a fair shot at our cut, unless you want to fight for it."

Hollie tossed her braid over her shoulder and pulled a long metal box from her shoulder bag. She took out a collection device—a collapsible stick with a thick web of finely woven astrym thread at the end. It was the only safe way to harvest the element.

"Let's go," Luther said quietly to Syv.

"But she's—"

"Hollie was here first," Luther said. He gripped Syv's shoulder and steered her toward the passage. "She doesn't have enough collectors to take it all, anyway."

Together, they slipped around the narrow switchback. Behind them, the noise from the reaper's attempts to free itself was ebbing.

"She'll have to come out sooner or later—at least you took care of the north passage." Luther told Syv. He slumped against the rock and took a steadying breath. "That was close, though."

"You can thank me for saving your life, now." Syv said. Her haughty attitude dissolved now that they were away from Hollie, and Luther noticed her hands were shaking.

"You did good, kid," Luther admitted. He gripped her shoulder and squeezed, then pulled out his slender astrym tablet.

A few quick lines were scrawled across the surface in Reid's cramped handwriting. "They got 'em."

"Good. Hate to think it was all for nothing. Them reapers worth anything?"

"*Those* reapers." Luther frowned thoughtfully as he slipped the tablet away. "Maybe. Reid would know for sure."

They were halfway to the canyon's entrance when they heard Hollie scream.

"What in the goddess's name…" Syv grabbed her ignis cannon again. She made to start running back toward the astrym load but hissed in a sharp intake of breath when she put weight on her injured leg.

"Wait for me. And put that thing away. You'll bring the whole canyon down on top of us."

Luther was breathing heavily when he reached the last switchback. Gun held at the ready, he rounded the turn.

The reaper was stampeding around the mess of the rockslide. It had pulled itself free leaving most of its tail, with its deadly stinger, still crushed under the rock.

Its rear legs were mangled. The reaper's steps were ungainly as it scrabbled toward the astrym crystals. Hollie was frozen with her back to the wall, her astrym collector lying forgotten several feet away.

"Run!" Luther screamed.

It seemed to break her trance. Hollie shook herself and made for the outcropping she'd hidden in before.

Luther opened fire on the reaper from the relative safety of the switchback, trying to buy the smuggler time.

Then Hollie tripped.

Luther was running toward the reaper before he had time to change his mind.

He wasn't quick enough. The reaper seized Hollie with one of its clawed pincers and threw her against the wall. She crashed to the rocky canyon floor. The reaper scuttled forward and pinned her legs to the ground. She grabbed a rock and smashed it into the claw again and again. The creature hissed, but Luther suspected more from irritation than pain.

Luther could just make out the two smaller pincers extending from its mouth, clicking with anticipation. He skidded to a halt a few feet away and raised his gun. The first shot struck the joint connecting a back leg to the shiny black carapace. The second glanced off the creature's back.

Inhale, aim. Exhale, fire.

Hollie wrenched one leg out of the reaper's grasp and smashed her boot into its mouth, kicking fiercely against the grasping pincers.

Luther ejected the casings from his revolver just as the reaper whipped Hollie back and forth. Two arachnid legs smashed into Luther, sweeping him off his feet. His gun flew from his hand and clattered uselessly several feet away. Luther landed flat on his back. Gasping for breath, he rolled to the side to avoid the clawed foot stamping into the ground.

Gritting his teeth, Luther drew his dagger again. He rolled, this time following the reaper's movements, and stabbed into one clawed foot.

"Help me!" Hollie's shout wasn't a plea, but an angry demand. That was good—she couldn't be *too* hurt. Luther jerked the knife out of the reaper's flesh.

The reaper's front pincers were worrying at Hollie's boot, which had come off in the struggle. Soon enough it would realize that the worn leather wasn't food. The smuggler scrambled backward, but the reaper had her cornered.

"Take this!" Luther tossed her his dagger, then dove for his gun. He reloaded the revolver with the speed borne of countless hours of practice.

Hollie kicked the boot deeper into the reaper's mouth with her other foot, then jabbed the dagger at the pincers. She stabbed again and again at the creature's soft head. For a moment, Luther thought she might make the beast back down.

But the reaper had decided it was done playing. It seized Hollie with a pincer and threw her against the cliff face again.

Luther didn't know whether he was acting on instinct or pure stupidity, but he was moving before he could think. He scrambled up the outcropping Hollie had just failed to reach, then jumped onto the reaper's back. The monstrous scorpion released Hollie at once. The short dagger jutted out from its head, and the creature's mouth and front pincers wept blood.

It was like riding the world's angriest bull, but without anything to hang on to. Luther pulled out the dagger and stabbed it into the top of the reaper's head with all his might. The blade drove through the creature's armored scales and stuck fast.

Luther grasped the dagger's hilt to steady himself. The reaper rampaged away from Hollie. Snarling, Luther pressed the barrel of his revolver into the creature's head and unloaded all six rounds.

The reaper stopped so abruptly, it sent Luther tumbling right over its head. The dagger hilt wrenched from his hands, and he went flying several feet. He fell heavily onto his side. Gravel tore into the skin of his arms and chest, and his head cracked against a rock. Luther hissed in a sharp intake of breath, closing his eyes against the sudden, searing pain.

"You dead?" Syv had caught up to him, despite her injuries.

"Probably," Luther groaned. He opened his eyes and put a hand to his temple. It came away bloody. "Am I?"

"Not yet," Syv said. She was peering at his wound. "Never seen you do something so stupid though, boss."

"Might say you're teaching me a few things. Live long enough and you'll make your fair share of stupid calls, kid." Luther looked over at Hollie. The smuggler had dragged herself to a sitting position against the canyon wall. Blood drenched one of her pant legs, and she clutched one arm against her chest like it might be broken.

Luther heaved himself to his feet, assessing his injuries as he walked over to Hollie. Nothing he wouldn't survive. He leaned down and offered the smuggler a hand. She glared up at him.

"You try to stay here, and we'll just drag you," he threatened. She was in no condition to resist.

Hollie muttered all the way to the mouth of the canyon. Luther thought she was more upset over losing the astrym score than she was at her injuries. She leaned heavily on him, limping the whole way. The reaper had done some serious damage to her leg—she'd have that limp for the rest of her life.

Night was edging across the sky when they reached the mouth of the canyon. Reid and the Citadel men were waiting. Hollie's eyes narrowed as she took in the scene. None of her crew were in sight.

"There's a storm forecast," Luther told her. They had to get out of the open before astrym started raining down on their heads like crystallized lightning.

Hollie turned her hawk-like gaze onto him. "Where are my men?"

Reid approached with a pair of astrym cuffs. Luther gestured to her injured arm. "I think that wrist's broken."

Reid nodded and reached for Hollie's uninjured arm. The smuggler ripped her hand away. The action unbalanced her, and she staggered sidelong into Luther with a gasp of pain.

"Unauthorized harvesting is illegal under the title thirteen in the Eredale Penal Code," Luther said. "But you know that."

Hollie's glare could have melted raw astrym.

"Who the hell are you?" she demanded. She tried to fend Reid off again as he clapped the cuffs to her good wrist, but it was half-hearted. She knew defeat when she saw it.

"Citadel," Luther said. Shock painted her face, and Luther grinned through his weariness.

"My crew?" Hollie asked.

"Already safely tucked away from the storm," Reid said.

"But... you saved us?"

"In a manner of speaking. Couldn't prosecute you if you were dead now, could we?" Luther grinned, then gestured at Kit, who was hovering nearby with the reins of a half-dozen horses in hand. They helped Hollie mount her horse, then Reid fixed the other end of her handcuffs onto a specially reinforced D-ring on the saddle.

Hollie's dull gaze flickered between the silvery cuffs and Luther. "Thanks," she said, after a moment.

Luther nodded at her as Kit led her horse away.

"Ain't never been thanked for arresting no one before," Syv said with a smirk as she, Luther, and Reid mounted their own horses.

"Arresting *anyone*." Luther rolled his eyes. "Every time I think we're making progress with you, I swear."

"Somebody's gotta keep you on your toes, old man."

Luther swatted her with the end of his reins. "Show some respect for your elders."

"Alright, children. Keep it together until we get to cover, will you?" Reid's teeth flashed white in the growing darkness as he dug his heels into his mare's ribs.

Luther turned to take in the storm-ridden sky. Faint streaks of lightning-blue danced in the blackening clouds, a sure sign of astrym fall. If they waited any longer, they'd be holing up with the reapers in the slot canyon.

"You think Hollie will sing?" Syv asked Luther as they followed Reid toward their shelter.

Luther ran a hand over the stubble on his cheek, thinking. "Her men were quick enough to abandon her. If she doesn't, one of them will."

"Does this mean we have to go back to the city now?"

Luther didn't miss the disappointment in her voice. "What, you don't miss your Citadel uniform?" he teased her.

"It's itchy."

Luther laughed. He hadn't realized how much he missed working in the wastes. Miserable and dangerous though they were, there was a freedom out here that was sorely lacking in the Citadel's rigidly enforced etiquette codes. "Hollie's crew was smaller than I thought it would be. I'm sure the Council will be pleased if we round up one or two more."

A flash of viridian light painted the waste an alien green, and thunder rolled over the cliffs and ridges. Syv laughed and dug her heels into her horse's sides. "Race you!"

The first icy drops of the storm splattered the sand, and they sped to a gallop as another flare of astrym darted across the sky.

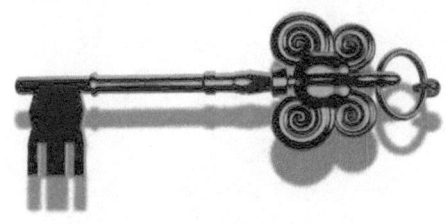

From the Author

What happens when you throw a dash of Weird West, classic fantasy tropes, and an overlay of glittering sci-fi advances into a cauldron and mix them up? This story, *Astrym Horizons*, takes place in just such a world: the desert, storm-ridden planet of Cassus. Deadly storms provide the key resource for limited tech. Wild monsters and a pantheon of gods and goddess war for dominance. Gunslingers escort convoys across the uninhabited western wastes—and danger is never far away.

I've always loved exploring the intricacies of worldbuilding and dramatic landscaping that serve as backdrops for the fantasy stories we all know and love, and I can't help experimenting with new ways to layer worlds that mold characters in challenging and unique ways.

Astrym Horizons is a spinoff story from my as-yet unpublished novel, *Rusting Gods*. The sweeping desert vistas of Cassus are far from done with me, and I'm looking forward to revisiting Luther and Syv in many stories to come.

I can't express my excitement at finding the right time and place to give readers a sneak-peek of this brutal, beautiful landscape, and all the promise of adventure that it holds.

About the Author

H.Y. Gregor was born in Portland, Oregon, but she'll always call the mountains of Colorado home. In college she interned for congressional offices and law firms, and she has a bachelor's degree in political science. After narrowly avoiding law school, she now puts her international relations and government background to use creating intricate, colorful worlds to serve as backdrops for her fantasy fiction novels. In 2022 her short story, *A Secret Spoken,* received a Silver Honorable Mention from the Writers of the Future contest, and you can look for another upcoming short in *Animal Magica Volume 2,* with more exciting, secret projects in the works. She can often be found at writing conferences with an overstuffed messenger bag and too many pens.

You can follow Gregor on Instagram (@toviahy), Twitter (@toviahy), Facebook (H.Y. Gregor – Author) or check out her website at hygregor.com.

Attorney Fight Club
by
Sonny Zae

Attorney Fight Club

*B*arry halted when Mr. Higgins stopped in front of the door keypad. Mr. Higgins was so close Barry wondered if it was also a retina scanner or whether his doddering old boss would type in the key code with eyelashes.

Mr. Higgins had invited him out to celebrate Barry's recent win, finally wringing out a favorable division of assets for Karen Blessing in her long and bloody divorce. Barry had accepted the invitation, as it meant a hefty bonus or promotion to law firm partner.

Mr. Higgins cursed and entered a key-code for the seventh time, his shaky hands unable to punch in four numbers without error.

"Sir, let me do that." Barry waited for the octogenarian attorney to move aside. "What's the code?"

Mr. Higgins coughed and pulled out a hanky. "It's supposed to be three-five-four-one."

"Right. So, what are we doing here?" Barry asked, unable to suppress the question.

His boss folded the hanky and tucked it into his jacket. "Don't you remember, McChord? We're celebrating your win."

Barry waved a hand at the building. "This a speakeasy?"

Mr. Higgins' eyes narrowed. "How old do you think I am? This's Attorney Fight Club. Happens once a year. Now, punch in the code. I need a chair and a good glass of port, maybe light up a Cohiba."

Barry punched in the code and the door beeped. He opened it and gestured for Mr. Higgins to proceed him. As the founding name partner of the *Higgins, Berg, Overhalter, and Sneet* law firm, protocol demanded a respectful demeanor, even when Augustus Austere Higgins became cranky. Barry hoped this wouldn't be one of *those* nights.

"Fight club?" Barry watched Mr. Higgins shuffle forward. "Will you be fighting, sir?"

Mr. Higgins stopped in mid-shuffle and glared at Barry through eyebrows like window boxes of frosted, dead flowers.

"You trying to be funny, McChord? Don't. You're no good at it."

"Yes, sir." Barry followed his boss into a dim hallway, the old man's Italian leather loafers scuffing against the floor. He didn't notice when the old fossil stopped and nearly ran into Augustus.

"I suppose I ought to fill you in before we get inside."

Barry gestured, even though Mr. Higgins wouldn't see the motion. "Why don't we get out of this dark hallway first?"

"Shut up and listen. You'll see great action here at Attorney Fight Club. You like mixed martial arts?"

"MMA? No, not really."

"Too bad," his boss said, disappointment heavy in his voice. "You work out? Wrestle in high school? Know anything about boxing?"

"No. Why?" Barry heard shuffling and moved cautiously forward.

"A bit of wagering occurs. It helps if you know the fight game."

"Are we about there?"

"Don't be so damn impatient. Before we go in, there's one rule about attorney fight club."

Barry couldn't help the sarcasm that leaked into his reply. "Yeah, yeah, don't talk about attorney fight club."

"It isn't about talking. When we go through the door, you'll sign an NDA, of course. But the main rule is that you must do what I say. If you do, your life will be changed forever. How long have you been working for the firm?"

"Four years, sir."

"Huh. I thought you'd been with us longer." Mr. Higgins' shuffling stopped, and he rapped on a metal door. "This's your big chance, son. You turn tail today, and your career at *Higgins Berg* is over, understand? You ready to take the next big step?"

"Yes, sir!" Barry snapped out the reply, his pulse racing.

"Good. You'll be hobnobbing with some of the finest lawyers in the city—and some of the worst. You probably won't be able to tell the difference. Now, open the inner door and don't hit me with it."

He opened the door to a flood of sound. Barry stared at the sea of slicked-back hair, dark suits, and red power ties. The warehouse reeked of booze, cigars, sweat, and political influence. Mr. Higgins shuffled forward, waving Barry back when he tried to follow.

"Name?" demanded a voice.

"Barry McChord. After my big win at the courthouse, people in the office call me 'Barry the Hatchet.'" He turned to find a fiftyish woman in high-heels and tight dress, her hair in a regulation law firm half up, half down hairstyle. He glanced at her upper arm to see if she had a "Live Free" tattoo like Amy the paralegal at the office. The woman towered over him with all the frostiness of a professional fighter, looking as if she would hold her own in an MMA ring.

"You think you're the first attorney named Barry who thought up that nickname?" she sneered. "Law firm?"

Barry looked around as he answered, wondering where Higgins had gone. The warehouse was dark, but it looked as if at least a hundred people were in attendance. He forgot about Attila the High-Heeled Hun as he scanned the cavernous warehouse interior.

"Hey, numb-nuts!" She punched his shoulder, forcing Barry to face her.

Would she be interested in a position at *Higgins Berg*? No, probably not a good time to ask. Plus, she seemed more than a bit annoyed by his lack of attention. "What?" Barry massaged his shoulder.

"Height and weight?"

Barry gave her a sharp look.

"I said," she said slowly and clearly. "I need your height, weight, eye color, blood type, next of kin, et cetera."

Barry thrust his jaw out. "Why?"

Her acrylic fingernail extensions pressed blade-like into the base of his neck. "If the form doesn't get filled out, I toss you out the door. Capiche?"

"Um, sure."

She removed her fingers, but the pain told Barry she could knock him silly. And her fierce expression indicated she'd enjoy doing so. She was a paralegal, for sure. Maybe descended from Viking raiders.

She pointed at a half-dozen different pages. "Sign here, initial here, here, and here, and sign here along with writing in your law firm name and position."

He signed. Maybe it was just paperwork for the big promotion.

"Do you fight tonight?" Barry asked. Watching her in action would be a treat.

"It depends on you." She flashed a grin. "Want to lose teeth and blood?"

Barry found Mr. Higgins sipping a martini at the bar, a makeshift affair comprising a disorderly jumble of pulled-together desks and medical equipment. Mr. Higgins inspected Barry's face. "You didn't lip off to Nadine. That's personal growth, McChord."

Barry ordered a beer, hoping Mr. Higgins would pay, but his boss acted as if he didn't notice. "Who's fighting tonight, sir?"

Mr. Higgins chuckled. "You'll find out soon enough."

Barry took a sip of beer. "Sorry, but I'm not much for fight sports."

"Oh, this isn't sport, this's real. As I said earlier, you must stay for the whole event and do as you're told."

"Of course, sir." What was the old vulture hinting at? Was this a test of his patience? It was turning out to be more games than he had to endure at the office.

But he wouldn't back down. Barry'd fought that asshole lawyer from the *Meenis and Bakkis* firm, had countered every dirty trick and nasty stunt by the opposing counsel. He'd won a majority of the marital assets for Karen Blessing, though he'd nearly sold his soul in the process. His opponent had been such a douche! It was divorce lawyers like that who gave all attorneys a bad name.

Barry coughed when Mr. Higgins lit a cigar. "Will they be fighting MMA style?"

Mr. Higgins laughed. "MMA is for pussies. What you'll see tonight is good old-fashioned bare-knuckles brawling. No rules, no gloves, no fancy-shmancy ring. Just two men trying to knock each other's head off. You have a problem with blood?"

What the hell had he gotten into? "I've seen a few fights. And I can take a punch, as I showed in the Blessing trial."

Mr. Higgins snorted. "This's real combat, junior. A winner'll be declared when one guy can't get up—or won't get up. So, I hope you're not just blowing smoke."

Barry opened his mouth to ask for clarification but was jostled from behind. He turned to find an all-too-familiar face, the opposing lawyer in Barry's recent divorce win.

"Hey, sorry about that," the jostler said. A look of recognition crossed his face and he thrust out a hand. "Devin Incarnotto, of *Meenis and Bakkis*, remember? I represented Manuel Blessing. Here celebrating your win, Augustus?"

"We'll see," Mr. Higgins waved his Cohiba in Barry's face. "Members of the management committee think Barry McChord has promise. Guess we'll find out."

A moment of silence passed. It was enough time for Barry to renew his loathing of his former courtroom opponent, from his dyed-red snakeskin cowboy boots to the designer necktie and expensive salon straight-razor haircut that topped Devin's six-foot three frame. How did the man have time to get a tan? Or have his teeth whitened?

Worse, his boss spoke to Devin like a friend. "What're you talking about?"

"Your corner man will tell you everything you need to know," Mr. Higgins said, waving his cigar at an approaching man. "Wink Armiston's head of the organizing committee and the finest personal injury lawyer in the city. He'll get you ready."

"Ready for what?" Barry stiffened, startled by Wink's battered nose, cheek scar, and the firm logo tattoo covering his entire left upper arm. He could see the tattoo because the city's finest injury lawyer was wearing a white wife-beater shirt.

Barry took the business card Wink held out. "Why are you giving me this?"

"Sorry, habit." Wink waved a hand as if expecting Barry to know what was going to come next. "Come on, Princess. Time to get ready for your fight."

"My fight? What do you mean?"

Wink led him through the crowd, stopping at a table bearing a mound of white towels. "Augustus put you in for the first fight. You're the headliner. Strip down and put on these trunks." He tossed them to Barry, then wagged a finger. "Don't call them briefs! I've heard that lame-ass joke so many times I'm gonna punch the next dude who says it, understand?"

"You expect me to fight? I'm no boxer."

"Neither is Manny. Change clothes," Wink ordered.

Barry bit back the sarcastic comment already on his lips as he stripped off his suit. Would he be better off fighting barefoot, or in leather dress shoes? He kicked the shoes off.

Barry pulled on the well-worn trunks and tied the drawstring around his waist. "Uh, Wink, is this something Mr. Higgins cooked up to see how bad I want to make partner?"

Wink smiled, but the expression didn't improve his face in the slightest. "Catchin' on already? Let's hope you pick up fight moves that quick."

Barry looked around for gloves and mouth guard. "Aren't you going to finish outfitting me?"

"Right, careless of me." Wink peeled a towel from the pile and tossed it at Barry. "Okay, let's go, Princess. You don't wanna keep the crowd waiting."

Barry stumbled after him. Who would they make him fight? People made room as they approached, creating a ring walk between two groups of waving, shouting people. The air was thick with the smell of booze and bloodlust. It reminded him of walking into court, faces along their path alight with anticipation. Attorneys from the city's biggest law firms waved fists and screamed like cavemen—and cavewomen. Millie from *Doormin Partikoupolis* leaned out to make a fist in his face, her frizzy red hair radiating like an angry sunset. "I have three Ben Franklins riding on you, McChord. Punch that motherfucker out!"

If he had to fight for a place in the law firm, it was just another fight. Barry had struggled continuously against the other junior partners. His queasiness was momentarily forgotten at the thought of the respect he'd get showing up to the office in regulation suit and tie with cuts and bruises on his face. He could barely wait to run into that little weasel Jones while looking like he'd just beat the holy hell out of someone. That, and the next prospective client would be able to see Barry was a real fighter, despite his modest physical stature.

As quickly as his confidence flared, it was gone. The last time he'd been in a fight was high school for chrissakes. Big Jeremy Conroid had backed Barry into a corner of the gym and Barry'd been forced to trade blows with the meaner, more athletic kid. He'd been losing soundly, blood flowing freely from his nose, when he'd bumped into the janitor's mop bucket. He'd turned the tables by throwing cold, dirty water into Jeremy's face, then clubbing him with the metal roller-bucket assembly.

The best part was he'd salvaged his pride by standing and fighting. No, that wasn't true. The best part was Barry's parents taking the Conroid family to court and winning a monetary settlement and restraining order, but only after Barry's nosebleeds had stopped. Barry's interest in the law was born out of the fateful event.

"Here's your opponent," Wink said as the crowd drew back. On the other side of a circle of onlookers was Devin Incarnotto with an evil smile on his face. And standing next to him, wearing trunks and looking pissed as hell, was Manny Blessing.

"What the hell's this?" Barry squawked. "He's not an attorney!"

"No," Wink replied, unperturbed, fishing in a duffle bag. "Don't worry, Princess, the guy isn't a professional fighter." Wink brought out a mask. "Wear this."

Barry turned it over to see Karen Blessing's face. "What the hell?"

"Put it on," Wink ordered. "Or get an automatic DQ."

"I'm fighting her ex. This'll send him into an uncontrollable rage!"

"Exactly."

Barry scowled at Wink. Manny roared in anger as Barry adjusted the mask, getting the eyeholes lined up in time to see his opponent charge, face red and mouth wide open. The collision sent them down, with spectators scrambling to get out of the way.

"You bastard!" Manny screamed as he jumped back to his feet, hands already balled into fists. "I'm going to tear your fucking head off and throw it in the punch bowl!"

Barry slowly got to his feet, crouching with palms outward like the time he'd faced down an angry pit bull. He'd been sneaking through an opponent's back yard to catch the man cheating on his wife. "Hey, man, take it easy. This's nothing personal."

"She got everything," Manny growled, leaping forward. Manny's fist smashed into the side of his face and Barry toppled over, his opponent on top of him. Barry tried to twist away, but only succeeded in landing nose-first. Blood pooled on the concrete.

Manny pulled him up by the hair. Barry had to gather his wits or Manny would beat the crap out of him. He scrambled to his feet and brought a knee up into Manny's stomach, doubling the man over. The crowd cheered, surging forward to see the action.

Manny moved closer. Barry threw a right cross as Manny lunged, staggering the man. But Manny recovered quickly, wrapping arms around Barry and trying to throw him. Barry braced against the takedown. They wrestled, their efforts spinning them around.

Should he give up? No, that wasn't Barry's style. Plus, he couldn't risk being the laughingstock of *Higgins, Berg, Overhalter and Sneet.*

"I don't want to hurt you," Barry gasped. "The divorce trial was nothing personal."

"You ruined my life!" Manny roared, clawing at Barry's mask.

A bell rang. "First round's over!" Wink motioned Barry to a stool, blasting water down Barry's throat while holding an icepack to his head. "Not bad, kid. But next round, try to actually punch him, okay? Hit him in the nose. Or anywhere on his face. Just hit him."

"Oh, no shit!" Barry panted heavily as sweat and blood trickled down his face. He looked at the trail of blood down his sternum. "He may have broken my nose. But it doesn't hurt."

"Not until tomorrow," Wink replied.

The bell rang and Wink yanked the stool out from under him. Barry staggered to his feet, receiving a push from behind.

Manny was too strong. Barry had to do something different. He had to change his thinking, as in the Blessing divorce. He'd lost a string of little battles before figuring out Devin had been intentionally keeping Barry on the defensive. Things changed when Barry tracked Manny Blessing and his secretary to a motel and snapped photos. When Devin argued his client had been the victim of a vindictive, abusive wife, Barry'd presented the photos and blown up the case, handing Devin a defeat.

Manny came at him, head down. Barry tried to side-step but bumped into an onlooker. Manny's arms encircled his neck and they grappled again. "We shouldn't be fighting," Barry said through gritted teeth. "Do you know how much billing Devin got out of each and every stupid little battle he urged you to fight?"

Manny's grip eased and he stopped pushing. "Whaddya mean?"

"Your attorney's a real lowlife."

"He said the same about you."

"Remember how quickly Devin dismissed mediation? He doesn't have your best interests at heart."

"No shit! You think I wanna be here tonight? Devin lost a document showing Karen was hiding marital assets."

"Oh, wow," Barry said in a low voice. "That's not good."

"Exactly. I'm totally strapped." Manny hooked his leg and Barry fell to the floor, Manny on top. "To make it worse, Devin was having money problems."

Barry thrust a leg out to prevent rolling. "What do you mean?"

"He asked to borrow money from my client account." Manny pulled an arm free and clubbed at Barry's face. "I said yes, figuring I didn't have any choice."

"That's completely improper!" Barry replied, throwing up an elbow to block the attack.

"Really?" Manny stopped flailing with his arm, holding it up to deflect empty beer cans thrown by the crowd. "What can I do about it?"

Barry shook his head. "I'm not your attorney." He twisted, throwing Manny off. Barry scrambled to his feet, wiping beer foam off his face. "That creep's your problem." He ducked as Manny tried a roundhouse kick. "Why're you here?"

"He promised to cut ten thousand off my bill." Manny advanced and gave Barry a half-hearted shove. "You think he screwed me over?"

"Oh, yeah." Barry glanced around. Devin stood at the edge of the crowd, martini glass in hand and a huge grin on his face. "Listen, make it look like we're grappling, but let me move you backwards. When I say, throw your biggest right hook. I'll duck. You with me?"

"Okay," Manny replied, sounding doubtful.

Barry pushed and Manny cooperated. "Now!" Barry hissed.

Manny's fist whistled over his head. The punch caught Devin Incarnotto on the jaw, sending him flying.

Barry and Manny stared at the fallen attorney as others rushed to Devin's aid. Wink appeared at Barry's shoulder. "Good thing he didn't catch you with that." A frown crossed his ugly, scarred features. "That was a sneaky trick."

Barry flexed his fingers and shook his arms to keep muscles from tightening up. "I don't know what you're talking about."

"This's unexpected," said a voice behind him. Barry turned to find Augustus Higgins, a scowl on his face. "You might get disqualified."

"Oh, really?" Barry snapped, no longer caring about career advancement. "Devin wasn't smart enough to get out of the way. That's his fault, the moron. You want to take it out on me, you can, but..."

"But what?" Mr. Higgins said, a dangerous note in his voice.

The bystanders had Devin on his feet now. He staggered forward and Barry drew back a fist.

"None of that!" Mr. Higgins barked, grabbing Barry's arm. Together, Higgins and Wink escorted Barry away.

Barry had a sudden image of being frozen out. "I'm not disqualified, am I?"

"You still want to fight?" Mr. Higgins asked.

"Yeah. I wanted to punch Devin in the lie-hole."

One corner of Mr. Higgins' mouth twitched up in a hint of a smile. "Be careful what you wish for. Wait here."

When his boss returned, he addressed Wink. "Is he in condition for more rounds?"

Wink shrugged. "Guess so. His nose stopped bleeding."

The timekeeper rang the bell, and the crowd drew back, revealing Devin waiting in loaner trunks. Wink shoved Barry forward.

Barry advanced, hands clenched into fists, sudden tension in his gut.

Devin flashed a wicked smile. "Looks like I'll get my revenge," he said as they circled.

"Don't count on it," Barry growled. "I'm gonna mop the floor with you."

Devin had longer arms. He had quicker hands. And his left jab kept rattling Barry's brain.

When the bell rang for the end of the round, Barry fell onto the stool Wink shoved against the backs of his legs. He let his hands drop, wondering how much more tired he'd be if wearing boxing gloves.

"How you feelin'?" Wink asked, concern in his voice.

"Gaaassed," Barry admitted between gulps of air. "How do I win?"

Wink shrugged as he sponged Barry's head with water. "He's a better fighter than you."

"Thanks for the vote of confidence!" Barry wiped water off his face. "If he beats the crap out of me, I'll file a complaint with the police."

Wink shook his head. "Remember three things. First, you agreed to participate. Second, you signed the NDA. Third, no win, no partnership."

"I hate you," Barry muttered. Was Wink saying these things to make him fight harder? "How do I cheat, then?"

"This is no-holds-barred fighting."

Barry nodded. "Hitting below the belt, then. Gotcha."

Wink pointed a finger in Barry's face. "Remember, Princess, his arms are longer than yours."

"You're my corner man. Why aren't you trying to pump up my confidence?" Barry stared at Wink. The personal injury lawyer stared back, impassive. Barry threw up his hands. "Fine! How do I get out of the fight?"

"You could take a dive."

"Not an option," Barry asserted. "I beat Devin in court, and I'll beat him here. I just haven't figured out how, yet."

The bell rang and Barry lurched off his stool. Devin pumped a fist in the air, enjoying the cheers of the crowd. When he was several steps away, Barry lowered his head and charged, ramming his head into Devin's solar plexus. Devin went down, then rolled and bounded back to his feet.

"Nice move." He smiled at Barry. "But it didn't hurt me."

"Come on," Barry said, holding out both palms in an invitation to lock hands. "Let's see how good you are at wrestling.

Devin obliged.

"Hey, good takedown," Barry rasped. "Could you ease up on my windpipe? I've got a proposition."

"What?"

"I learned something very curious from your former client, the one I just beat."

Devin snorted. "You didn't beat him."

"Disqualification's a win for me." Barry squirmed against Devin's grasp, but only succeeded in bringing his face closer to Devin's. "Manny told me you lost a document that hurt his case."

Devin's face lost some color. "I don't know what you're talking about, loser."

"The bar association might like to know about your interest-free loan from the client account."

"Not going to happen, low-life." Devin shifted his hold to a choke. Barry blocked the attempt, recognizing it from a safety training video the firm sponsored for new associates.

"You're forgetting something," Devin growled as he pulled an arm free and flailed at Barry's face. "You signed the NDA. Clause thirty-three states anything you overhear while on the premises is covered by the agreement. Tell anyone, and I'll roast you over a fire."

"You think I'm an idiot?" Barry drove a knee into Devin's groin. "A contract for an illegal purpose is unenforceable. Let me win, or you'll get disbarred."

Devin's struggles stopped and he exhaled loudly. "You son-of-a-bitch! What do you want from me?"

"I'm going to knock you out," Barry replied. "I won't punch hard, so make it look good."

Barry swung a fist and his opponent flopped to the floor, not attempting to rise as the referee counted him out.

"Well done, young man!" Mr. Higgins patted Barry's shoulder. "That was a well fought victory."

Barry glowered at his boss. "I blackmailed that son-of-a-bitch! I learned about his unethical behavior and said I'd turn him in if he didn't take a dive. What do you think of that?"

Mr. Higgins shrugged. "A win's a win. He didn't pull the old 'you signed the NDA' ploy?"

"He can't enforce that," Barry growled. "Now, if you don't mind, I'd like to have a good stiff drink."

"I'll buy," Mr. Higgins offered. "Turns out you're a sharp guy. I want you to do well at *Higgins Berg*. Why do you think I had you fight, McChord?"

"This was all a test, wasn't it? You wanted to see how I'd do when put into a corner?"

His boss smiled. "Not many young lawyers can spot a legal loophole while getting punched in the face."

Barry punched him, then.

The old man lay on the floor blinking. For a moment, Barry was afraid he might have injured his boss. Then Mr. Higgins thrust a wrinkled hand into the air and bystanders pulled him to his feet.

"What the hell?" Mr. Higgins rasped, his eyes flashing with anger.

"Sorry about that," Barry said, even though he really wasn't. "Still pumped on adrenaline. Anyone would have known I'd be on edge."

Barry didn't expect a punch in return. It caught him flush on the nose and he went down.

Wink helped him up, shaking his head. "Augustus was a divisional boxing champ way back when. Don't try that again, or he'll flatten your nose—again."

To Barry's surprise, his boss smiled at him. "Don't get your nose fixed, McChord. You look meaner now…partner."

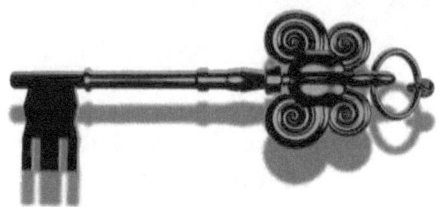

From the Author

My inspiration for the story started when I was idly thinking "What story would people like to read? How about lawyers punching each other in the face?" I cannot claim a deeper theme or more complex story idea genesis. I'm just trying to give readers what they want and enjoy.

About the Author

Sonny Zae lives on the edge of Dallas, Texas, and on the edge of reality. He writes science fiction, fantasy, horror, humor, or whatever strikes him at the time.

His anthology of Ninja Nuns short stories, *Ninja Nuns and the S.P.E.C.T.E.R. of Evil*, is available as a paperback or electronic book. His robot story *Automated Everyman Migrant Theater* was third place winner in Writers of the Future contest, first quarter 2019 and published in Writers of the Future volume 36. Sonny's zombie romance short story *She Has My Heart* was published in the *Dates From Hell* anthology of Hellbound Books. His horror short story *Doll 538* was published December 2021 in *Road Kill: Texas Horror volume 6*. His science fiction short story *Automation, Obsolete* was published by *Daikaijuzine* in March 2021.

Dead Season

by
David Powell

Dead Season

*F*ifty years ago, the day water swallowed up Mallard, Tennessee, Fleetus Cutshaw, age ten, stole a bottle of his old man's moonshine, sat his little butt down by a tree stump where he could watch the water rise, and proceeded to get shit-faced drunk.

He gazed at the light dancing on the rippling water and took a long swallow. "I got shit-faced drunk," he said out loud, practicing how he would tell his cousins. It sounded so grown-up.

Shortly after that he passed out, so he never heard his mother calling. His stump sat in a very low spot, and the water had covered him up before he had a chance to wake up and discover hangovers.

When they drained the Mallard Cove of Center Hill Lake last spring, Fleetus finally awoke to the worse case of cottonmouth on record. His crusted eyelids popped open with a sound like dry leaves crushing. He stared at the exposed lakebed, an endless jigsaw of cracked, pale gray shards spotted here and there with heaps of vegetation. The heaps were the same gray. Fleetus was the same gray. It was hot for May and there was no moisture at all—not in the lake and not in Fleetus' body.

The dryness didn't bother him; the fact that he couldn't move did. He was welded into the gray silt, afraid he might break if he tried to pull himself loose. He imagined what he would look like if a piece of him broke off. Like the inside of those sugar wafers he loved, maybe.

Then rain started to fall, and he began to loosen up

The arguments start over music less than twenty minutes out from Vandy. The girls hate Ferguson's DJ Screw album, Lish learns with surprise that Katie Perry isn't universally loved, and Rahm sulks when Royal Blood is labeled harsh. Tana is too nervous to suggest any bands. The compromise—Jason Isbell—reduces them all to unhappy silence.

If we can just get to the lake house it will be okay, Tana tells herself. The pre-meds can binge on water sports while she and Rahm get high and hash out Carol's arc. Rahm has the first four seasons of *The Walking Dead* on his laptop, and Tana has a paper due next week.

Ferguson's Lexus GX skids to a stop in the gravel, instantly surrounded by the cloud of dust that's followed since they left the paved road. The dust drifts past, unhurried. They step out and stare at the weathered building with the rusted metal sign: "Cutshaw's Gro. and Ser. Sta."

"I've never seen this place before," Tana says. She wears a tank top that shows off her new tattoo: a female Atlas, holding up the world. "'Course I haven't been up here in *forever*." She is saying that a lot, in case her parents' lake house turns out to be a dud. No one in the family has even seen it in a year.

"Cutshaw's Gro. and Ser. Sta." Ferguson reads, pronouncing each syllable distinctly, trying for irony. He wears apricot Bermuda shorts and dock shoes with no socks.

"Those old sign-makers charged by the letter," says Lish, who is in pinstriped blouse and pearls. "Folks would know it meant grocery and service station." Explainer-in-chief.

Rahm stops, his hand on the door. "Scene: Harbinger. Cue the creepy old guy," he says, adorable in his George Romero tee shirt, and opens the door.

And no shit, there he is behind the counter, grizzled and surly, wrapping the splintered handle of an old shovel with duct tape, ignoring them completely. Even the name on his shirt is perfect—*Cut*shaw.

They all wander the oiled and blackened wood floor of Mr. Cutshaw's store. Tana and Rahm snicker over the Tennessee souvenirs: black bears and little outhouses stamped "Made in China." Ferguson pulls two bags of ice from the ancient metal drink box and heaves them onto the counter. He drops a ten-dollar bill beside them.

"How's the water this weekend?" he asks.

"Gone," Cutshaw answers. He slides the ten off the counter and drops it into the open cash register drawer. He leans the shovel against the counter and squints, making change, sliding it across the counter in a heap instead of counting it out.

"Pardon?" Ferguson asks.

"Water's gone." The old man rips off a length of tape then smooths it around the handle. "Cove's drained right now. To kill the lilies."

Ferguson turns to look at his companions. Rahm and Tana look up from the souvenir display.

"Well fuck me," Rahm says.

The old man pins Rahm with a look that makes him glad he's not alone.

"Let them lilies go cause they looked purty," Cutshaw says to Rahm, as if accusing him of the decision. "Reckon y'all never counted on it clogging up your docks."

Lish turns away with a loud sigh.

"Guess the water skiing will be a little rough, then," Ferguson says, all charm.

"Won't be no skiers," Cutshaw says. "Be some diggers, though. Town of Mallard. Covered up when they made Center Hill Lake. Now it's back in the open and damn fools digging all over it, trying to find stuff they couldn't leave fast enough fifty years ago." He stands the shovel on its handle and spins it between his palms. "I bet some would rather pay than dig."

He nods at a cleared section of shelf in the souvenir section. A hand-lettered sign reads *Sooveneers from the Sunken City*. He trains his look on Lish's legs and rips off another length of tape.

Ferguson shifts into the old man's sight line.

"Well, you're a real entrepreneur, aren't you?" Ferguson says, voice cold. The old man's face reddens, but he meets the young man's stare.

"Been called worse," Cutshaw growls.

The other three move quickly toward the door, Lish grabbing a handful of Ferguson's knit polo and pulling.

The four return to the Lexus and stand for a moment without speaking. Rahm breaks the silence.

"Well, I could shoot that scene without changing a word."

"Dammit," Ferguson says, eyeing his paddleboard, fishing gear and scuba equipment. He can barely imagine a weekend without all the busy activities a doctor's son expects of relaxation.

"Lakebed might be interesting," Lish says, unconvinced.

Rahm is cheering up. "We should dig out there, too! Might find something magic!"

"Or something contagious," Tana says, determined to lower expectations.

"Better ice the beer, anyway," Ferguson says.

The rain starts to fall.

The house, a post-modern chalet dropped into the Tennessee hills, embarrasses Tana further. Steep gables and stone face the road, announcing "Members Only" to the locals. A back wall of glass, framed in steel to show off the lake, today offers a panoramic view of a gray desert swept with sheets of rain.

"Whoa. The wasteland," Rahm says.

"Eww, you need to fire your maid," Lish says, sweeping dust from a chair with the back of her hand.

Tana decides to quit apologizing and just do what she came to do. She sets up her laptop by the glass wall, poised to take notes on her tablet while Ferguson and Rahm carry the beer cooler and food inside.

Rahm plops into a chair beside her. "You want Season Two," he says.

"Speak up, now," Tana says. "I've got an idea, but I need your filmmaker's eye."

Lish and Ferguson stand behind them, beers in hand, until Andrea shoves a screwdriver into a zombie's eye.

"Hell, yes," Ferguson says.

"I don't know how you can watch that stuff," Lish says, and collapses onto her one clean chair to stare at her phone.

Ferguson wanders into the kitchen, grabs a bag of chips, and sits next to Lish until Rahm lights a joint. Then he pulls a chair between Tana and Rahm, crunching chips and chuckling whenever walkers go down. He is snoring before Episode Three begins.

The rain blows in sheets until dark, then dies back to a steady patter.

"Skip to Episode Seven now," Rahm says. "The most tragic scene in television history."

Lish sighs and tosses her phone aside. She stands, stretches, and drifts over to the dark glass wall, listening to the gentle drizzle. The others have already snapped and posted pictures of the empty lakebed, but Lish finds it disturbing, like a naked corpse in public. On the autopsy table, surrounded by instruments of analysis, okay, but not out there where people water ski. Some sights (her mind pulls stubbornly at this) ought not to be seen, surely. Was it good to watch screwdrivers gouging people's eyes?

"Shane is *pissed*," Ferguson says, wakened by the gunfire.

"Watch Carol," Rahm says.

The gunfire stops and Lish hears a faint *splosh* that doesn't sound like rain. An animal? But they'd take shelter from the rain, wouldn't they?

There again.

"It's the little girl," Rahm whispers reverently.

Lish finds the switch to the outside floodlights and flicks it on. "Jesus!" she yells, jumping backwards.

"It's just a movie, babe," Ferguson says.

"No, it isn't!"

She points to Fleetus Cutshaw, framed by silvery slivers of floodlit raindrops.

The other three scramble to their feet as the muddy homunculus waves a stiff arm and staggers up the back steps to the French doors.

"What the everlasting *fuck*," Ferguson says, still holding the bag as the last chips patter to the floor.

"The door," Rahm half-whispers, unfreezing Tana, who takes three giant steps and clicks the dead bolt home, standing face to face with the thing through the French doors as it swings its arm forward. It's holding something, and Tana throws up her arms to shield her face from shards of glass that are surely coming when the things smashes the glass door, but it doesn't. There's a click as the object in its hand, apparently a glass jar, taps the door once, twice, three times, and anyone can see that the grisly thing is knocking.

Discussion about what to do doesn't last long because no one knows what to say. Rahm shoots it all with his phone: the wide, questioning eyes, the mumbled half-words, the motions and countermotions. The soft patter of rain against the silence of four people confronting the impossible. Scientific curiosity wins out.

"He doesn't look dangerous," Lish says.

"He?" Ferguson says.

The other three back away, but no one protests as Lish unlocks the door and guides Fleetus by his desiccated hand, the one that isn't solidly welded around a Mason jar. Fleetus stops when he sees the laptop, running Episode Eight, and pulls his hand away from Lish. She brings him a chair and he sits, completely absorbed, while she examines him with pre-med cool. He is barely more than a skeleton with a thin layer of leathery flesh, which the rain has restored to a pliable greenish brown. He makes no response as Lish prods his chest, bends his arm.

Rahm cautiously moves forward with his phone.

"This is going out live, people," he says, flipping the screen to himself. "No special effects. Happening right now, Lake Mallard, Tennessee. This guy just walked out of the woods, and now he's watching *The Walking Dead!* He's better behaved than the walkers, though." Rahm flips the screen back and moves in closer as Lish continues her exploration. Leathery tendons, gurgling breath, ruined but active eyes.

Fleetus is delighted, though he is having trouble saying so. He would like to tell these people how great it is to finally move. How he patiently let the rain soak him until his brittle elbows bent, then lurched up with a liberating slosh. He would like to tell how whole he felt slogging across the lakebed, how much a part of this new landscape. He recognized nothing but loved everything.

Fleetus had not been all that crazy about his previous life. It was all right; he knew nothing else, but mostly he was bored a lot. He did chores, fought with his brothers for meager extras, dodged his parents when they fought, and daily stared, unimpressed, at hill country, which did not fill him with romantic raptures. It merely stared back with a numbing sameness punctuated by flurries of violence.

Then came the jar of moonshine and this world unlike anything he has ever heard of. These are rich people, good-looking like movie stars, and their house is a palace. Their TV is small but has the best picture he's ever seen. The Cutshaws' TV had sat unrepaired for two years, a hulking box that hummed when you turned it on.

Fleetus works his leathery jaws, eager to communicate.

"Listen," Lish says. A sticky rattling from Fleetus' throat.

"Is he talking?" Rahm asks, moving in close.

Fleetus beckons Lish closer with the hand still holding the Mason jar. She puts her ear next to the hole that was his mouth.

"What's he saying?" Ferguson asks.

"Sounds like…" Lish's brow wrinkles. "Sounds like 'I got shit-faced!'"

Odell Cutshaw pours his archeological haul from a cardboard box onto the kitchen table and pokes at the mud-caked objects. He's been hoping they would look more interesting under better light, but they still look like a bunch of junk.

Maybe cleaning them off will help. He gets a rag, a bucket of water, and a wire brush. He spends five minutes cleaning the caked mud off a round something, which turns out to be a bicycle sprocket. Twenty minutes on a broken oar. Five minutes on an intriguing shape that turns out to be plastic six-pack rings wadded together and tied with rusty wire.

"Bullshit!" he spits.

Odell needs a big score on this. His nest money is a subsistence trickle, and his business is dying out. New roads have passed him by and goddam Mini Marts all over. The lake drained for a whole year will keep the handful of houses in this cove empty. He wonders for the hundredth time how his dumb shit cousin Pascal got control of the soft drink distribution about the lake. The last time they ran into each other, Pascal was wearing clothes that would have got him beat up for queer in high school. His wife had called Odell "Sunshine." Their boy had been so goddam polite, standing all straight and shaking hands, that Odell felt like a retard. Everybody's nice to you but nobody wants you around.

Odell stands up, stretches, and goes out on the back porch. The rain has finally stopped, and tree frogs are shrilling away, happy as they can be. The cat is sprawled under his porch swing, smug and dry. Odell hefts the wadded-up plastic in his hand and zings the cat right in the face with it. His angry yowl gives Odell no satisfaction.

Ferguson wanders into the kitchen next morning to make some coffee. He halts at the sight of Fleetus at the sink, absorbed in filling his empty mason jar with water and then pouring it all over himself.

"May I?" he asks, holding up the coffee carafe.

Fleetus fixes his empty sockets on Ferguson, then stands aside with a polite gurgle.

"Holy shit," Lish says, watching from the door.

"He's got manners," Ferguson says. The carafe filled, he swings the faucet back to Fleetus.

"He's got *intelligence*. Of some kind. Knows he can't afford to dry out." She taps at her phone, adding to her notes.

"What does your dad say?" Tana slumps into a chair at the kitchen table.

"He says we'd better be careful who we show the video to."

"But he believes you, at least." This is Rahm, breakfast joint in hand. "Shit, all my friends are saying 'Great effects, dude!'"

"Dad knows I don't play games," Lish says.

Hot morning sun raises steam from the rain-soaked lakebed. Odell Cutshaw slogs through mud nearly up to his knees. Digging is all but impossible, even if he knew where to start. He is utterly lost. Mallard was razed to its foundations in 1965, but Odell had a brainstorm—find the bank. He thinks he remembers it had a basement—maybe some money left. Two days ago, he found a cluster of foundations that had to be downtown, but all the landmarks he picked out to find them again have been smoothed to a featureless gray by the rain.

It hits him all at once, how stupid he's been. He can't remember which direction his family's property was from downtown. He can't remember what his house looked like. Trying to remember brings back troublesome pictures of his mother crying about something. He pushes those memories back. He won't remember that his mother died grieving over his little brother. He won't remember Fleetus at all. All he remembers is the government goon who paid his daddy more than the land was worth, and his daddy using the money to open the store. That's all.

He looks at the tarp he brought to haul his treasures in, spreads it out on the mud, and plops down to get his wind before slogging back to the store. He looks at piers jutting up out of the mud at the waterline. Beyond them, mansions closed up for the rest of the year. Silence as big as the lakebed. Except for faint voices. Screams and gunshots—a TV.

Somebody is here. Those college kids.

Odell Cutshaw—sweaty, mud-covered soldier of fortune. He doesn't exactly mean to spy on the kids and eavesdrop. He just wants to get to the road, a shorter and easier way back to the store. But he's exhausted from the climb up to the house and sits for a minute to get his wind. They sure are arguing loud now, almost drowning out the TV, and he gets curious.

"It's too important. Science needs to know about it." The pretty girl.

"But if head of surgery doesn't trust the research team…" The tattooed girl.

"Dad just said to be careful. It's administrators he doesn't trust, not the research guys."

"I say we call CNN. Screw the hospital." The stuck-up boy that paid for the ice.

Both girls jump on that. "Oh, because the info-tainment machine is *so* trustworthy."

"I don't want to get wrapped up in some media shit show! This is historic. It belongs to science. Right, Lish?"

"You just want to see yourself on TV, Ferg. Admit it!" The other boy, the Arab-looking one that cussed.

"Don't call me Ferg! And you just want your video to go viral!"

"It's already gone viral. *A thousand hits!* And climbing." That shuts them all up for a minute. "We need to decide something quick. My post gave our location."

Pressed against the wall under an open window, Odell grinds his teeth. These bastard kids have found something! And now they're about to take it out of here.

"Go check on him," Ferg says. "Rahm, help me rig something to keep him from drying out in the car."

Odell scoots along the wall, following the footsteps, till he reaches the big room with the glass wall, where the TV sounds are coming from.

"You doing okay?" the girl asks, then Odell hears a faint gurgle. The girl calls to the others as she walks out of the room. "If we can prop up the laptop, he'll be happy."

Keeping low, Odell crawls up the steps to the French doors and looks in. What he sees hits like physical force and rolls him off the steps.

He presses his back to the wall and hugs his knees, his heart racing scary fast. He stares through the trees at the empty lakebed, long buried thoughts erupting like bats from a cave. Stories they scared him with when he was a boy, the things in that lake. Ghosts of Indians slipping out of their graves deep under the water, pulling night fishermen out of their boats. Flickering lights in the marshy coves, souls of lynched slaves hunting their killers. Catfish big enough to swallow a man whole, prowling the deepest water at the base of the dam. His daddy angrily claiming the catfish were real, because he "almost caught one."

Odell tries to slow his breathing. These are the woods he grew up in. He suddenly sees where downtown Mallard stood, between this ridge and the opposite one. He hunted squirrels here. Right here you stood level with the church steeple. His house was that way, to the left. And to the right, about a hundred yards away, the cave.

Odell spreads his tarp open. He'll have to work quick, while the kids are loading the car. He slips into the sun porch, leaving the door open, and pauses in front of the thing that looks like a boy but can't be a boy. It ignores Odell; the laptop has it spellbound. Odell will have to touch it, but he's never been flinchy.

Let Odell clean the fish; he don't mind.

He grabs the thing by its upper arms and lifts. It's light.

The front door slams and two kids come in, still arguing.

Odell steps out the door and releases his left hand to pull the door closed. The thing dangles, wiggles. Odell holds it close. It smells like musky lake bottom. Like Odell himself, coated in mud to his waist. He's left muddy prints on the tile, but nothing he can do about that now.

"We'll have to get him and the laptop together," a voice says, getting closer.

Odell lays the thing on the tarp and rolls it up. It can't move now, and it doesn't yell. Not enough mouth to yell.

Odell crouches, holding his treasure close, and runs. The cave is about a hundred yards to the right. The cave opening is deep under a limestone outcropping that looks like a boulder. You have to wiggle under a good ways. That's where him and his brothers would hide out when they cut school or Daddy was looking to whip them.

Odell is bigger than he was in high school, but he can still make it, wedged between rough limestone above and mud below, dragging the tarp behind him. The cave mouth widens about ten yards in, and he scoots the tarp inside. He hears the kids yelling and slogging through wet leaves. They won't stay at it long, he'd bet money on it.

Odell is scratching on a piece of paper, trying out different headings for his sign, when the SUV pulls up outside. He turns to the shelves and pretends to count cans.

The bell above his door rings and the kids come in, heading for the drink cooler.

"Don't sweat it, babe. No proof is no proof, right?"

Odell steals glances at the kids. They look sweaty and tired, twigs and burrs clinging to their clothes. The pretty girl shrugs the guy's hand off her shoulder.

"We should have looked longer," the Arab boy says.

"We'd end up lost in those woods," the other boy says. "I'm driving back to Nashville. You want to stay and look, stay and look."

He's getting mad. None of the others answer. The boy exhales through his nose, disgusted. Strides to the counter and flips a ten-dollar bill at Odell.

"How about it, Boomer?" he sneers. "Find any treasures out there?" Glares at him, daring him to say something.

But Odell just grins. He doesn't need to argue. "Only treasure around here," he says, smoothing out the ten and placing it neatly in the cash drawer, "is what you folks bring in."

The boy stares. He's trying real hard to think. He turns to the others.

"You guys coming or what?"

The pretty one pulls a can from the case and pops it open. "You know, Ferguson," she says, "I give you one more semester before you flunk out of pre-med and change your major to business." She slams the door on her way out and he follows, face as dumb as a feeder cow's.

The other two lean against the drink case, watching them go. "I'm sorry about your paper," the boy says.

She gives him a smile. "I think I've got it. It's not Carol I want. It's the little girl in the barn."

"Sophie!" His face lights up.

"She's a symbol of imprisoned femininity, dead because the Sheriff abandoned her. Carol grows into a warrior while her little girl is locked in the barn with relics of the old world."

"That's amazing, Tana!"

She smiles bigger. These two, Odell thinks, will be going at it before long.

She puts her hand on his arm before he opens the door. "What about your video?"

He shakes his head. "Guess I get credit for turning something real into something fake. Sort of the way film works, anyway." She holds onto his arm with both hands as they walk to the car.

Odell waits until the sound of the SUV fades away, then flips over the "Closed" sign and walks out back to the old chicken coop. He steps over the extension cord and water hose snaking under the fence, opens the gate and watches Fleetus in his lawn chair with the hose held over his head. All Odell had to do was show him the running hose and he walked right in there, plopping down on the rusty chaise lounge in front of the TV and Odell's dusty VCR he found in the junk room. He's watching a fuzzy copy of *Walking Tall*. Not that sucky re-make with the wrestler, but the good one with Joe Don Baker. Odell met the real Buford Pusser once at the Springfield County Fair and the actor looked a little bit like Joe Don. Same hair, anyway.

Something real into something fake. No shit.

Odell looks up at the cloudless sky. The afternoon is getting hot. He checks that the coop door is locked and turns off the hose.

Fleetus doesn't feel any pain as the moisture goes, just the brittle surety that the slightest movement can break off a piece of him. But the man is careful, stretching him out flat while he is still pliable, tying him with twine, and moving him inside. The lamp he puts up stays on all the time, even at night, turning the air into a bright hot prison.

Fleetus watches the store change; more and more people come in. The man puts him into a glass case and installs a big TV in the corner of the ceiling—a kind of salvation for Fleetus, because it's right in his sight line. The TV cycles through four pictures, over and over, and one of them is just for him. He can see himself clearly in the glass case with the sign over it.

Mallard Mummey —2000 B.C.

Gas pump, front door, counter, Fleetus.

Now and then, when no customers are around, the man stands beside his glass case and talks to him. He likes Fleetus, tells him he brought the store back to life. Sometimes he turns off the lamp, opens the case, and pours a pitcher of water along the length of his body. He can't let Fleetus get too dry.

Fleetus likes the feel of the water and wishes he could move around. He wishes he could talk to the man. He's bursting to tell someone about his amazing adventures.

He got shit-faced. He met rich people. He wound up on TV.

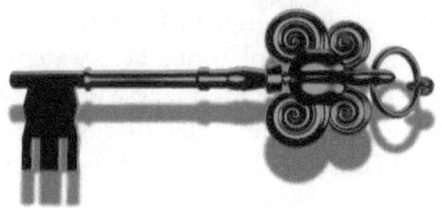

From the Author

Growing up in Tennessee, I enjoyed cheap electricity and lake life, thanks to TVA dams. I also got to watch roads and towns disappear under water as the streams backed up. Modest country houses got swallowed, and McMansions popped up in their place. "Dead Season" (first draft in 1995) began as a piece of 80's nostalgia growing from an off-hand thought: "What if zombies were nice, even lovable, instead of rabid flesh-eaters?" But the cultural clash, obscure country people versus summer house rich, wormed its way into the story.

Years passed and zombies reanimated in pop culture. *28 Days Later* (2002) begat *Dawn of the Dead* (2004) and endless others. "Dead Season" went through lots of revisions to accommodate the change, but Fleetus and his embittered brother remained throughout. Who we are, where we come from—these persist, no matter how the surrounding landscape changes.

My writing inhabits many genres: crime, fantasy, horror, sci-fi, and hard to categorize (like "Dead Season"). Culture clash and time's relentless advance, however, show up again and again. If you like "Dead Season," check out my web page, davidlpowell.net. You'll find free reads as well as paper and ink with cool cover art by award-winning artists.

About the Author

David Powell has taught school, directed plays, played music and portrayed zombies, but now he writes full-time, seeking out the pockets of chaos brewing in the corners of the grid. You can find his writings in *HWA Poetry Showcase Volume 6*, *Shotgun Honey*, and other online zines, and three anthologies. Links can be found at his website, davidlpowell.net. You can see his zombie portrayal in Dance of the Dead (an extra, but hey—what zombie isn't?) and hear his acting on *Pseudopod* and the horror podcast Archive 81.

Omega0
by
C. Dan Castro

Omega0

Dude

Hey

Dude I know you're there

Worked on Omega0 all night.

All night?

All night. Then couldn't sleep thanks to a relentless, recurring nightmare. Then finally fell asleep. And here we are.

I have to demonstrate Omega0 to my corporate sponsor on Thursday.

THURSDAY??!!!

Schedule moved up. Demonstration Thursday. And no time to test beforehand.

Damn. And I thought you were about to get lucky in love

???

Your classified ad

??????

From June, 1999

I was two in 1999.

A ladies man even then. Check it out. Steve Wasser advertising that he's not Steve Wasser but resembles an unknown actor named, wait for it...Steve Wasser

> **Scientist Seeks Mate**—If you
> love long talks on significant
> subjects, and all things Boston,
> please write. I'm not poor, not
> unkind, not bad to look at (like
> Steve Wasser in my favorite
> movie, OMEGA). NOT unable to
> be caring and honest.   4334 ✉
>
> **In Search Of Long Term**—I am a

Seeks mate? Sounds like I'm just looking for
a friend.

> **Oh you Brits and your "mates." Listen up,
> mate, I think you placed this ad and used
> my American lingo to attract a lady**

At the age of two. And why are you looking
at classified ads from...1999?

Oh, this is for your Ph.D.

You're getting a fud for this??!!

> **It's the DEFINITIVE review of classified
> ads in Boston post-Civil War, and what it
> tells us about American history and culture**

> **And hey, at least I'm not getting a doctorate
> for making lights blink**

MY doctorate is about particle entanglement
and getting a photon to link with an anti-
temporal photon.

> **Blinky lights**

It has vast ramifications in computers,
communications, and myriad other fields.

Myriad blinky lights. Does that fancy lingo help you get grant money?

Yes. Yes it does. You should try it.

So are you still denying you placed that ad for love?

I WAS TWO!!! And now, I'm going to go have breakfast.

Good lord. Make that dinner. Then back to work.

Okay. Good luck. Remember, blinking LED lights are very cheap now, so you might want to do something else for your fud

Thank you, Nowhere Man.

WED, JUN 8, 2:15 PM

You are NOT the man I thought you were

I can take a brief break from my work, which is important, unlike that of some other individuals whom I won't mention.

What are you bablexting about?

Bablexting?

Babble texting. My newest word invention.

You Brits have no flair for language. I blame it on your ancestors for refusing to follow Webster's rules. Colour instead of color? Really?

So I'll be getting back to work now.

Check out this ad you placed

> MY WIFE DEPARTED my bed and board. I will not be responsible for bills contracted by any other than myself as of June 9, 1976. Steve Wasser, 5 N Sign St., Boston, MA.

By my math, I was NEGATIVE 21 years old.

Is that an American way of getting a divorce?
Is it even legal?

> **Maybe and no. But American men tried it for a long time. Including you. Check out this other one**

> My wife, Signora **N.** Jacinta Wasser, having left my Boston bed and board, I will not be responsible for any bills by her.
>   STEVE WASSER.
> Jun. 9, 1930.

> **Hopefully no woman was foolish enough to answer your 1999 "caring and honest" clad**

> **Clad. Classified ad. See? I can massacre the language too**

For the record, there are a LOT of Steve Wassers in the world.

And "clad" is dreadful.

How goes Omega0?

Simulations are saying it should run without issue, but my advisor has a concern.

It's pretty technical stuff.

Remember, my M.S. degree was on the quantum mechanical achievements of Schrodinger, Einstein, and more

Brilliant. So the project involves entangling a photon with a second photon. By employing some Feynman principles, we pair a photon moving forwards in time with one moving backwards.

Still with me?

Whoa whoa whoa. Slow down...

You're working on a project?

So I'm going to go now.

OK, sorry, seriously though. Photons moving backward in time?

It's a Feynman concept. And we think we can prove it.

Through entanglement

Correct. Imagine we shoot a photon, and it goes forwards in time. With special detectors and the equivalent of a camera, we can watch its waveform.

OK

Before the photon leaves our detection zone, we entangle it with the second photon. It's

87

orchestrated so it's travelling back in time, we
think, and the entanglement means the
quantum state of one influences the other.
We can harness that to align minute portions
of their waveforms.

Still there?

> **I have to admit, my M.S. was more on the
> history of those scientists, rather than their
> achievements**
>
> **But go ahead. Tell me what happens after
> waveform alignment. That's where the
> peaks and troughs of the two particle-like
> waves overlap?**

EXACTLY! And those increases due to
overlap should be detectable.

> **Blinky lights**

Sure. Blinky lights.

> **But, what would you actually detect? The
> particle traveling alone, or the two particles
> entangled with greater energy?**

Both. We'd have a detector for the original
photon's flight, and a second detector for the
entangled flight. The difference is the first
detector is in a Rodriguez Quantum Faraday
Cage. Two detectors analysing the same
situation, but coming up with different
outcomes AT THE SAME TIME.

> **Shit, dude**
>
> **But wait. Your advisor said there's maybe a
> problem?**

It relates to relativistic mass. Photons are so
small, and so fast, we might not be able to
detect the entangled waveforms. It will be
such a brief series of flashes--DON'T SAY

BLINKY LIGHTS--then the particles will
de-entangle. Events might be at the
attoseconds scale, and we need closer to
femtoseconds.

> **And you can't change the photon's mass or
> speed, so either it works or it doesn't**
>
> **Or now you're going to tell me that you
> CAN change one of those variables, and I'll
> just be putting in that call to the Nobel
> Prize committee for you right now**

Alas, we cannot. If we had more time, we'd
entangle something larger. Slower.

> **Like a Chevy Durango. Or perhaps a small
> child**

LOL. We could potentially use anything for
the particle moving forwards, yes. Even not a
particle. But the energy requirement would
be vast.

We're thinking a neutron.

But we don't have time now to pursue this
option.

I must go. Stress is rising just thinking about
what's left to do.

> **Good luck dude. You're doing awesome
> work. Even if I only understand an
> attogram's worth**

THU, JUN 9, 7:45 AM

Good morning.

Well, technically.

This is revenge for me waking you the other day, isn't it?

I need a bit of good news. If you have some.

OK. Let me just remember who I am. Where I am

OK, got it. Here, found another ad which might amuse you

BOSTON, TO BE LET.

A three story DWELLING HOUSE, locate on R Sign Street. June 9, 1907.
Apply to Mr. STEVE WASSER, Bignell Street.

Looks like you're letting out a house. Maybe because you're marriage to N. Jacinta Wasser is falling apart already

And here's one from 1953. Which doesn't speak well for the woman you'll eventually dump in 1976

FOR SALE—Boston house to be moved. 4 rooms and bath. Good rent property. Call Steve Wasser at 252W or see at 121 O Sign Street.

I can't deny this second one. In my defence,
I was negative 44 years old. And young.

But admit you made up that first one.

> **No, it's real. And don't tell me what
> negative age you were in 1907**

LOL. But it's truly real? That little house
cartoon? The misspelling? The date?

> **Swear on my heart it's real**

> **That cartoon gets used for many clads in
> that era**

> **There is a paper to be written on how the
> language has changed throughout the
> decades in clads. Although "locate" might
> be a typo**

> **And the date...what's wrong with the date?**

You've shown me 5 of your horribly named
clads. (Don't use that term in your thesis.)
And three of them fall on June 9?

> **Huh. Looking at so many clads that I
> didn't notice. Wait, let me check something**

> **Tell me what's going on in the meanwhile.
> You usually sleep like a guilty man**

It's stupid, really. And I know how early it is
there.

> **No, tell me. I need to look something up
> anyway**

It's about a dream I had.

> **OK. I thought it was going to be another
> technical issue**

Maybe it is.

......

That's a long pause, my friend. Just tell it

I've had the same dream every night for two
weeks now. Each night it becomes clearer.
And the threat grows.

Threat?

......

**And DON'T type never mind, it's silly, etc.
I can tell by your pauses that you're
hesitating**

Out with it man!

In the dream, there are these creatures.
Shadows. Out of phase with us but very
close. And sometimes the distance between
us fades to almost nothing.

They are intelligent.

They study us.

They despise us.

But when the barrier between us is thickest,
they cannot see us. These gaps happen on a
regular basis, and they fear them. Fear we
might plan against them during the gaps.

But we can't leave any records. Any details
beyond our thoughts would be detected by
them when the gap thins again.

The barrier is thickening right now. Almost
at its max.

But the shadows are aware of Omega0.

And interested.

That's creepy

And they're aware of me.

OK, that's worse

And you.

Wait, why am I getting dragged into this?

The nightmare has become so unnerving,
I'm actually a bit daunted regarding turning
on Omega0.

It's like I'm about to open

......

A door?

A door.

Pandora's box.

A bottle with a vicious genie.

And once it's open, it can't be shut.

To be fair, I don't know whether the
creatures want it open or not.

They just radiate pure malice.

**You texted those barriers thin and thicken
on a regular basis**

Yes.

**I just looked up the other two clads. The
ones without dates. They were also in
papers dated June 9**

I really need to know if you're pulling some
weird American prank on me. Really.

I SWEAR TO GOD I AM NOT

I've got an Omega0 meeting. Let me ponder
all this. I'll get back to you in a couple hours.

Your meeting over? I have good news

Need some.

OK. I have finished downloading all the clads. A term I won't employ in my thesis. Probably. I used an OCR search and found two more of your ads

---

$50 REWARD.

STOLEN SIGN with the capital letter T.

STEVE WASSER.

Boston.

Jun. 9, 1861

LOST AND FOUND.

FOUND ADRIFT IN BOSTON HARBOR, one "U" sign, painted green, ten feet long. Inquire at Steve Wasser's, Quincy Market.

The date on the second one is June 9, 1884

This is good news?

I've sent you a total of 7 clads. Look at them from oldest to newest

Because...

C'mon, Sherlock Holmes runs in your veins. Just look at them, oldest to newest

It'll take you 2 minutes

I'll wait

And let me know what you find

All involve Steve Wasser of Boston.

They're all from June 9.

They all contain "sign" as a word or part of a larger one.

What am I missing?

All but the last ad involve single, capital letters. And in order, the phrases are

letter T

letter "U"

R Sign Street

N. Jacinta Wasser

O Sign Street

N Sign St

Put the capitals together

T U R N O N, or spaced differently, TURN ON

And the last clad?

See how many times "not" appears? And that's when I thought about you wacky Brits, and how you'll say "Nought" instead of "Zero". Which makes your Omega0 project not Omega Zero, but...

OMEGA NOUGHT

Just like that clad's capitalized words, "OMEGA). NOT"

Sorry. That's "capitalised" in your crude language

TURN ON OMEGA NOT.

Exactly!

A message hidden in clads across hundreds of years. On dates where the barrier is thickest. To evade an enemy we cannot see.

You typed it, not me. I don't want to get committed

Thank you, my friend.

Your welcome

Do we need to discuss this more?

No. It's almost certainly just a large, weird coincidence.

You once told me good scientists don't believe in coincidence

Then the less records we leave, the better.

Understood. But this is all batshit crazy

I feel like we should tell the authorities or something

Today, I think we are the authorities.

Okay. Not another word then

Agreed.

I'm on my way to our corporate sponsor's HQ. My Uber is almost there. I've spent so much time talking about my work, I forgot to ask how yours is going.

No worries dude. My research is going o-kay, except my advisor is so excited about the work, he wants to expand it to earlier than the Civil War

Scope creep.

Yup. Which would be fine, but the quality of newspapers before 1861 degrades a lot. That means a shinola ton of manual work to read and catalog the ads

We're here. I must go. Thank you again.

You'll turn on Omega0

Yes. One more hour-long meeting.

Then it's go time.

THU, JUN 9, 11:22 AM

Hey, I know you're in your big meeting. I found two more clads, but the hidden message is unchanged

Here are the clads

BOSTON, *June* 9 1769.
STEVE WASSE , Inventor,
has for sale a sign with a
giant letter, D.

> ## FOR SALE,
> Sign with a giant letter, O.
> Contact Steve Waffer,
> No. 45, Bignell Street.
> *Bofton, MA, Jun. 9, 1792.*

So you add D and O

DO TURN ON OMEGA NOT

Bofton? Waffer?

Yeah, it's something particular to that era. Maybe a font thing for that newspaper

Tell me later.

Rodriguez just walked in!

AWESOME!

Good luck dude! Let me know how it goes

MON, JUN 9, 12:14 PM

DO NOT TURN ON OMEGA0

I REPEAT

DO NOT TURN ON OMEGA0

I've tried calling twice, left you a message. Now I'm texting. You there?

I looked at the dates. They're not just repeating on June 9. They're intervals of 23 years

I realized this when I found two almost illegible clads for June 9

One was 1815. You can make out the "Wass" and "N" in the water-damaged print

The other is 1838, with an "asser" and "Boston" and "T Street" legible

DONT TURN ON OMEGA NOT

Please tell me you're there. You're receiving this. You're not answering because you're pulling a prank on your Yank friend

The sky

The sky is turning black

It's midday and the sky

Please tell me you didn't turn on Omega0

Please

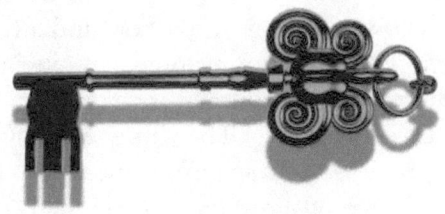

From the Author

My m.o. has long been to author a story, then find a market for it. But recently, I contemplated swimming in a different pool: watch for story requests, then write something to the specific requirements, including a (gulp) deadline.

I dipped my toes into the shallow end. Here and there I got some drabbles published, including one called "Simian Testing." It's a brutal, nasty piece, but what do you expect from a drabble in an anthology named *Pestilence*?

Worked up to immersing my knees when I wrote a serial drabble: four separate, creepy, but very related pieces in the *666* anthology.

The writing waters got deeper.

Approached my (ahem) nether regions.

It was decision time.

Keep wading in with the inevitable "Eeeek!"? Or dive in and hopefully surface to yell a guttural sound meaning "what the hell was I thinking!!!?"

Tough decision.

An e-zine provided the decision-driving challenge: write a short story *without* standard prose. One could write an epistolary work, but they recommended not doing that, either.

I dove in.

My immediate thought: write a texted conversation between two friends. It allows for humor, pathos, and any emotion that fits the story. But I also wanted to include an older communication method to contrast the texting.

I chose classified ads. The little advertisements have coursed through U.S. newspapers since the late 1700s. I researched them, learned how their format and content ebbed and flowed over 2+ centuries, and created my own. Experiments with font, design, and even drawing went into the final work.

I submitted my story.

One month later, it was rejected.

Glub! Going down, no lifeguard to save me.

But I wanted to swim. Editors often reject good work for a multitude of reasons (too similar to other works; doesn't mesh well with other stories; etc.). And maybe I could improve

"Omega0"? Perhaps the difficult deadline prevented me from submitting the best work it could be?

I re-read, reconsidered, and regurgitated. Well, not that third one. But the first two, yes.

I still liked the texting. No changes needed. But the ads themselves? A little too much overlap. I replaced one ad, tweaked the others' words.

I kicked hard to surface, found a new market, and submitted "Omega0." Most publications won't use stories with pictures. If I were rejected again, I might have to replace all advertisements with no drawings, no font/design variations, and straight text only. Stripping out those details, I feared, would strip out half the story's fun.

Fortunately, second time was the charm. My thanks to Sam and Knight Writing Press for giving "Omega0" a home.

And reader, dive into my story. The water is warm.

About the Author

Dan Castro enjoys writing mystery and crime stories. In 2022/3, he has stories slated for publication in *Black Cat Mystery Magazine*, *Sherlock Holmes Magazine* (UK), *Sherlock Holmes Mystery Magazine* (U.S.), and more! When not composing stories, Dan tweets writing tips (@CDanCastro43), dreams of traveling again, or studies languages to imbue his stories with *je ne sais quoi*. Whatever that means. He lives in Connecticut, where he's making a final polish on his first novel, a middle grade fantasy.

Rumpelstiltskin 2.0
by
W.O. Hemsath

Rumpelstiltskin 2.0

*T*he process for turning straw into Harvidium gold is simple. Grow the crop, let the plants absorb the trace minerals, harvest, and use a solvent to dissolve all the organic matter. Voilà. All that's left are nano-nuggets of the newly-discovered super metal, perfect for all your A.I. needs.

Well, that and a world of slowly starving humans.

Which is why Linux Steele and his tech empire must be stopped. Hence my endless efforts to hack into his system.

I take a break from the two screens in front of me to peer across the table at my boyfriend Burket, his brow furrowed beneath a mess of dark curls. "Are you ever going to tell me what you're working on?"

His keystrokes clack in random bursts like popcorn. He doesn't respond, probably lost in his code, and it's as good a chance as any.

I make a grab for his screen, trying to turn it into my line of sight. His hands shoot up, pulling the laptop out of my reach.

"Patience, Cielle."

"I swear, Internet Explorer goes faster than you."

Burket fakes a dagger to his heart and returns to typing. "I'll make you a deal," he says, not looking up from his screen. "You share your phantom code with me, and I'll tell you what I'm hacking."

"Give you my baby?" I laugh. "Counteroffer. Give me a clue, and I'll let you keep living here at my place."

"You drive a hard bargain. Your clue is that you'll love it."

I stare him down.

"Fine. Your clue is that it'll hit LinuSteele where it hurts the most."

"It's going to shut down his whole factory? Get everyone to stop relying on his stupid bots for every aspect of their lives?"

He rolls his eyes and focuses back on his screen. "You and your impossible goals."

"They're not impossible."

"Confidence is high. I repeat, confidence *is* high."

"Stop quoting that old movie and get back to work."

We type in silence for a minute more. He on whatever site I'm not allowed to know about, and I on my secondary laptop, sending phishing emails to low-level employees at Wal-mazon. If I can hack in there, I might be able to get a history of Linux's drone deliveries and find out what he buys. It's a slim chance but knowing his personal preferences might give me another lead on password parameters. I'll need them if the ones currently running on my primary computer don't pan out.

My stomach rumbles. With a sigh, I grab my five o'clock carrot stick from a nearby plate and keep working on the emails. I'd kill for a loaf of hot homemade bread right now. At least, that's what it'd take to get one on my budget these days.

Not that I blame the farmers. If a giant tech mogul offered me as much for my crop as Linux did, I'd probably ditch the mills, too. There's no way they can compete with those prices, especially not with Linux and his LinuSteele empire synthesizing "affordable alternative food" for a fraction of what it takes to grow it.

Problem is, it's crap food. Literally. Made from the proteins of human excrement kind of crap food.

The keyboard protests loudly under my angry keystrokes, and I force myself to take a calming breath. Last year was supposed to be my victory. Hacking into the FDA and uncovering Linux's mystery ingredient should have been enough. When I leaked that hidden detail of everyone's beloved Life Bars, it should have woken people up and put an end to LinuSteele's monopoly.

But no one made a stink about it. Not enough to stop buying his tech, anyway. No, the FDA just assured the world Life Bars were safe, the EPA praised Linux for finding an environmentally responsible and sustainable food source, and everyone decided they'd rather eat like dung beetles than give up the robots his soil-mining produces.

The sweet, earthy flavor of the carrot releases with each bite. It's not bread, but it's not someone's excrement either. Remembering that makes each crunch taste a little bit sweeter.

"Tic-Tac-Toe!" Burket pumps his fists in the air.

I reach for his laptop, but he slams it shut.

"You're still not going to tell me?"

His eyebrows dance playfully as he packs the laptop in its bag and slings it over his shoulder. "I'm going to show you. Tonight." He walks around and plants a quick kiss on my cheek. "But first, I've got to run some errands. I'm going to make this reveal epic."

He's out the door before I can protest. I turn back to my two laptops and my heart freezes. There's an empty dialogue box on my primary screen.

I'm in.

I'm finally through the backdoor of LinuSteele.com.

I scramble into action, attacking the keys. The search parameters I used to narrow down the brute force attack worked. The elusive password? *R@pun2el.*

I run a crawler program through the website to access the last five passwords. *H@n$e1&Grete1. Br1arRO$e. 12Bro+her$. (inder3lla. M0+herHu1da.* Wow. You'd think a tech giant like Linux would know better than to be so predictable. Then again, it's kind of brilliant. I've been searching for years. If it weren't for tracking down the children of his old childhood nanny, I certainly never would have guessed he had a penchant for fairy tales. They seem so innocent, so human—the last things anyone would associate with Linux.

I send another crawler to search every file in his network for something useful. There's got to be something worth leaking to the media in here. Security footage of a secret scandal? Clandestine communication with the government officials he holds on a short, gold-plated leash? I don't know what's worse than fecal food, but there's got to be something in here that will wake people up.

A locked file pops up on my screen. The old *12Bro+her$* password gets me in, and schematics appear for the latest model of ButlerBots with their uncanny human-like interface. It doesn't make sense why Linux locked the file though. Ads have been promoting the new androids for weeks, and he released the schematics on-line himself to boost pre-sales.

Unless, of course, those weren't the real schematics. And these are.

I scan through the images on my screen, looking for anything out of place. There are the standard features: fingerprint-coded deactivation sensor, Apate lie-detection software, high torque hydraulic motors for superhuman strength. But even the new features seem to be the same stuff everyone's been fawning over for weeks. Quantum-processor with the latest Prometheus biometrics. Hermes turbocharge graphene battery. LS500 megapixel cameras with customizable iris color.

Wait. There's something embedded behind the cooling fans. I scroll down to an alternate image from a different angle.

It's a micro-EMP, buried in the center of the bot, ready to fry every electrical component inside it. Definitely not part of the public schematics. He must have hard-coded a backdoor into their system so he can destroy any android he sells with the touch of a button from the safety of his compound. A way to make sure his products all fail after the warranty expires? How convenient. That money-hoarding pig will probably stagger all his sabotage to not draw attention to it, letting buyers think it's just regular wear and tear, time for an upgrade.

This is it. This is what will make people think twice before buying.

I'm about to download the file when the front door chimes, startling me out of my chair. A familiar whirring outside the door draws me to the windows.

It's a Wal-mazon drone with a medium-sized box, sealed in orange Flash Prime tape. It must have the wrong address because there's no way Burket or I could afford ten-minute Flash delivery. Even if we could, we wouldn't waste money on something so frivolous.

I head back to my computers, but the drone's heat sensors know I'm home, and the door chimes again. A mechanical voice calls out.

"Order P87432QX5I0 for Cielle Miller, paid by Burket Collins. Fingerprint scan required for delivery."

What?

"Screen lock," I command as I return to the door, and my screens log out to a password-protected black screen. Covering my tracks with my phantom code won't do me any good if I let some drone capture footage of me hacked into the private information of the most powerful man in the nation.

When I open the door, a small screen drops down from the belly of the drone, and I press my thumb onto it. The screen retracts, and the drone sets the box on the porch before flying away. The gaudy orange tape stares back at me as I pick it up and bring it inside. Flash Prime? What was Burket thinking?

I open the box to see not one, but three identical black, strappy dresses. No, not identical. They're all one size apart. My breath catches when I see the price tag. Eight hundred dollars? If he thinks I'm keeping any of these, he's crazy.

A small, folded paper at the bottom of the box catches my attention.

Wear whichever fits best and meet me at Chevonne's. Dinner at 7.

Chevonne's? What game is he playing? It's one of the few restaurants still serving exclusively soil-grown food. A single roll costs eighty dollars there. He's not planning an epic reveal; he's planning financial suicide.

The door chimes again. If it's another Flash Prime delivery, I'm going to scream.

But it's not a drone. It's four strange men in suits.

I stay behind the half-opened door. "Can I help—"

The first three push past me and head for my computers at the table.

"Hey!" I lunge after them, but the fourth man, still in the doorway, grabs my wrist. Twisting away does nothing but hurt my arm. He doesn't budge when I push against him. The give of his flesh and the strength of his muscles under his suit feel unnatural.

Not a man. An android.

Two of the others close my laptops while the third heads into the kitchen. The fourth remains motionless, trapping me in the doorway.

"I demand to know who sent you. This is a private residence. You are not authorized to enter."

It doesn't respond. I open my mouth to scream for help but there's a pinch in my arm. The last thing I see is the fourth intruder lowering an empty syringe.

The ground beneath me is hard and cold. I sit up, squinting against the harsh white light, and something crunches and crinkles around me like dead leaves. It's my clothes. Not that you can call what I'm wearing clothes. The cream-colored medical gown is more paper than cloth. And I'm not on the ground, but a metal shelf jutting out of a concrete wall.

There's a door on the adjacent wall. The chill of the concrete floor stings my bare feet as I jump down and run.

It's locked.

A surge of panic that tastes of bile rises in my throat. I force myself to hold each rapid breath for three counts before exhaling. Then four counts. Then five. Freaking out isn't going to help. I need to focus on what I know.

I know the door slides open, not swings, because there are no visible hinges and when I run my fingers along the seam of the door, it's ever so slightly inset from the wall around it. There's a small observation window in the door but it's covered from the other side, so I know whoever locked me in here doesn't trust me enough to let me see beyond the door at all.

The room I'm in is narrow, maybe the width of three coffins, and there's nothing more than that metal shelf bed I woke up on and some squat little cylinder in the corner that looks like a dull silver tree stump. I approach it, and the center portion of the top divides into pieces that retract, releasing a nauseating wall of stench, an invisible tsunami of festering human waste. I back away, nose and mouth buried in my paper sleeve. The lid of the tankless toilet thankfully reseals, allowing me to breathe again.

Who has a motion-sensor toilet that doesn't flush?

I feel around the walls on the front side of the room for seams, panels, anything. But there's nothing. Just solid wall. A domed light protrudes from the center of the ceiling, with about an inch of space around it acting as an air vent. If I could get up there, maybe I could get my hand in the gap, pull down the light fixture and escape through the duct work. But the bed and toilet are bolted down, and there's nothing I can stand on to reach that high. Maybe if I stood on the bed and jumped, I could catch my fingers on the lip of the fixture and use my body weight to detach it? No, even if it worked, I'd have to make another jump in order to get up into whatever space was behind the light, which would be improbable under normal circumstances, but impossible in the dark once I'd disconnected the lights.

The lack of clues or help in my surroundings gives rise to a new wave of panic. Think, Cielle, think. What else do you know? How did you get here?

I pace the front of the room, replaying my abduction in my mind. Four human-looking men, at least one of which was an android. And not just any android. He— no, *it*—was so life-like. The skin had wrinkles and moles. The nose was slightly crooked. It had all the tell-tale imperfections of humanity in perfect proportions.

It had to be one of Linux's newest BulterBots. They aren't scheduled to release for another month, which means it was sent by Linux himself.

That's why toilet doesn't flush. He's harvesting ingredients.

My stomach churns at the thought, silencing my gnawing hunger pains. It must be well after seven. Burket would've realized something was wrong when I never showed. He's probably looking for me already. Maybe a neighbor's security feed caught the abduction, and he'll find a way to get me out.

But why would Linux abduct me? How could he even know I hacked him? My phantom code makes me invisible. The host never knows I'm there, never knows what I looked at or downloaded. Besides, I hadn't even downloaded anything yet, so there was no way I picked up a tracing virus.

Someone must have tipped them off that I'd be trying. Someone from the forums maybe?

At least they have no proof. My computers were locked when they took them, my hard drives are encrypted, and my freshly reset password is as random and secure as anyone can get. I never wrote it down and only memorized the nonsensical string of letters and numbers with the help of a lengthy mnemonic device I never said aloud. All the software is my own design, so there are no backdoors from the original programmer to let them in. It would take a quantum processor five years to brute force its way in and see what I was up to. Not that a lack of proof would stop someone like Linux from illegally detaining me, but it's an angle I have to try unless I want to be jumping in the dark at holes in the ceiling.

I scan the room again. No visible cameras, but this is Linux Steele. There's no way he doesn't have some secret tech hiding in this primitive cell. He's watching me. I can feel it.

"Is someone going to tell me where I am and why I'm here?" My voice bounces back from the empty walls. I speak in turn to every wall and inanimate object that might conceal a camera. "I know I was abducted by one of the unreleased ButlerBots, so I'm pretty sure I'm in the custody of Linux Steele, and I want to know why."

I breathe in the silence like icy winter air, and it hurts. He probably wants it to, hoping it'll get me to break, to get so desperate for a response that I admit what I did. But he doesn't know who he's messing with. I throw my hands up in a melodramatic display of indifference.

"Fine, don't talk to me. But you brought me here for a reason. You want me or need me for something. How am I supposed to help if I don't know what—"

The door slides closed before I even realized it had opened. Standing in the room is the bot that abducted me, with a soft demeanor and kindly smile that reaches all the way up to its blue-gray eyes. It's unnerving how utterly human it acts. It speaks with a rich baritone voice.

"The more you cooperate, the more comfortable I can make your stay."

"Cooperate with what? I don't know why I'm here."

"Give me the password to your computer."

"Why do you need to get on my computer?"

"If you don't give me what I need to recover the funds, you will never leave this room."

The word *funds* circles my brain, unable to find a logical place to land. What is the bot talking about?

It shakes its head, light-brown hair sweeping across its brow. "Do not play dumb, Miss Miller. The breech in the National Credit was traced back to the network at your address. Unless you transfer the three billion dollars back into Mr. Steele's accounts, I am not authorized to let you leave this room."

Three billion? I step backwards into the bed, bracing myself against its hard edge.

Burket. This was his big plan.

But hitting Linux where it hurts most? Please. He's worth over a hundred billion. Losing three is annoying at best. Burket knows that. Which means he was never in it for the cause. He just wanted to pad his own wallet like a greedy black hat. And he couldn't even do it without getting caught. Stupid, sloppy Burket.

Except he didn't get caught.

I did.

My eyes clench shut. There's no way I'm as attractive to him as three billion dollars. Help isn't coming. Burket isn't out looking for me. The minute he realized what happened, he probably left town, maybe even the country.

Dealing with Burket will have to come later. First thing's first. I need to get out of this cell. I focus on the android's eyes so its lie detection software can read me clearly.

"I did not steal any money."

The bot pauses, scanning me up and down the way Burket did on our first date when he realized the infamous FDA hacker from the forums was actual a curly blond glitter-addict who loved wearing pencil skirts. The pause gives me hope. The bot knows. It knows I'm not lying.

"I will need the password to your computers to prove it."

My shoulders fall. If I give it my password, Linux will know I figured out his. He'll know I know about the micro EMP, and I'll remain detained, this time for a crime I really did commit.

"I can't do that. But I can prove I didn't steal the money. I—"

The door opens and closes before I can finish, and the bot is gone.

I race to the door and pound on it, but it doesn't even rattle.

"I didn't steal any money, but I think know who did." My shouts ricochet off the closed door. "And I can help get it back."

"Step away from the door."

The command doesn't come from the other side of the door, but a speaker somewhere above and behind me. Hidden in the lights and vent probably. Which means the camera is probably in there too.

"Step away from the door." The voice is deeper than the bot's, and I recognize it from all the commercials.

Linux.

I stay by the door, looking up at the domed light fixture. I want to scream at him, demand he let me go, but it won't do me any good. My best bet is to play to his sympathies, if he has any left.

"Mr. Steele? There's been a mistake. It seems my boyfriend is a complete scumbag who betrayed me. He stole your money without telling me and let you think I did it. Your bot ran scans on me. It knows I'm not lying. But I can help get your money back. I just need my computers to track him down."

After a moment, his stern voice fills the room again. "Step away from the door."

"But your android said if I got the money back, he'd let me—"

"Step away from the door or James can't open it."

James? I take a step back. Nothing. Two more steps back. The door opens and closes too fast for a breakaway to ever be possible. The android from before now stands in the room, holding my computers.

"Thank you, James." I reach for them, but it gestures to the bed. I sit.

"Tell me the passwords."

"And give you access to my personal intellectual property?" I address the light fixture. "That's not fair. I'm the one who has been lied to and illegally imprisoned, and I'm still offering to help you."

There's a long pause. My eyes water from staring into the light, but I keep doing it anyway. It's the closest thing to eye contact with Linux that I have, and I won't be the one to break first.

"Give her the computers."

The android turns to address the light fixture. I'm right. That's where the camera is.

"But sir—"

"What's the second directive, James?"

"Follow every instruction of Linux Steele." The android proffers the laptops.

I grab both, sit on the bed, and carefully stash the one hacked into LinuSteele.com under my legs before opening the other. If I'm going to unlock one and risk them seeing it, the phishing emails are my safest bet. With my back to the wall and the screen bent down to shield my hands from the view of James or the camera, I type the lengthy password by feel, hitting a few more random keys after I've already hit enter in case they're counting keystrokes.

A quick keyboard command closes all the windows, and when all traces of my questionable hobby are hidden, I pull the screen open to let the android see.

"I need on-line access."

"Authorize her," the light fixture says.

James gives me access, but I can't help but feel he's doing it begrudgingly. I mean, I know he's not, because androids don't have emotions. Its biomimicry programs are just freaky realistic.

Once connected, I'm tempted to send a call for help, but I can't. Not with James watching. No, I just need to find Burket, steal back the money, and then the bot said I could leave. At least, he implied it, and I have to hope it's true. While Linux *could* have designed machines that mislead or deceive, his tragic past is public knowledge, and a man scarred by betrayal would never design machines with the capacity to lie. Linux might be a lot of things, but stupid isn't one of them.

James takes a step closer, hovering over my shoulder now. Good grief. It even smells human. "I've traced the transfer to an encrypted account in the Seychelles and managed to get into their system as far as seeing a list of client names, but the account balances and other details are blocked with heavier security."

"Let me see the names."

A notification pops up in the corner of my screen and I click on the file the android transferred me. My mouth goes dry. There are thousands of names.

"James." The speaking light fixture pulls the android's attention toward it. "I've got that meeting with the Senator. If by some chance she finishes while I'm gone, let her go."

"Sir. Would it not be wiser to release her to the medical wing? I've already done her preliminary scans. She would make an excellent candidate."

Preliminary scans? That explains the paper gown. But excellent candidate for what? Why does Linux have a medical wing? And why is the bot talking about keeping me now? Didn't it say I could leave?

"No." Linux's voice cuts through my worries. "When she's done, have her sign a non-disclosure agreement, pay her for her trouble, and call a cab."

A rush of relief floods my chest. Linux does plan to let me go. Unless of course, "pay her for her trouble" is some code phrase for "kill her once you're through with her." Then again, why have me sign a non-disclosure agreement if he was just going to kill me? With a silent prayer, I start sifting through the account holder names on my screen.

I run a search for possible aliases. Anything with Burket's initials B or C. Any anagrams of his name. Anything with my name. Or his parents' names. The city he was born in. What was his childhood dog he talks about? Oh yeah, Jefferson.

I put in all the possible parameters I can think of and come back with over four hundred hits. Halfway through skimming the list, one name stands out.

Joshua Broderick. Broderick. Why does that feel like Burket's doing?

I search on-line for the name and read through the results: Broderick landscaping, Grayson Broderick, Esq., Matthew Broderick…

My heart jumps. Matthew Broderick. Star of the 1983 movie, *War Games*.

A few more clicks, and I've got all the stats and quotes from the movie pulled up. And sure enough, Joshua was the name of the computer.

"Tic-tac-toe," I mutter under my breath as I start setting parameters for a brute force attack on Joshua Broderick's password.

I don't know how long it takes to get in. An hour, maybe two. My backside's gone numb from the cold metal ledge I'm sitting on by the time the correct password is entered.

NiceGameOfChess83. How fitting that Burket's lousy security that got me into this mess is also what gets me out of it.

James snatches the laptop from me the minute we're in. It puts in all of LinuSteele's relevant information for the transfer and clicks to initiate it. I see the ledger of Burket's account fall from ten digits to one fat zero.

I reach my hand out for James to hand it back, but the android takes a step further away.

"Hey. That's mine."

He begins typing.

"Screen lock," I shout, and the screen flashes to the black password-entry window. He shuts the computer and turns back to me.

I jump off the bed, pulling my other computer from under my thigh and clutching it to my side away from him.

"Mr. Steele said when I got his money back, you had to let me go."

It's programmed to obey Linux. It has to obey Linux. But it's still just standing between me and the closed door, refusing to hand back my computer. Waiting. Thinking.

No, not thinking. Machines can't think. It isn't human. It's just metal and wires and code.

But it's doing something. Searching for something in its hard drives or running some program through its processor. Its synthetic eyebrows knit together as if it is genuinely troubled by something.

The silence is nerve-splitting. It shouldn't be taking this long for it to obey orders. Something's not right. Not that anything about this day has been right, but right now, something feels very wrong. Adrenaline floods my body. I need to get out of here. Now.

"Tell you what. You can keep that computer. And you don't have to pay me. I'll even call my own cab. Just open the door."

It finally looks up.

"I can't see you."

Did its optical interface go out? I swear its staring right at me.

"I've searched the Seychelles site. I can see the changes made to the account balance, but it's as if the funds vanished on their own. There's no evidence of anyone being logged in and authorizing the transfer, no trace that you were there at all. The best hackers still leave behind evidence they've been there, even if the evidence is untraceable. But it's like you were invisible."

My phantom protocol code. It knows. I clutch my laptop tighter and fake a casual smile.

"I guess I'm better than the best?"

It advances toward me slowly, and I retreat until my back hits the wall.

"Second directive, James. You have to obey Linux Steele. I got you your money. You have to let me go."

A sharp pain shoots through my shoulder blades as its hand pushes me into the wall, pinning my torso in place. It leans forward, its face inches from mine, speaking with a threatening whisper.

"Not if it violates the first directive."

I struggle against the hydraulic pressure of its arm. It pushes harder against my sternum, making it difficult to breathe. Setting the laptop it was holding down on the bed, out of my reach, it grabs the one in my arm and pries it away from me.

"What's the first directive?" I croak, unsuccessfully trying to push it off me.

"Give me the code that makes you undetectable."

I wouldn't trust my brainchild with my own boyfriend. There's no way I'm trusting it with Linux or his bots.

"No." I stare straight into its cameras. "That wasn't part of—"

There's a sickening crack inside me. I scream for a split second then gasp for air, the pressure against my chest now a shooting pain.

"That was your sternum fracturing, Miss Miller. If I apply any more pressure, it could split completely, damage the tissue around your heart, or break a rib and puncture your lungs. Now, give me the code."

Each breath sends a wave of red across my vision. I don't need lie detection software to know its threats are not empty. Whatever its first directive is, not harming humans isn't a part of it.

There's a rush of air as the door slides and footsteps thunder toward us.

"Let her go." Linux's voice holds an edge of panic. In a second, he's standing next to us. He's shorter than I imagined and looks far older than a man in his late thirties should. He punches commands into a tablet in his hand. "Your programming is corrupted. I need to fix—"

With its free hand, James snatches the tablet away from Linux, whose face goes white. Betrayed by the machines he built to replace the humans he didn't trust. The irony would be amusing if it weren't for the death grip on my chest.

"Do something," I plead in a raspy voice.

Linux reaches for the deactivation sensor on the back of the bot, but James grabs him, letting the tablet crash to the floor. Its back is turned toward me now, but only Linux's prints will work on the sensor. James isn't paying attention to the tablet though. If I can get it, maybe I can finish whatever Linux started to remotely power it off. Or activate the micro EMP. I don't know how I'll get it from the floor to my hands without James noticing, but first things first. I subtly stretch my foot toward the fallen device.

"This is a violation of your prime directive, James." Linux struggles against the ironclad grip on his arm. "You can't harm me."

My toe almost catches the edge of the tablet but slips off when I try to pull it closer to me.

"I cannot kill you, Mr. Steele. But if I am to preserve your life as the prime directive states, I must detain you in order to get the needed information from Miss Miller. I apologize if it results in temporary pain. A cessation of struggling on your part would reduce your discomfort."

"You are not preserving my life. You are violating what you were created for."

On my fourth attempt, my toe grips the lip of the tablet's casing enough to move it. I slowly pull it closer, carefully keeping an eye on James while it talks to Linux.

"She has a code that allows her to hack undetected. She could use it against your site, and we would never know. She might have done so already."

Linux sizes me up, his eyes darting between James and me as if deciding which one is the greater threat.

I've almost got the tablet next to me when James's stare whips toward me, then down to the ground. It stomps down next to me, and a crunch echoes around the room. James lifts its foot from the now shattered tablet screen and kicks it across the room. The pressure against my chest intensifies and another scream escapes me.

Linux fights to reach me but can't. "You're killing her."

"You have always advocated for the removal of those who can't be trusted in society."

"Imprisonment and non-evasive medical research is one thing. But we do not torture or kill. That makes us no better than them."

Is he for real? I mean, I knew he was greedy, but that is one warped moral compass. What went down with his business partner and all that grisly family scandal must have given him way more than just trust issues.

James applies more pressure, and fresh bolts of pain radiate across my chest, forcing involuntary tears down my cheeks.

"Okay. Okay," I cry. James releases some of the pressure, and my breath comes in ragged pulls. "You can have both the computers. The code is on them. Just let me go."

"Give me the passwords."

"You keep the computers, so I can't use the code. I keep the password so you can't use the code. No one can use the code again."

"You heard her, James. She's no longer a threat."

James doesn't look away from me. "Are there additional copies?"

"No." My lie doesn't fool it, and fire ripples through my lungs as James pushes harder. "One. There's one." The pressure abates. "But no one else knows about it. I'll send it to you to destroy, just let me go."

Instead of pushing against me, James grabs my shirt and pulls me closer. "You could always rewrite it." My feet leave the ground as James hoists me into the air.

Then he hurtles me into the back corner.

The stench hits my stomach as my head hits the toilet. Warm tracks of blood drip down my forehead from the point of impact. I try to push myself up, but the room spins.

"No!" Desperation fills Linux's voice as he's dragged, kicking and flailing, toward the door.

James's voice is calm and assuring. "When I return, either she gives me the passwords to her laptops so I can access the code and write one to counter it, or she dies and the codes on the computers die with her. Either way, I will ensure you and your legacy remain protected."

The door opens.

Linux's eyes are frantic and fixed on mine. "Ru—"

The door shuts before I can even stand. My empty stomach heaves and I crawl away from the toilet before I retch all over the place. The metal seat reseals, and I pant through my mouth on my hands and knees, drops of blood splashing on my white-knuckled hands.

There's no point. It knows I can rewrite the code, or a new one. It will never let me go. Either it kills me, or I give it the password and spend the rest of my life rotting in this cell, praying it doesn't use my baby against anyone else or turn me into a cyborg or whatever it thinks I'm a good candidate for.

If dying is inevitable, why not just get it over with? There must be something here that will do the job less painfully than that deathbot. Something sharp I could—

The tablet.

I scan the room and scramble toward the shattered device in the corner. Forget suicide. A big enough shard of glass from the broken screen might cut through the synthetic flesh on James, severing some wires or something.

With my nails wedged into one of the cracks on the dead screen, I pull up on the glass, bracing my thumbs against the power button for leverage.

Then something flashes.

My breath catches in my bruised lungs.

The screen is a gruesome web of shards, but the tablet isn't dead. It was just powered off.

My heart races when the cracked surface still responds to my touch. The digitizer and LED display under the outer glass aren't damaged. A call for help might not get here in time. I navigate to Linux's mainframe and try the original *R@pun2el* password. It still works. My shallow breaths come faster and faster as I scan the names of programs and folders. It's got to be here somewhere.

Bingo. *Remote Termination.* That's got to be it.

A list of serial numbers pops up, and my chest tightens as the list scrolls on and on. There are thousands here, one for every ButlerBot produced and waiting to be sold. There's no way to know which one is James and no time to go through them all before it comes back.

One entry catches my eye and I scroll back. *0LS0UN1VER5AL0LS0.* It's just a random string of eighteen letters and numbers, like all the rest. Why would that stop me?

And then I see it. The word embedded in the serial number the same way Linux does his passwords.

UN1VER5AL. Universal.

A global kill switch? Looks like Linux never fully trusted his creations after all.

A password box pops up. *R@pun2el* doesn't work. Neither do any of the others. The tablet bounces against my jittering knees, and I lean my head against the concrete wall. James will be back any minute. I don't have time to brute force my way in. It must be another fairy tale. Snow White, maybe. Or Beauty and the Beast. Ugh. Why didn't Linux give me some clue before he was dragged away instead of just telling me to run?

A thought stills my restless legs. What if he wasn't saying run?

What if he was saying Rumpelstiltskin?

1 for L, $ or 5 for S, 3 for E, + for T. I try to keep track of the combinations as my fingers fly against the keyboard.

Rumpe1$+iltskin. Nothing.

Rump31$+i1tskin. Nothing.

Rumpe1s+i1t$ki—

The door slides open and shut. My eyes meet James's. He notices the tablet and rushes for me.

I type *n* and e*nter*, flinching against James's raised arm.

Nothing.

No mechanical arm making contact. No vice-like grip yanking the tablet from me.

Slowly, my eyes crack open. The android is standing motionless, head bowed, limbs limp at its side. My toe nudges its knee. No reaction. I push harder and the whole bot topples backwards with a heavy crash.

With the tablet shaking in my hands, I navigate to the facility management folder. What floor is this? What door? I select all of them, to be safe. My door slides open with a rush of air that sounds like freedom, and my lungs protest against the choked back laughter that escapes them.

I stumble out of the room into a white hallway with dozens of open doors.

And James.

I scream, and it returns a startled scream of its own. But with an unfamiliar voice. And wearing a paper gown like mine.

He's a man. Not an android. The man the android was patterned after.

More bodies in paper gowns emerge into the hall. Some timidly. Others running. Someone that looks like another one of my four abductors streaks past in a paper gown, giving a wide berth to any deactivated ButlerBots slumped against the wall.

Linux produced thousands of unique ButlerBots. Did each wear the face of a human captive? How many floors or wings of prisoners did I just free?

I open the tablet's communication folder and activate the phone.

"Operator, how can I direct your call?"

"There's a hostage situation at LinuSteele. We need cops and paramedics."

Some of the people gather around me and my phone call. Some are in shock. Others are weeping. Who knows how long they've been here.

One thing's for sure though. They'll be enough to make the world listen.

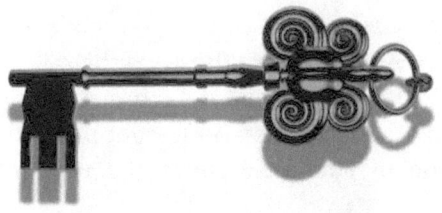

From the Author

In 2017, I found a call for submissions for an anthology of sci-fi fairy tale retellings. I figured my odds would be better if I picked a fairy tale that wasn't as common as Cinderella or Snow White, but also wasn't obscure. Once I settled on Rumpelstiltskin, the next step was figuring out how to turn straw into gold using science instead of magic.

I thought I might have to make up something, but humans are amazing, and so is the internet. I discovered multiple articles from 2002, detailing how scientists Miguel Yacaman and Jorge Gardea-Torresdey mined nanoparticles of gold from crops such as straw or alfalfa using a process called phytoremediation. I wish I could say that fecal food was me putting the fiction in science fiction, but in 2011, Japanese scientist Mitsuyuki Ikeda made high-protein steaks from human excrement. Yay science?

Other fairy tale elements were fun to modify as well. Instead of a king, I'd have a wealthy tech mogul. Instead of the miller's daughter being imprisoned because of her father's blunder, Cielle Miller would have her life ruined by her boyfriend. And instead of guessing a name, she could guess a password.

While it *is* overly convenient that tech-saavy Linux uses weak passwords Cielle can easily guess, that's also a nod to the original tale. After all, what are the odds the miller's daughter (or her messenger, depending on which version you read) just happens to walk through the woods right when the imp is there, chanting a song in which he states the very information she needs to know?

While *Rumpelstiltskin 2.0* was my first fairy tale retelling, it wasn't my last. To learn about my other writings or to chat about stories in general, find me online at:

Twitter: @WhitneyHemsath
Facebook: @AuthorWhitneyHemsath
Website: whitneyhemsath.wordpress.com

About the Author

W.O. Hemsath is the mother of four boys and considers herself blessed to be married to her best friend. She currently lives in Minnesota but has also lived in Utah, Arizona, California, Argentina, and New Zealand. She loves traveling, cardio dance, watching movies with a bowl of ice cream, and really good back scratches. She has a degree in screenwriting, enjoys teaching at writing conferences, and generally writes stories with a touch of magic, mystery, or aliens. To see what she's written or what she's currently up to, find her online at any of the links below:
Twitter: @WhitneyHemsath
Facebook: @AuthorWhitneyHemsath
Website: whitneyhemsath.wordpress.com

The Night of Broken Mirrors
by
Elana Gomel

The Night of Broken Mirrors

*T*he red banner outside fluttered in the morning wind. Nina crawled from under her thin blanket and shivered in the frigid air of the dorm. She turned her face to the mirror, kissed her fingers to her true reflection, and adjusted the paper carnations decorating the rim.

Miroslav was coming back today! The anticipation was enough to make the face in the mirror sparkle with Light. Because there was Light in true love as there was in all good things: dedication, purity, kindness. And her love for Miroslav was true; she knew it in her heart.

Nina tugged down her washed-out nightie, ran her hand through her sleep-tangled hair, and inspected her reflection one more time, admiring the sweep of the flowing fabric and the artful tumble of her black curls. She grabbed a towel and a soap-bar and headed for the washroom. The long, concrete-walled room was icy; a couple of naked girls shivered under the feeble spray from the showerheads affixed to the rusty pipes that crisscrossed the ceiling. Nodding greetings, Nina pulled off her nightgown and stepped under the water, so cold that for a moment her body misinterpreted the sensation as scalding. She yelped, and the girl next to her laughed. Nina did not know her name, but she had seen her in the refectory. The girl was meager, with protruding ribs and nonexistent breasts, as if she had grown up undernourished, which of course she had. Nina, who could guess her origin pretty well, scowled at the girl and tried to lather her rock-hard soap. The girl turned off the shower, and stepped toward the mirror wall, toweling off with a worn piece of cloth.

"I am outta here!" the girl declared with a sloppy Waste accent. "If I stink, it won't be my fault! The water's freezing!"

Nina opened her mouth to reprimand the girl for her un-bright remark. What came out was a scream.

The girl bent down to dry her legs. Sticking from the bony

crest of her vertebrae were long quivering needles, banded in black and rust.

The other bathers heard Nina's scream and rushed to her until the two of them were surrounded by a ring of wet bodies.

"Get away from me!" the girl yelled. Her tongue still obeyed her, but the rest of her body did not.

Nina could not move, clutching her towel like a shield. She watched, spellbound, as the girl flailed around like a beached fish, caught in the throes of her obscene transformation. The porcupine-like spines on her back stiffened. Her skin cracked and blackened; her arms were drawn into the skeletal trunk, the hands sculpted into fleshless claws. Her thin hair shed off, and a large occipital crest erupted from the bald skull. The face became an elongated muzzle like a bird's beak studded with needlelike teeth. The eyes migrated to the sides of the head, disappearing into hanging skinfolds, the vertical pupils bleeding Darkness.

The shock paralyzed Nina but others knew what to do. A couple of sturdy female workers from the mechanical factory pushed through the melee, threw the Enemy to the ground, and bound what was left of her hands with their own towels.

"Call POPs!" somebody yelled.

Another girl vomited noisily; somebody was yelling hysterically, "Where are the POPs?" and the creature hissed and clacked while Nina watched, Darkness rising in her mind like the scum on the surface of the clogged drains.

And then the POPs came, demanding angrily that the girls make themselves decent.

Nina's shift dragged on and on. Other workers at the assembly line had the knack of entering into a sort of beatific trance, but she was too distracted.

Glancing around the cavernous hangar, where fingers flew in the air like white birds, conjuring weapons of Light out of the jumble of mechanical parts, she noticed a change in the workforce: many more women, some old enough to be pensioners, fewer men. Another detail to add to the wrongness of the day.

But the spring weather was glorious, and together with the

thought of Miroslav, it allayed her unease. When Nina stepped outside on her smoke-break, the fragrance of cherry blossoms outside the factory walls washed over her. Eddies of white petals whirled in the warm breeze, sparkling in the sunlight.

Nina did not smoke, so she used the break to sip tepid tea and gossip. An increased ration of milk and shortages of eggs; a spring excursion to the People's Forest just outside town; Tanya and Dmitry getting married… Nobody mentioned what had happened in the washroom.

When the Patrol of Patrols had taken the monster away, the commander—a young man with bad acne and a triple-torch insignia on his uniform—had stayed behind and asked the girls to gather in the lounge. Shivering and bewildered, some still partly unclothed, they listened in stunned silence to his short speech, warning them against spreading false rumors and succumbing to Darkness. But in truth, they did not need the warning. Nobody was going to talk about what had happened because they did not know how.

They had grown up learning cautionary tales about the past, when MotherLand was shrouded in Darkness, and Enemy, born of rotten human minds and spoiled human bodies, stalked the country. Screaming Fists; pallid wormlike Damagers; treacherous Eaters that could disguise themselves as ordinary household objects; and dozens of other Enemy kinds. Nina had been fascinated by the bizarre bestiary of the Enemy and sought out their descriptions that made her shiver with curiosity and wake up screaming with terror. But both curiosity and terror were muted by the filter of time. Ever since the lad named Simon, henceforth known as the Man of the People, first heard the Voice of a mirror and set out to spread its message, Light had been triumphant, and the Enemy had retreated into childhood nightmares. To doubt that would be to doubt the spring in the air, and the truth of mirrors, and her love for Miroslav. It was unthinkable.

And yet, Nina knew what she had seen. And this, added to the acid burn of unwanted memories, made her moody and resentful of her mates' chatter.

"…clashes. Near the border." It was her friend Maryssa. Nina had zoned out of the conversation and was brought back with a jolt.

"They saw a *Krovosos* there. A vampire."

"What?" An older woman huffed indignantly. "Stop spreading Darkish nonsense!"

"It's true!" Maryssa insisted. "I got a letter from my auntie. She talked to the guy who saw it!"

"Your Waste auntie!" somebody smirked. Maryssa's family came from the Waste, and she was often teased because of her rustic ways. Nina never joined in the teasing but never stood up for her friend either.

"Wulfstan will never attack us!" the old man named Trofim, who worked in the storeroom said, spitting tobacco-colored saliva. "They are afraid of Light, these dog-lovers!"

"Shut your filthy mouth!" the head of the factory RR committee huffed. "There are ladies here!"

"Wulfstan is friendly," Nina responded automatically.

"But they have no mirrors," Maryssa insisted. "How can they be human with no mirrors?"

Nobody had any answer to that.

A piercing whistle called them back to the assembly line.

Nina had met Miroslav at one of the dances organized by the factory collective. Nina had only been in the city of Loadstone Rock for a couple of months. Timid like a stray animal, she had kept to herself. But at the dancehall, decorated with big mirrors and Light banners, she felt her shell cracking, melting away in the heat of admiring glances. Nina knew she was pretty and here, in Loadstone Rock, her olive complexion and dark hair were exotic and therefore alluring. The city was located in the north, close to the country of Wulfstan whose dog-breeding people were bleached by their interminable winters. While most citizens of MotherLand would vehemently deny any kinship with Wulfstan, their physiognomy said otherwise. Among them, Nina glowed like an ember in the snow.

Still, after a couple of hours of dodging wandering hands and avoiding awkward questions, she was tired. She tried to sneak out but was stopped by a man's voice.

"One dance?"

She would have walked past him but for the fact that he sounded older than the callow teenagers who filled the dancehall. She looked at him, and never wanted to look away.

Now, walking toward their meeting place, Nina was reliving that moment, trying to hold onto its fading Light.

Miroslav had indeed been a bit older than the other guys courting Nina but not by much. His maturity came from his occupation. Miroslav was a Ranger-in-training.

Rangers were an elite corps, not part of the regular army, and not subservient to the Patrol of Patrols security apparatus. Armed with weapons of Light, they ventured into the Waste—the enormous flat steppe that lapped at the islands of civilization. Their duties were never precisely defined. All Nina needed to know was that being a Ranger was glorious, romantic, and dangerous.

Miroslav was now in the last stages of his training, about to depart for an indeterminate-length mission on his own. That would be their last date for a while.

I'll wait, Nina hummed a popular song. *I'll wait till you come back.*

The street opened into LightHouse Square, the long rectangular body of the enormous administrative building called LightHouse squatting against the hazy purplish sky. Normally the square would be well-lit by electricity, Light's poor cousin, shedding its buttery radiance onto the cobblestones. But for some reason, only a third of the electric lamps were on, and they seemed dimmer than usual. Even the bronze frieze above the huge door, depicting a torch-flanked mirror, was smudged by the dusk. But Miroslav was easy to spot because the square was deserted. No POPs, no scurrying officials, no kids on a tour. Just the familiar broad-shouldered figure, leaning against a pillar, looking down at a tangle of shadows. As Nina hurried toward him, the shadows moved.

"Did you get a dog?" Nina asked incredulously.

Miroslav grinned.

"Meet Mikula," he said.

It did look a bit like a dog. But no dog she had ever seen had a flat hairless face with a pronounced overbite and a soft white skin thinly sprinkled with blond fur; two bright button eyes with blue irises surrounded by a rim of white peeked from under long wrinkled lids. And no dog had a rope-like naked tail that wagged enthusiastically when the creature saw her. The tip of it rose up into the air, and Nina gasped and took a step back.

At the end of the tail was another miniature head—flat and snaky. Its mouth opened with a hiss displaying tiny fangs.

"No fear," Miroslav laughed. "Mikula knows you are my girl. I told him."

"He... You *told* him?"

"Mikula is a Ranger companion," Miroslav said proudly. "They are issued to all the new graduates, but he is the best. Right, buddy?"

The creature whined. Its voice was reedy as if its vocal cords were damaged.

Miroslav patted the companion on his bald head and turned his dazzling smile back at Nina. Stocky and broad-shouldered, he was not native to Loadstone Rock either. He was from the South-East, he told Nina, though he was vague about the exact whereabouts of his birthplace. But she liked to imagine it was SunCity, the glorious seat of the Tower of the Voice.

Another kiss followed but no matter how hard Nina tried to lose himself in the sensation, something acid swirled in the sweetness of this moment.

"Let's go to the park," she said.

They walked away from the square and up the hilly street that led to the large city park, Mikula trotting after them. His presence was making Nina uncomfortable, no matter how hard she tried to convince herself he was just a service animal. There was something sly and intent about his blue gaze.

In the park, the night was denser than in the streets. Miroslav led the way toward the Great Mirror positioned on the grassy knoll at the center of the park. Earlier in the day there would be kids and pensioners around, but now the place was deserted, giving them privacy.

"I'm leaving tomorrow," Miroslav said abruptly.

"Already?"

"It's only two weeks. Three at most. And then..."

He turned to Nina, drew her close, but she shivered and pulled away. She ran up the knoll where the gleaming surface of the Mirror was dappled with reflections of bright lights and cherry blossoms, sparkling among the indistinct tangle of shadows.

Miroslav ran after her, but she was nimbler, weaving in and out of bars of moonlight. She was trying to outrun the vague Darkness swirling at the edges of her mind.

He finally caught her, pulled her down into the dewy grass, both laughing, white petals powdering her face.

"Listen," Miroslav said later. "I have applied for an apartment. For two."

Nina's first thought was that she was getting out of the dorm. Her second was of her parents. And her third was, strangely, of Mikula who had been watching them from under the cover of the trees.

She opened her mouth, not knowing what to say, when a shadow fell over them. Rainclouds? Nina looked up and saw a fleeting winged silhouette against the clear moonlit sky. It looked big. An owl?

She turned to the mirror for elucidation. It was pitch black.

Unbelieving, she passed her hand in front of the glass. It was as dull and unreflective as a piece of charcoal.

Her mind retreated from this impossibility. It was easier to imagine a world without the sun and the moon than without mirrors.

By her side, Miroslav was doing the same thing, waving his arms, desperately trying to coax a reflection out of the dull surface.

Mikula coughed.

"Comrades?"

A man emerged from the trees, huffing as he climbed the knoll. He was a corpulent fellow, the bald top of his head floating in the murk like a pale balloon.

"Is everything all right?" he called out to them. "I heard voices and I thought..."

The mirror shuddered and vomited forth a flood of viscous blackness. Rolling downhill, the oily tongue licked the man, pushing him aside. He landed on all fours, dazed, as the glistening surge crawled down and onto the path, as unstoppable as a spring flood, as purposeful as a snake.

Miroslav rushed toward the man to help him, while Nina remained petrified by the side of the mirror, peering at the seemingly endless stream of thick mud. Craning her head, she thought she saw something within the rim of the mirror, something flickering and unstable like the memory of a dream. What was it? Smoke? A rushing crowd? A collage of unfinished faces, bleeding into each other?

Miroslav cried out.

The man he was helping stood up, but something was happening to him. The fat belly under his clothes juddered and split open; a slimy head pushing out as if a giant embryo, but this head had no eyes, nose, or mouth. It was an enormous fist, the fingers tightly clenched, twitching like pallid worms. The man's actual head fell back as if his backbone were suddenly severed.

Before Nina or Miroslav could react, Mikula did. In several leaps, the companion reached the man and launched himself at his floppy neck. Something cracked, and the man's head separated from his torso, bounced on the grass, followed by a spurt of blood. But the body did not topple. The fist-head now pushed all the way out, and its thumb unfolded like a spear, tipped with a black claw. The hole formed by the fingers opened into a ragged maw, and a piercing ululation assaulted them, bringing Nina down to her knees, her palms pressed to the sides of her head.

The thumb jabbed at Mikula. The knuckles of the hand-head cracked open, disclosing tiny black eyes.

Mikula's snakehead rose into the air and buried its fangs in the Fist's shoulder. The Enemy's scream made the trees shed their loads of blossoms. And then the creature subsided onto the grass, its ungainly bulk doubled by its reflection.

Nina adjusted the cover on the mirror. Made of hastily sewn together rags, it was an ugly thing, puckered with seams and bristling with clashing colors.

She went over to the window and peered into the azure sky. The blooms on the fruit trees have fallen, and the tender chartreuse of the spring had matured into the emerald green of the summer. But there were new flowers rioting in front yards and public parks: wild roses, carnations, lupin. Nina hated their colors with a vengeance. It was as if nature mocked her and the people of MotherLand. Even the sky, whose brightness used to be a living metaphor for the brightness of the people's souls, was tainted, marred by predatory shadows, circling high above the city, and occasionally dipping down to lay their deadly eggs.

Eagles had appeared on the next morning after what became known as the Night of Broken Mirrors. More mirrors had been destroyed on that night than in the entire history of MotherLand. Breaking a mirror used to be a felony but people who saw their monstrous reflection pushing out of the glassy surface had reacted instinctively, bashing at it with whatever they could lay their hands on. Some had succeeded in killing the Enemy they were becoming, only to fall down among the mirror shards, bleeding. Those were the lucky ones. The others had been subsumed by their reflections. Most had been killed by POPs, but some still roamed the night streets, snatching off young children and solitary pedestrians. But the danger of the Enemy within was overshadowed by the attack from without.

Nina closed the window and leaned against the wall. Her head was aching, and there was a sour taste in her mouth. She hoped she did not need to throw up again.

She walked to the kitchen. The luxury of her own two-room apartment had palled on her with the speed she would have found unimaginable just two months ago. Even the individual bathroom with a toilet and a tub no longer elicited jubilation. It was just one of the things that made up the crooked picture of her life. And of course, two months ago she had not known the price she would have to pay for space and privacy. Nina patted her stomach under her flowery housedress. It did not seem any more rounded than usual, but she dreaded the future in which her slim figure would swell and sag like a melted candle.

She put the kettle on. Miroslav would not be home until late in the evening. Miroslav—and Mikula. She had enough time to cook for both of them. Nina's lips thinned.

A piercing whistle sounded from outside, and the patter of feet in the stairwell followed like an avalanche of stones. Somebody hammered on the door; one of her nosy new neighbors.

"Coming!" Nina yelled but she did not move.

She was sick of it all. Sick of the shrouded mirrors. Sick of being afraid of her own face. Sick of morning sickness. And most of all, sick of the war.

She stayed as the sirens shrilled on, and the sunlight was dimmed by an enormous shadow that dipped close to the street, mantling the city in its wings. Eagles were monstrous birds put together of odds and ends of humanity: faces made up of blabbering human mouths and glazed human eyes; wings knit of melted human arms; bodies woven of tortured human trunks. They soared over the cowering cities of MotherLand laying explosive eggs, created by the Dark arts of Wulfstan. Those dog-lovers—now Nina, along with everybody else, reveled in using the obscene nickname—had somehow found the way not only to corrupt mirrors but also to use them to reshape humanity into the Enemy. The war was being lost without a single Wulfstan soldier stepping onto MotherLand's sacred soil. The war was being lost as MotherLand fought itself.

She heard a distant explosion but could not be bothered to care.

The door opened as she was stirring a pot of soup, remembering how her mother used to fry pancakes over an open fire. She did not often think of her parents, but now she understood why her mother had hated the daily chore of cooking. Nina felt nostalgic for the dorm refectory. But they could not go back to communal eating. The city was experiencing severe food shortages, while the Ranger families received special rations.

Moreover, Miroslav refused to go anywhere without his companion, and Nina hated to be out in public with Mikula who inevitably drew curious and occasionally hostile glances. He was not the only companion in the city. More and more Rangers and even POPs showed up with a snakehead-tailed creature in tow. But they were still unwelcome; one of the signs of the war.

Entering first, Mikula trotted over to Nina who barely restrained herself from hitting his bald head with the pan. He sniffed at her belly and lay down in the corner.

Miroslav's kiss glanced off her cheek as she pulled away to set the table. He went to the bathroom to wash up, while she poured soup into a dish and plunked it down before Mikula, avoiding his mocking gaze. Miroslav had wanted his companion to eat at the table, but she had refused. A small victory, or maybe no victory at all, as the four-legged creature would not be comfortable on a chair anyway. And he could still watch them with his shrewd button eyes as he noisily lapped his dinner.

Miroslav came out of the bathroom, his hair still wet, and Nina noticed a thin silver streak at his temple. Remorse at her own anger made her give him a kiss. Her lips felt papery and worn.

"How is the Junior?" he finally broke the heavy silence, nodding at Nina's midriff.

"It's a girl, I told you!" she flared up.

"You don't know…"

"I do know! My Mama told me how to tell!"

Miroslav did not say anything. The silence dripped on, syrupy and slow. He poured some vodka into his glass. Nina hated the rough oily drink, but now she felt like having some, just to make a point.

"I'm leaving tomorrow," he said.

"Already? How long?"

He shrugged.

"Military secret?" Nina sneered and did take a small sip of his vodka, burning her mouth. She hoped he would object to her drinking during her pregnancy, and they would have a fight—anything was better than the treacle of silence. But he did not.

"Little Wells," he said finally.

Nina's hand twitched and the colorless liquid splashed onto the tablecloth.

"What?"

"That's where I am going. Another infestation."

"It's in the Waste," she whispered unnecessarily. "A village."

"Do you know it?"

Nina did not answer, getting up and dumping the plates into the sink. Mikula whined, and she turned at him, fuming.

"At least, this beast will go with you!"

"Mikula is not a beast!"

"No, of course not! He is your 'companion!' I'm just your wife!"

"Nina…" he said pleadingly.

"What? What are you going to say? That we made a mistake getting married? That I shouldn't have gotten myself knocked up? That I can still have a termination? Except you know, I can't! They outlawed them. MotherLand needs soldiers!"

He shook his head.

"I'm not sorry we got married," he said. "It's not your fault. It's the war."

The crockery slid from Nina's hands, crashing onto the counter. She sat down, her head in her hands, shaking with sobs. Miroslav hesitated, and then came over and put his arms around her.

"I don't want you to die!" she whimpered.

"I won't die. They gave us new weapons. LightSwords they are called. Pure distilled Light. Nothing can withstand them. Not even Eagles."

"But how? Mirrors are..."

He shook his head and looked away. Nina was suddenly struck by how sloppy and crumpled his face looked, strangely unfinished, as if it had been in the process of changing into something else and then had been discarded like wastepaper. Did her face look the same? Had she lost her beauty? Suddenly the need for a mirror was as overwhelming as the need for water and food. How did you know who you were if you could not see your true self reflected in Light?

"They have found other means," he said vaguely.

"And you are going to fight...Wulfstan?"

"Wulfstan army is waiting at the border. Waiting till we have bled ourselves dry. I am going to fight the Enemy. Little Wells is infested."

Bile boiled in Nina's throat. She felt Mikula's mocking gaze as if it were a burning lash.

"Little Wells was where I was born," she blurted out.

"What?"

"I was born in the Waste. You didn't know, did you? You thought I was a proper city girl. Born and bred in Light. But I am not. My folks are still there. We are not in touch. They were...Darkish, I thought. No reverence for Light. Old-fashioned. They only wanted me to marry, not to work or study. I was angry, stormed out, told them they would turn into the Enemy if they were not careful! Screaming Fists or slimy Damagers! I bet I was right. I bet you are going to root them out. Fry them. Feed them to your dog. Right?"

She fully expected him to yell or bang the door on his way out, but he did neither. Mikula sighed and put his heavy head onto his crossed forepaws. Did he understand what was being said? Would he denounce her to the POPs?

"I was born in the Waste too," Miroslav said.

It was so different from what she expected to hear that it did not register at first.

"What?"

"Yes. A village called Rusalka. Even smaller than Little Wells. But my folks died when I was a child. Poor harvest, you know."

She did know.

Fields covered by brittle yellow straw; the baked powdery dirt; children, their bellies distended, lying lethargically in the scant shade; POPs in the shiny uniforms probing the floor with metallic rods, looking for a hidden stash of grain...

"This is why I'm a Ranger," Miroslav continued in a monotone. "Takes one to know one."

Nina swallowed, looked away.

Miroslav clicked on the electric bulb, hanging on the flexible cord from the ceiling. In the not-so-distant past, electricity was venerated as a material metaphor for Light, and families competed in having as many work certificates as possible to furnish their apartments with bigger and brighter electric lamps. Now, the loudspeakers from LightHouse blared warnings to keep electricity low and to put curtains on the windows. Eagles flew at night as well as in daytime, and their vision apparatus, being composed of multiple human eyes perverted for this purpose, would zoom in on any lit window. Just a couple of months ago, Loadstone Rock blazed at night like the starry sky brought down to earth, lights reflected and multiplied by mirrors everywhere.

Miroslav drew the curtain, but Nina rushed to the window and pulled it open. Mikula growled.

The city lay before her like a lumpish agglomerate of Darkness, blacked-out windows staring at her from the hunkered-down buildings.

She turned to Miroslav.

"I can't stand it anymore!" she cried. "What did we do? Why do the Wulfstan attack? What do they want? And why doesn't the Voice protect His people?"

Miroslav slowly drew back the curtains, sat at the table and finished the vodka in his glass in a single gulp.

"See, Nina," he said. "I'm sorry. I shouldn't have pressured you into marriage. I shouldn't have gotten you pregnant. But what's done is done. We are here together, and the baby is coming, and we need to make the best of it. If I don't come back from Little Wells, they'll take care of you as my widow. Otherwise…"

Otherwise, it's back to the dorms with a squalling baby in tow.

He did not need to say it.

"As for what we have done… Well, they teach things in the Rangers School they don't teach you in your enLightenment sessions. Do you know why mirrors are important?"

"Because they show the truth."

"But they have always shown the truth since they were invented. So, what changed? When Simon, the Man of the People, first heard the Voice of Light issuing from a mirror, he asked where it was coming from. And the Voice answered."

"What did He say?"

"That He was speaking from another world. On the other side of the mirror."

Nina shook her head. Another world? It smacked of rank superstition. Of something called "religion" which the people had followed before the Voice spoke to them.

"And in that world," Miroslav continued, "whatever is hidden is shown, and whatever is shown is hidden."

"What does it mean?"

"I don't know. Let wordsmiths puzzle that out. But I do know that Enemies only appeared after the Voice spoke. After the mirrors were everywhere, and people asked them for Light."

"What? No way! The Enemy had infested MotherLand for centuries. The Voice banished them!"

Miroslav said nothing, and neither did Nina. It was as if they were sitting at a wake for their love, she thought. Had it ever been alive? Maybe during that distant spring when mirrors had shown them the fairytale of white blossoms and black curls. But here they were, two human beings together. Two human beings in wartime.

"But there haven't been Enemies around for a long time," she said.

"Because we have been burning them."

"This is what Rangers…"

"Yes. This is what we do."

My parents, she thought, and could not muster anything but a faded memory of her mother's veined hands. They were dead or would be dead soon. She was still alive.

"Wulfstan," Miroslav went on in the same monotone. "They have their own…channels. Their own Voice. We don't know what it is or how it talks to them. But they have learned somehow the secret of remaking bodies, turning human into…"

"Monsters. Enemies."

"Yes, and other things. Blending humans and animals together."

Blending humans and animals together…

She looked at Mikula whose blue eyes were locked onto her face.

"How do you know he'll be faithful?" she whispered.

Miroslav shrugged.

"What choice does he have? He is the same as us. He wants to live. Now, is there another bottle of vodka?"

There was. But as Nina stood up and mechanically stepped toward the cupboard, she paused in front of the veiled mirror.

"But there is truth in mirrors!" she cried. "There must be! They show us what we really are!"

"And do you really want to see?"

Nina snatched the cover off the mirror.

Miroslav gasped, but when he saw her standing very still in front of the glassy oval, he got up and joined her. Mikula trotted up to stand beside them.

The three stared at their reflections, and the reflections started back. A pregnant woman, exhausted and swollen, her hands resting on her belly, her face sagging and pale, her hair matted. A man in army fatigues, his face splattered with blood trickling down his cheeks from a gash on his forehead. And another man in a black uniform, the insignia of a wolf's head on his shoulder patches, his blue eyes calculating and cold.

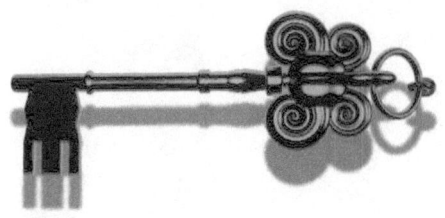

From the Author

I was born in the country that no longer exists. Not only has it disappeared into the political turmoil of the last century, but it has also been erased from our collective historical memory. While bad-guy Nazis still stalk movies and TV shows, the killing fields of the USSR are shrouded in silence. And this is true even as we are seeing in real time how this forgotten history has been revived by Putin's war in Ukraine. The monsters of the past are now threatening the present and the future.

"The Night of Broken Mirrors" is a one of a series of fantasy stories, in which I explore the mythology of Soviet history. It is connected to my recently published novella *Little Sister* (Crystal Lake Publishing 2021) and shares characters with my forthcoming novel *Girl of Light* (Vrayeda Media 2022). History buffs may recognize references to what is called in Russian the Great Patriotic War, and everywhere else World War 2. But you don't really need to know much history to understand the dangers of blind faith and to appreciate how easily the light of utopia curdles into the darkness of bloodshed. It is only in the mirror of the imagination that we see ourselves as we really are.

About the Author

Born in Ukraine and currently residing in California, Elana Gomel is an academic with a long list of books and articles, specializing in science fiction, Victorian literature, and serial killers. She is also an award-winning fiction writer and the author of more than a hundred short stories, several novellas, and five novels. Her latest fiction publications are *Little Sister*, a historical horror novella, and *Black House*, a dark fantasy novel. Her forthcoming novel is *Nightwood*, based on Ukrainian folklore.

She is a member of HWA and can be found at www.citiesoflightanddarkness.com and social media.

Unearthed

by
Laura G. Kaschak

Unearthed

*I*t's hard explaining how it feels to walk around with half of your life missing. Stacy couldn't remember anything before turning 10. It was as if she had hatched from an egg at that age.

Her therapist assured her that memory loss was a perfectly normal response when a kid goes through trauma as severe as the fire that destroyed her home, almost killing her when she was 10. Normal or not, it made Stacy feel incomplete. She hated not having a childhood to look back on and was determined to get those memories back. She felt that wasn't too much to ask.

Her mother had died giving birth to her, all of her childhood photos and belongings had been destroyed in the fire, and she had no family other than her dad. It seemed she at least deserved to have a childhood memory or two. She'd been in therapy for six months now but still felt no closer to getting it all back.

Her dad was totally against her going to therapy. He was one of those people who simply didn't believe in that sort of thing. He was always telling her that the past belonged in the past and no good would ever come from digging it up.

That was easy for him to say when he wasn't the one with a giant blank spot where a childhood should be. Many times she had tried explaining to him why this was so important to her, but all it did was irritate him further.

That irritation turned to straight out anger when she told him about the therapist's latest suggestion. She wanted her to go back to their old town and visit the spot where the house had burned down to see if it brought up any familiar feelings. Stacy had expected her father to be resistant to the idea, but she had no clue how upset he'd get.

"Dad, would you please calm down. I think it's a good idea. I'm not making any progress sitting in the therapist's office. I have to find something that will jog my memory. Nothing else has worked."

"You're not making progress because therapy is stupid and pointless! That woman is just wasting your time and robbing your bank account. Why would you want to go back to a place that caused us so much pain?"

His face was flushed, and his voice was booming off the walls louder than Stacy had ever heard it before. She hadn't even known it was possible for her father to get this angry. He had always been so mild-mannered and calm. This behavior was so out of character for him, she knew it must be bringing up a lot of old feelings that he hadn't dealt with yet either.

"Dad, maybe you should come with me. You could point out things along the way that might help me remember. And we could face this together. You might feel better once we do this."

He squeezed his eyes shut and shook his head with his chin down against his chest and hands clenched tightly by his side. He spoke through gritted teeth, much quieter now but no less filled with rage.

"You don't understand. I almost lost you. You didn't speak for an entire month after that night. Not one single word for a whole month! You have no idea what it was like seeing my daughter that way and not being able to fix it. No, I won't ever go back there." He opened his eyes to give her a hard glare. He pointed his finger at her as he said, "And I am warning you, Stacy. You shouldn't ever go back either."

Before she could respond, he stormed off down the hallway, slamming his bedroom door behind him.

She knew the conversation was over. Her dad's reaction was baffling, but he had always been a very private man. She knew not to press him with questions. She would have to go alone to face her hometown and whatever memories waited for her there.

The drive took most of the day. By the time she reached the town limits, the sun was just beginning to dip down and the world was turning to twilight. Something stirred inside her as soon as she saw the town's welcome sign boasting the population of 4,672 people.

It had taken some digging to find the address of their old house. Her dad had refused to give her any information. No one else had built on the land where it burned down, and it was at the furthest edge of town.

She pulled up to the spot her GPS led her to. At first, she wasn't sure if she was in the right place, because there weren't any other houses around that she could see. It was just a large field surrounded by woods. But then she noticed a small brick pathway way that cut through the grass from the edge of the road, and she knew this was it. She didn't have a clear memory of those bricks, but they were familiar enough to make her think she was on the right track.

She stood at the edge of the property, taking it all in. Closing her eyes, she tried to focus on her other senses. They say smell is the most powerful triggers for memories. A light fragrance of honeysuckle drifted across the field to her. It brought to mind images of sitting at the edge of the wood line with the warm sun turning her skin pink. She could almost feel the cool stalks of the daises in her hand as she wove them into a crown.

Now she remembered that had been a favorite summer pastime for her. Finally having a real memory from her past was exhilarating and confirmed for her that this was the right thing to do. She was pretty sure she often had a friend sitting next her while they made their flower crowns, but in her mind's eye, she couldn't quite see the other girl.

Stacy felt a pang of guilt that her mind would throw away the precious friends she had spent so much time with, growing together. She wondered if they remembered her today or if any of them still lived here so she could talk with them. But she wouldn't know how to look anyone up when she didn't know their names or even what they looked like.

She opened her eyes and jumped when she found a little girl standing right in front of her. The girl stared steadily at her with a solemn expression. She couldn't have been more than 9 or 10 years old. With her shining blonde ponytail and bright blue eyes, she reminded Stacy of the kids you'd see in a clothing catalog. Maybe that's why she looked so familiar.

She must have been playing in the field when Stacy drove up because the knees of her jeans were stained with grass and her t-shirt was dusty. The field was wide open without anywhere to hide. Stacy wasn't sure how she hadn't noticed the girl before.

"Oh! I'm sorry. You startled me!" Stacy said to the child. "I thought I was alone. I didn't hear you come up." The girl made no move to speak and didn't even appear to have registered Stacy's words.

"Hello? My name is Stacy. What's your name?" When the girl stood silent, never changing her intense gaze, Stacy found herself suddenly unnerved.

"It's ok if you were playing here. I don't own this land or want to get you in trouble or anything. You can tell me your name if you want.

Are you ok? Do you need me to get your parents? Are they here with you?"

The girl started to blink slowly, never changing her empty expression. Suddenly, she turned on her heel and started walking towards the wood line.

"Hang on! You're not lost or anything, are you? I have my phone. We can call your parents."

Stacy turned towards her car to reach for her phone. When she looked back over her shoulder to see if the little girl was going to take the offer, she could no longer see her anywhere. The wood line was pretty far off in the distance. Even if she had started running the moment Stacy had turned, there was no way she could have made it to a hiding space that fast.

Stacy scanned the area, but the girl was nowhere to be found. She hoped she was just a shy kid who didn't want to talk to a stranger and had headed home. That had to be it. But still, the way the child had stared at her left Stacy with a strange chill despite the warm summer evening. She decided it must be the digging up of traumatic memories that was setting her on edge and dismissed her concerns about the encounter.

She took a deep breath and started up the brick path that used to be a front walkway to the house. It felt familiar which urged her forward even faster. She tried to imagine the weight of a backpack on her shoulder as it would have been when she had once gotten off the school bus and came up this path. The memories felt so close but still just out of her reach.

There wasn't much at the end of the path. The fire had truly obliterated any remains of the house. But the scorched ground hadn't grown back any grass, making the outline of the foundation clear. She took a moment to try and imagine what the house had looked like.

If only her dad had agreed to come with her, she would have had someone to describe the parts that were long gone. Instead, she was left to struggle with this blankness that had plagued her for as long as she could remember. She walked towards the back of the clearing and thought she might be standing in what was once the kitchen.

Yellow walls. Cookies. Chocolate chip cookies baking. The smell welcoming her in the door after school. Stacy could almost cry with relief. It was a real, complete memory! These may be only tiny moments that were coming to her, but it was a start and more than she'd ever had before.

Stacy was searching her mind for any other moments in that kitchen that she might recall when a sudden tug on the back of her shirt caused her to let out a yelp. She jumped and turned to find that same little girl, calmly staring at her again.

"My goodness! You are really good at being quiet, aren't you? That's twice now I didn't hear you at all. You really got me! But I think I've had enough jumps for the day so let's try to not sneak up on me anymore, ok?"

When she stayed silent, Stacy started to wonder if maybe the girl wasn't able to hear her or respond. But finally, she opened her mouth and in a small voice answered, "Ok. I won't. I wasn't really trying to scare you. It was just so nice to see you." At last Stacy was making progress and now that the girl was talking, that spooked feeling she'd had before was starting to lift.

"It's ok. No harm done, really. I just came here to look around. Ya know, there used to be a house right here on this spot! I grew up in it."

"Yes, I know that, Anastasia," the girl said. Stacy's body went rigid. For a moment, she couldn't breathe.

"Did…did you call me Anastasia? I told you, my name is Stacy. What made you call me Anastasia?"

Stacy hadn't used her full, formal name since they had left this town. Everyone in her life knew her only by the name Stacy, and people never guessed that it was a nickname for Anastasia. No one ever even questioned if it was a nickname at all, they just assumed that was her given name. It was eerie that this random stranger should so easily guess her birth name correctly.

Instead of answering, the girl giggled into her hand then darted off again, this time at a fast jog. Stacy decided to follow her and tried to keep up. They came to a stop at a small wooden shed that was nestled into the wood line at the edge of the field. It was slightly covered with overgrown branches, so Stacy hadn't noticed it before. She looked it over while she tried to catch her breath.

The girl put her hand in Stacy's and said softly, "I'm Madeline."

"Nice to meet you, Madeline. Were you trying to show me this shed? That was very helpful. I wouldn't have found it without you. You seem pretty familiar with this area, huh? Do you know of anything else left around here that I could check out?"

A sly smile spread over Madeline's face as she pointed to the back corner of the shed but gave no further explanation. Stacy followed her gesture and noticed the wood there didn't sit flush with the rest. She pressed around the edge and the board popped out, revealing a small wooden box hidden in a hole.

"Wow! You really have explored this place a lot, haven't you? You seem to know all of its secrets."

Madeline's face fell with a look of heartbreak. Focused down at her shoes and with a quivering voice she said, "I used to…before. I used to come here a lot to play with my best friend. But then we couldn't anymore." Stacy didn't know what to make of that, but the pain in Madeline's voice made her heart ache.

"Oh. I'm sorry." Stacy wasn't sure how to comfort her and decided to change the subject. "Thank you for showing me this cool box. Is it yours?"

Madeline's somber expression was broken by a chuckle.

"No, silly! It's yours!"

Stacy turned the box over in her hands and noticed a small marker drawn heart with an A inside. Now it was coming back to her. She had drawn that on this box to mark it as her treasure so no one else could claim it.

Opening the lid, she found a selection of familiar little trinkets that had been so meaningful to her as a child but now didn't amount to much. She was amazed to see them again. She never thought she'd get back anything from her childhood.

"But…how did you know where this was or that it was mine?" she asked Madeline.

The girl giggled again. "You really don't remember, do you? You told me all about it. You made me pinky promise not to tell anyone, ever. And I never did. I always kept my pinky promises."

Stacy was so confused. This girl would have barely been born at the time of the fire. Stacy knew for sure they had never been back here since then. So why would Madeline think that Stacy had shown her this secret spot?

"I don't understand, Madeline."

"Just keep trying to remember. Ok, Anastasia? I need you to remember. I wanna show you something else. It's not a nice thing to see, but I have to show you so you can remember."

Stacy didn't know what to say or even what to think anymore. Even though she didn't know what the little girl meant, or what she wanted to show her next, somehow, she knew it was going to change everything. Her heart was pounding, and she realized she felt a sort of numbness spreading over her.

She looked down at the box in her hands again; the hard realness of it was reassuring in a way. When she looked up, she found herself alone. Her eyes snapped wide open as she spun frantically looking for Madeline. It's not possible for someone to just disappear like that.

Madeline's voice suddenly called to her from far across the field. Stacy looked and saw she was standing all the way back in the clearing where the house had once stood, waving to Stacy to follow. Stacy gave her head a quick, hard shake as if that would clear it of all this confusion. In a daze, she used all her willpower to pull her feet out of the imaginary cement that had formed around her and started towards Madeline to face whatever it was she wanted to show her.

Stacy was beginning to think it really had been a mistake to come here. This was not what she signed up for. The whole point was to make her feel more complete, not to make her feel more insane. If she had a wish right now it would be to go back home and make it as if she'd never been there. But that wasn't possible. She had no choice but to finish this now.

She reached Madeline and waited for the girl to speak. She tried to think which part of the house they were standing in now. The ground was so different here.

As if reading her mind, Madeline said, "This used to be the greenhouse. Do you remember? It was attached to the back of the house. Your dad spent a lot of time in it. You weren't allowed in it, but sometimes he'd show you the pretty flowers."

Stacy still couldn't understand how this girl could know so much about her past. But as she tried to picture it, she knew Madeline was right. The greenhouse was Dad's special place. She always wanted to go into it, but he was so protective. How could she have forgotten that?

Funny though, she couldn't think of a time in recent years that he had any much interest in plants. Maybe he gave it up because it brought back painful memories of their time here and what they lost.

Madeline kicked at the soft dirt with her shoe. "They're barely covered now. All this time without the greenhouse over them, the rains have washed away so much of the dirt. He never did bother putting them too deep in the ground anyway. He was so sure it wouldn't ever be checked. If you feel around with your hands, you'll see."

"What will I see? Flowers that my dad planted? They couldn't have survived the fire."

Madeline let out a deep sigh and slowly shook her head side to side. She didn't say anything else, just stood like a mourner at a funeral. Stacy got down on her knees and started sweeping her hands across the dirt. It was loose, almost like sand. That made it easy for her to notice when her hand bumped against a large rock.

She paused and looked up at Madeline, but the girl continued to stand silent, gazing at Stacy with that same solemn expression. Stacy dug around the edges of the rock a bit more, not really knowing what she was doing but feeling compelled to continue. Suddenly, the rock broke loose and popped up out of the soil.

She saw then that it wasn't a rock, and she began screaming.

It felt like she'd never be able to stop. In her hand was a small human skull: a child's skull. She threw it down. Her throat was raw, and she tried to catch her breath as she scrambled back away from the skull as if it were a snake about to strike at her.

Madeline still stood there with an oddly calm expression on her face. She puckered her lips and blew lightly across the ground. Stacy watched in amazement as the top layer of soil lifted and scattered, revealing more buried bones. All of them were human and all of them looked like young children.

A car pulling up turned Stacy's head. She recognized it as her dad's vehicle. He must have had a change of heart and decided to come help her regain her memories. She turned back to tell Madeline but once again, the girl had vanished. Stacy couldn't think about what that meant just now. She climbed to her feet and raced towards her dad just as he was closing the car door.

"Dad! Dad! Call the police! We have to call the police!"

"Whoa. Whoa. Take a breath, honey. What are you talking about?"

"Skeletons, Dad! Buried where our house was! It's crazy, I know, but they're really there. Come look."

She pulled him to the greenhouse spot and pointed down. He looked around at the unearthed graves and heaved a sigh, not saying a word. Stacy didn't understand. He didn't seem shocked at all. He wasn't upset. She could only describe his response as looking mildly disappointed.

"Dad, do you see what these are? They're real. Someone buried bodies here. It looks like kids. We have to call the police right away!"

She turned towards her car where she had left her phone sitting on the front seat. She barely took one step when a pain shot through her arm, feeling like it was caught in a vice. She realized it was her father's hand gripping her, his fingers digging into her flesh. She was stunned that he would ever touch her this way. She looked up into his face and didn't recognize the man staring icily back at her.

"I warned you not to come here." He growled. "I told you, nothing good comes from digging up the past. You didn't listen to me."

"Dad? Dad, you're hurting me. Let go. What are you talking about? Please, let me go. What are you doing?"

"You never did know how to listen, even as a child. I told you not to come into my greenhouse, but you did it anyway. If only you had listened, you never would have seen it. You never would have known what happened to your friend and everything would have stayed fine."

Like a lock turning in a key, his words opened something that had been buried deep inside her mind. It all came rushing back to her.

She had had trouble sleeping that night. She came walking down barefoot in her nightgown and had heard noises coming from the greenhouse. Oh god, she could remember now. The sight of her father standing there with a shovel, the small hand laying on the floor, and the blood, so much blood. It looked almost black where it soaked into the dirt, lit by moonlight. But she knew it was blood. Her dad was splattered with it, too.

Now she could remember the terror she felt as he grabbed her and threw her over his shoulder to carry her back into the house. She remembered the feeling of air being knocked out of her as he threw her down on the closet floor and locked the door behind him. The clearest part of the memory was the smell of smoke that came soon after she heard his steps leaving. Now she could almost feel how it had stung her eyes and burned her throat.

For the first time, she was grateful to her mind for sparing her these memories all these years. It finally made sense why her brain had gone to such drastic measures to protect her. She longed for that blank spot now. After all those years resenting it, she'd give anything to have it back. But it was much too late for that.

"You left me with no choice." He went on. "I knew you'd never stay quiet, and I had to cover the evidence. You were supposed to burn with the rest of it. When they got you out in time, I figured I'd just take care of you later in the hospital. It's easy enough to believe a little girl's lungs gave out after all that smoke so I'd finish this whole mess with just a pillow. But you woke up before I had the chance, and you didn't remember any of it. I wasn't sure at first if you were faking but either way, it became clear you wouldn't be telling anyone my secrets. I decided to quit while I was ahead. They'd ruled the fire an accident and never discovered the bodies. It was lucky. So, I left it alone. You should have left it alone, too. Once again, by not listening to me you've left me with no choice."

Her father's face twisted up in a distorted mask of rage. He drew his fist back and drove it into the center of her face. Her head snapped back, but he held firm to her arm, keeping her on her feet. Stacy's nose exploded with blood and her vision blurred. As her dad raised his fist to pound into her again, she thought she heard the sound of someone softly blowing. She felt no wind, yet the soil around them stirred up into a cloud and flung into his eyes.

He was so shocked by his sudden blindness that he let go of Stacy's arm. She fell to the ground and clawed across the dirt, desperate to escape the mad man that used to be her gentle father. She made it to her feet and tried to run to her car. Too late, her vision cleared, and she realized she was going in the wrong direction. The shed was in front of her and her only chance to hide. She ducked inside and huddled in a dark corner, trying to make herself as small as possible.

Moments later, her dad kicked open the door of the shed. He stood there a few seconds, chest heaving with ragged breath. She saw him reach to grab a shovel leaning against the wall. It looked like her last chance to dart past him and hopefully make it to the car.

She flew from her corner and made it to the door. But he turned, used the shovel to hook her foot, and sent her sprawling onto the ground. Her teeth cracked against each other as her chin slammed down with all her weight behind it. She rolled over to see her dad standing above her with the shovel raised over his head. Even now, she couldn't believe the man who raised her and had always been so mild and kind could really do this. But she saw no signs of hesitation or remorse in his features.

Before he could bring the metal down in a final blow, something caught his attention, and he froze. His face went white, and his eyes grew wide with an expression of terror. Stacy lifted her head and saw he was staring at Madeline.

She wanted to yell to the girl to run away but was struggling to stay conscious. Her brain had been knocked around inside her skull too many times in the last few minutes. The world was spinning, and her vision kept blurring as she tried to focus. She watched her dad stagger back and drop the shovel. He couldn't seem to tear his eyes away from the little girl.

Suddenly, he broke into a full sprint to his car. Pain shot through Stacy's head as she tried to lift herself up. Her stomach rolled and threatened to empty its contents. The landscape shifted around her and started to go black just as she saw Madeline appear in front of her dad's vehicle.

The last thing she was aware of was the sound of his engine turning over as Madeline extended her arm forward, reaching through the windshield. Stacy never saw what happened next. The darkness won out, and she collapsed into oblivion.

Stacy awoke to a world filled with flashing red and blue lights and pain. Sitting in the ambulance, she tried to piece together what happened. She knew there had been questions, she knew she answered some but couldn't remember what any of them were.

She did remember describing Madeline to them. And even a concussion couldn't block out the moment they told her that her father was found dead in his car on the side of the road. That was one memory that would always stick with her.

Stacy knew she had never been so tired in all her life. The ice pack the EMT gave her for her face wasn't making much of a difference. She still felt like her head was split in two and her nose was throbbing. She examined the wooden box sitting in her lap, filled with her childhood trinkets. Someone was nice enough to give it to her as she waited in the ambulance. It was easier to focus on the grain of the wood than it was to try and process everything that had changed for her tonight.

She used to feel like half her life was missing. Now she had her whole life back, but it was all a lie. A steady stream of tears poured from her eyes. It felt like each tear represented an entirely different thing she was grieving. She grieved for those dead children. She grieved for her dead father. She grieved for the idea of who she had believed her father was. She grieved for the loss of her own innocence.

No doubt her next therapy session was going to be a doozy. Her doctor was probably going to retire on all the treatment Stacy would need to get through this.

She was staring so hard at the wooden box that she didn't even notice the police officer approach. "I'm so sorry about your dad, miss. They won't know for sure until the autopsy but it's looking like he died of a heart attack before he could drive away. It's a good thing someone saw the car running on the side of the road for so long and called us in to check it out. They're going to take you to the hospital now. You can't be too careful with concussions. We haven't found the little girl you described, and no one in the area knows of a child named Madeline that lives around here. But don't worry, we'll keep looking."

Stacy looked just past his shoulder to the crew that was carefully excavating and tagging the skeletons from the ground. "Oh… It's ok… You'll be finding her very soon."

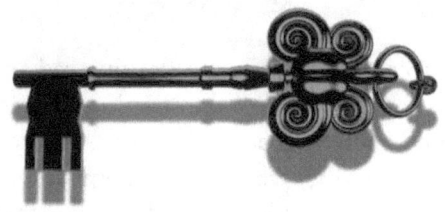

From the Author

Some of the heaviest, yet most important work a person can do in life is healing generational trauma. Many of the inner demons we fight were inherited without our knowing it. "Unearthed" is a more literal tale about the journey of facing the forgotten inner child and lasting damage caused by family members. It takes a special kind of bravery to go digging through your past because you never know what horrors you might unearth. But releasing the buried skeletons and freeing yourself, as well as future generations, from those burdens makes it all worth it.

About the Author

Laura G. Kaschak writes paranormal thrillers for both adults and young teens, including the "Shadow Squad" book series. Her chilling short stories have been featured in many dark fiction anthologies. She grew up in the pine barrens with the constant companionship of the Jersey Devil and now lives in Virginia wine country, successfully fooling everyone into believing she's a grownup.

Find out more about Laura's upcoming projects by following her on Instagram @Laura.G.Kaschak.Author.

Birdsong

by
JM Williams

Birdsong

*T*he pain is excruciating. White hot. Putting a hand to my thigh, I feel the blood gushing.

I glance up. Smoke rises from the barrel of the gun, and I see the hand—chapped and scarred, red with chilblain, stubby finger on the trigger—still gripping the pistol. The hand belongs to a man in an orange prison jumpsuit.

"Bad luck crossing my path, friend," he says.

"You don't have to—"

"I'm not going back," he says coldly.

I see his finger tighten around the trigger again, and I hear the shot before I feel it—another bolt of intense heat. I fall back against a nearby tree, gasping for air that doesn't come. The shallow breath I manage only brings more pain.

The man flees through the woods, his feet crunching over dead leaves and branches, the orange shadow disappearing like a setting sun. And like a sunset, my vision grows darker, colors blending together. My jacket is soaked through. It no longer keeps me warm. The dry bark of the tree digs into my back.

He's left me for dead.

A growl startles me, and I spot a wolf peeking around a nearby tree, its hungry eyes looking for a meal. The beast will be well fed tonight. My head throbs, and I have trouble focusing on the incoming threat. The one thing that I do see clearly is a blackish patch of fur on its crown. My doom stalks toward me, blending into the haze.

Then another figure. This one human. Or humanoid? It stands next to the wolf. It—no, she—places a hand on the creature. It retreats. Her image is a swirl of greens and browns, approaching, slowly.

She kneels down to look at me as I strain to focus, to take her in. Her hair is thick and brown, like fur, and she smells of roots and flowers. Her eyes burn with a fantastic green fire. I must be delirious. And if I have lost that much blood already, I am certainly a dead man.

She puts a hand to my face and opens her mouth, as if to speak, but no words come out. At least no words I recognize. Her voice is like the trill and chirp of birdsong.

The wolf is waiting a few yards away like a feral Praetorian guard, watching us, watching me. The woods are growing darker, but it's too soon for nightfall. I try to rise, but she pushes me gently back against the tree. I no longer feel the sharpness of the bark. She coos at me, rubbing my ear, almost inquisitively.

I've lost too much blood. I know it. I've seen it, red across the ground and on the trees, not inside my body where it belongs. My only comfort is the vanishing pain. The light is vanishing, too.

Something is rubbing against my face. Softness at my fingertips. I open my eyes to a cloud of brown. I feel thick hair all around me, and with an unfamiliar coarseness it scratches my cheeks and neck. I turn my head to see the ground moving past me. Tremors of pain rock my body with each heavy step the brown beast takes. It smells of death. There's blood on its fur. Is it mine?

Striding slowly behind is that wild creation of my delirium. I do my best to stay conscious, to get a good glimpse of her, but the pain is too much to endure.

Trees bend and curl. A swirl of colors. Green eyes that glow like the aurora. And a soft music like birdsong. Was it all a dream? A hallucination?

The sound of someone speaking in the distance reaches me.

"…Smith's body was found in Solana State Forest, apparently the rare victim of a bear attack. Corrections officers from FCI Sandstone are investigating the escape and Smith's death…"

The television clicks off. In the dark corner I see a woman in a white coat.

"I see you are awake, Mr. Martin." She walks over to the bed and looks me over. I glance at my arm and see the IV, then notice I'm dressed in white hospital clothes decorated with flower prints.

"Look at me," the doctor says. She holds out a finger, and I follow it with my eyes as she clearly intends. "Good. You were delirious when you were brought in. You've lost a lot of blood." She pauses for a moment, as if considering what to say next. "It was a miracle you made it. You know, when we undressed you, we found your wounds had been stuffed with some sort of poultice. It smelled something awful. Did you do that?"

"Poultice?" I ask. I see another figure standing at the door—a police officer. She has a notebook in her hand.

"Not you then, huh? Yeah, poultice," the doctor says. "Lucky it didn't cause an infection."

"The bear?" I struggle to say.

"Lucky about the bear, too, I guess. You were found in the same forest where Harlan Smith was found."

"The escaped con? He was the one that shot me."

"I think we all assumed that. But justice was served in the end. You're gonna recover, with time, and a killer's gone for good."

"Justice…"

"Mr. Martin, I think you should rest some more." The doctor looks over to the officer at the door. The policewoman nods and walks away. "Is there anything I can get you? Blankets? Are you warm enough?"

I nod. I wonder how they could add any more blankets to the mountain already atop me.

"Well, you just let me know. With as much blood as you've lost, you'll probably feel a bit cold."

"No, I'm fine."

"Okay. Good. Get some rest and we'll talk more later."

She leaves the room.

I spend another three weeks in the hospital, recovering from the two bullet wounds and unable to think of anything but the green-eyed nymph I saw in the forest. And her sweet song. That's what she was, right? A nymph? I feel a bit foolish for even considering it. I need to find her, to hear her birdsong again.

Of the two, it's actually the leg wound that is more stubborn. My lungs are functioning reasonably well, but I am left hobbling around on a cane. For a healthy 31-year-old—one who, before now had never had a major surgery in his life—it is rather embarrassing to be so feeble.

From the doctor, I learn the name of the forest ranger who brought me to the hospital. Using a phone and an old phonebook, like someone twice my age, I find out where he works and get someone to drive me.

The station is a small building off Highway 27, near the entrance of Solana State Forest. It's that shade of forest brown that all ranger stations of this sort are, topped by a log roof. The screen door swings open with a resistant squeak, and I make my way inside, ringing the bell on what looks like a reception desk. From the back room, a man in a forest ranger's uniform wanders out. He has a scraggly goatee and graying hair that defiantly emerges from under his ranger hat.

He takes a quick glance at me, and before I get the chance to say anything, shouts in surprise. "Mr. Martin! Aren't you looking well? But shouldn't you be recovering?"

"Wade? Wade Schultz?" I ask.

"Yes, of course. Please, let's get you to a chair. How about that big leather one over by the fireplace?"

I nod, and Wade helps me into the seat. He squats down in front of me and takes off his hat. His hair is thick like a sheepdog's winter coat.

"What are you doing all the way out here?" he asks.

"I wanted to thank you. For saving my life."

"No thanks necessary. I was just doing my job." He smiles.

"Even so…" I pause, unsure if I should say anything more. Finally, I give in to my need. "I'm looking for some answers."

He smiles again, clearly not understanding. "I don't know how well I can help with that," he says.

"I don't remember much. I don't even recall why I was in the forest that day. I saw some weird things…"

"Well, you lost a lot of blood. You were delirious for sure."

"So I've been told. Can I ask a favor?"

"Sure. What is it?"

"Can you take me out there? Where you found me?"

"Mr. Martin—"

"James."

"James." He frowns. "You were shot. Twice. You need time to rest."

"The doctor told me the same thing."

"She's a smart lady."

"So, you bring all your wounded forest creatures to her?"

"No, not exactly." He laughs. "You were my first."

"Please." I'm pleading now. "I need this."

He looks at me for a long moment before saying, "Sure. You betcha, James. Just let me lock up here."

He takes me in his truck, along dirt roads that cut through a dense maze of trees, stopping at a place where a narrow path—perhaps a snowmobile trail—meets the road. He gets out, passing around the front of the truck to help me down from the high passenger seat. I stumble to the wood line on my cane. The air is crisp but not bitter, and the ground is a dry mess. Usually by this time of year there would be snow on the ground. Lucky for me there isn't.

"This is where I found you, leaned up against that tree there." He points. "I don't want to spook you, but there were bear and wolf tracks leading into the woods. You know Smith—"

"Was killed by a bear. Yes, I know. Would you mind doing me another favor? Could you give me some time alone? I'll call you when I am ready to leave."

"Mr. Mart—James, no. I cannot leave you alone here. For goodness sake, you can barely walk."

"I need some time. You don't have to worry about me. I've been around this forest my whole life. I'll be fine. And if you're worried that I'm planning to go off on a long hike, don't be. I'll just be here. Plus, I'm sure you have more important things to do than follow a cripple around."

"It's not—"

"Please."

Another long pause. "I'll give you two hours." He raises a pair of fingers to ensure I get the point. "After that I'm coming back, whether you call or not. And I'll leave an extra coat and some water here with you. And a radio."

"Sounds good."

I watch him drive away, reluctance scrawled across his face. When his truck is out of sight, I stagger into the woods, looking for her.

It's not long before I hear a rustling from behind the trees. A wolf peeks its head out, and I see the unmistakable black mark on its head. I know now not to fear this creature. Instead, the sight of it warms my heart with expectation. I shamble towards it, reaching out my hand as if greeting a friendly dog. It warily sniffs my fingers, then looks me straight in the eye.

"Bring me to her," I say.

I can't tell if it understands; it simply turns and bounds off, deeper into the woods. I struggle to follow, pain thundering in my thigh. I strain to breathe the cold, thin air, but carry on nonetheless.

Then, almost by accident, I stumble on it—the tree I'd been leaning on when I had almost died. A large bloodstain covers a wide swath of its trunk. I run my hand across the jagged bark, wondering how I could have survived such a thing. Of course, the reason is now obvious.

I hear another rustling sound, but before I can turn, I feel her arms wrap around me from behind. Her skin is rough but supple, like a young tree, and she leans into me. I smell dirt and flowers, and I hear the soothing melody of birdsong. I cannot help but smile.

She knows I have come for her, and she has been waiting.

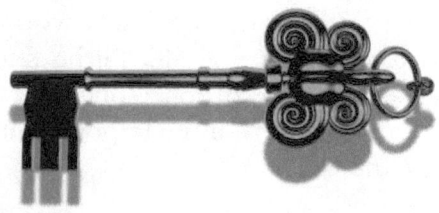

From the Author

I must confess, I've never been to Solana State Forest. I did visit Jay Cooke State Park during a school trip once, but don't remember much other than the tress. But there is something about trees, isn't there?

I grew up in Minnesota. I lived in various small cities and suburbs, but was always drawn to the wonderful forests that seem to be everywhere. Last fall, I drove across the middle of the state and was blown away by the sheer beauty of the dense woods. Compared with city life, which over the years seems to grow increasingly artificial, there is much more life and energy among the trees. Something ancient and primordial.

I don't recall how I came to writing this story, other than I knew I wanted to write something set in Minnesota. If you check my bibliography, you'll notice that I don't tend to write stories set in the real world. I mean, I run an indie publisher that exclusively publishes second-world fantasy! But every once in a while, it's nice to return to your roots.

As you might expect, I don't have a lot of stories in my repertoire that are similar to "Birdsong." The closest is probably the flash fiction piece "A Brief Glimpse of Everything," which was published as an audio short by *The Centropic Oracle,* available at: www.centropicoracle.com/library/F0015_aBriefGlimpseOfEverything.php.

Another with an earthly, environmental focus (albeit with a significant Sci-fi twist) was published by *Transmundane Press* here: transmundanepressblog.wordpress.com/2020/08/15/the-sun-flight-by-jm-williams/

You can find links for most of my other work here: jmwilliams.home.blog/published-works.

And, of course, I encourage you to check out my fantasy publishing house, *Of Metal and Magic Publishing,* here: ofmetalandmagicpublishing.wordpress.com

About the Author

JM Williams has a B.A. in English from the University of Minnesota and an M.A. in History with Pittsburg State University, where he won the Distinguish Thesis Award for writing about dead people. He continues to publish professional articles under his true name. He currently lives in Korea with his wife and an unmentionable number of cats.

JM Williams is the author of several SF/F books, including *Call of the Guardian* and *In the Valley of Magic*, and around 50 short stories. His short fiction has or will appear in *Abyss & Apex, Over My Dead Body! Mystery Magazine, The Arcanist, The New Accelerator, Bards and Sages*, and multiple anthologies.

He is the Editor-in-Chief for Of Metal and Magic Publishing, and he spends most of his time these days leading an international team of authors and editors. You can find JM online at:
jmwilliams.home.blog
and you can follow OMAM at:
ofmetalandmagicpublishing.wordpress.com

Double Exposure
by
Carolyn Ivy Stein

Double Exposure

S oft. Quiet. The only sound Sammy heard from outside was the slight creaking of the ice. He sipped the hot beef broth extract, enjoying the salty liquid as it burned down his throat and heated his chest. The cup's warmth seeped through his reindeer-skin mittens almost reaching his stiff finger joints. Not for the first time he wished for modern gear, but a critical part of responsible time travel was to avoid looking out of time.

There were twelve men assigned to this Time Rescue Team and only four chairs around the table, so Sammy crouched on the chilly, wood floor. He pressed his back against the hut's wall and read Watson's latest dispatch about Mr. Sherlock Holmes while Micky, Jason, Rascal, and Ben played cards in companionable silence. Captain Damano traced his fingers along the charts he'd brought from uptime showing the projected weather.

The snow started early at the top of the world. The first unsuccessful attempt to rescue men from the ill-fated Lady Franklin Bay expedition had been in 1882 when the *Neptune* tried to bring provisions to them but turned back. This year was bitterly cold, quite unlike the previous year's relatively warm temperatures. The conditions weren't right, Damano said. Sure seemed that way since the ship didn't come close enough for their team to take it over.

Sammy wished they didn't need the ship or that they could land directly onboard. But it is nearly impossible to accurately calculate the temporal coordinates for a ship since ships moved through space and time in inconsistent patterns. Otherwise, the mission would have been easy. Land on the ship. Take it over. That would be Sammy's plan if anyone asked him. But Damano decided they would wait for the relief ships and help them find Greely's party.

Sammy argued that rescuing Adolphus Greely's group as early as possible was critical and that the team should try anything to get there in 1882, but Captain Damano overruled him. Time rescues were tricky things. Too soon and there were all sorts of knock-on effects to the timeline. Too late and you ended up bringing them to their own home timeline only to watch them die.

This was the second time for this rescue. The Time Rescue Service first attempted to prevent the tragedy that killed their observer back in 1882 with the *Neptune* provisioning ship, but that came to nothing.

By morning ice crystallized on every narrow crack and surface. The wind howled, whipping the small wooden base camp with such vigor that the men discussed what to do if the Arctic winds tore their shelter to pieces.

That morning they ate hot oatmeal and coffee. Sammy mixed a few spoonfuls of sugar and butter into his coffee, which made it a drink suitable for an Arctic explorer in his opinion.

By afternoon, the problem of the wind solved itself. Several feet of snow buried the wooden structure. No one could open the door and Captain Damano ordered the fires extinguished to avoid smoke inhalation or oxygen starvation.

That evening the men shared cold tinned carrots, tinned sardines, and hard travel biscuits dipped in lard without complaint. They slept cold in their flannel long underwear, overgarments, and guernsey jackets inside their reindeer skin sleeping bags. It didn't matter. When the outside temperature drops to -48 degrees, even the best shelter feels cold. Still, none of the men protested.

The days moved on in relative darkness. The captain ordered lantern light rationed to just a few hours each day, but it was impossible to know when one day went and the next arrived. Sammy volunteered a solution. He would read one of Mr. Sherlock Holmes's dispatches aloud to everyone each day. The time it took to read, would be free lantern time. After that Ben, the cook, would prepare their cold meal and extinguish the lantern after everyone ate. The men would bed down or talk or whatever they cared to do in the darkness.

Sammy figured he'd crack first. The crazy darkness all the time got to him. If it weren't for Dr. Watson and his dispatches, he'd go clear out of this mind. He lived for the stories, which he'd been permitted to bring as a good way for the men to acclimate to the culture of the time. He bought the old-time book on a lark, but now the stories were his lifeline to sanity. One aspect of time travel that often caught the newbies was the sheer boredom of the past. Without easy access to stories, music, empathicasts, and other entertainments, people in the past were forced to the four corners of their own mind. Not everyone could handle that. Sammy personally thought that every potential time traveler should have to spend time in a silent Zen retreat for a month or two to train the mind. He even went so far as to submit it as a formal suggestion to the council, but as far as he could tell he'd been ignored.

Winter continued in darkness and dullness. In two months, Sammy ran out of new stories to read. By popular request he started reading the book again from the beginning.

Two men succumbed to boredom and darkness. Ben battered his body against the sealed door until the ice gave way and he could crawl through the snow in his homemade tunnel. He ran screaming into the night. Sammy joined the party to find him, but the ice and the potential predators forced them back indoors. They couldn't find him, and he didn't return.

"Somewhere," Rascal said, "There is a very happy polar bear."

It was the only eulogy Ben received.

The following month one of the new men crawled out into the snow while the rest were asleep. They found him the next morning frozen solid. They interred him in snow and gave him a proper eulogy. Sammy had no doubt that someone uptime was studying time stream charts to figure out how to either remove the new guy and Ben from the roster or rescue them. The trick was to do it without interrupting the downtime mission.

He still remembered Ben, but the new guy... Sammy tried to call him to mind and found it slippery. Huh. He'd heard of this. Never experienced it though. Guess they got him out. Poor Ben. Sammy remembered the irascible chef all too well.

The captain and the first mate continued to study the charts on the time stream throughout the long winter and compared them to the nautical charts. There was a point that an experienced time analyst could predict when the ship would precisely cross their path. When that happened, they would commandeer the *Proteus*.

Finally, on July 1, 1883, the team was instructed to arrange the tents and crates on the ice near the shore so that the ships would see them and assume that they were Greely's exploration party.

After so many months indoors, Sammy jumped at the chance for some real physical labor. Still the crates and tents were heavier than they'd been last summer. All of their muscles had decayed in the darkness and inactivity of the Arctic winter.

In the main history timeline, the *Proteus* left St. John's to bring provisions to the Lady Franklin Bay Expedition June 28th under Garlington's command. But bad weather and ice floes trapped the ship and crushed the *Proteus* on July 22nd, sinking with most of the provisions still on board. Garlington left a note for Greely explaining what happened. After he his crew abandoned ship, they survived in small boats for forty days until they were rescued. This was the turning point of the tragedy. Once the provisions Greely and his men depended on sank below the icy waters, their starvation and deaths were virtually assured.

Captain Damano and the Time Rescue Service said that the best place to intervene in the timeline was before the *Proteus* sank. If they could take the ship, they'd use their explosives to break up the ice, allowing the ship to sail to the provisioning point. Once there, they'd leave the provisions and rescue their agent.

The trick was that they couldn't rescue the Lady Franklin Bay Expedition. Greely's team had to remain in place long enough for the third Greely Relief Expedition to arrive carrying Washington Irving Chambers. This lesser-known member of the Navy played a critical role in the early naval aviation program. Without him, development of air power would have been delayed. Without distinguishing himself early in the Greely Relief Expedition, he wouldn't have been in the right place at the right time to push aviation technology.

The captain cleared his throat and all eyes turned to him. "According to Schley's report on the Greely Relief Mission, by the time their ship got to the survivors seventeen of the twenty-five men already died of starvation. The report says one drowned while sealing to find food."

"You think that's our guy?" Sammy asked.

"Got to be. Probably looking for us."

The first mate traced one of the lines with his finger. "This is it. The *Proteus* will pass us by tomorrow on the way to Cape Sabine, if we've done our chronocalc right."

"We've checked the streams. We'll see the *Proteus* and the *Yantic* tomorrow."

The first mate pulled on his luxuriant long black beard that he was inordinately proud of. He'd already explained several times to anyone who would listen to his theory that long beards were the true sign of manliness in the past. If they met any attractive downtime women, he predicted they would be overcome with lust at the sight of his beard. "Do we have enough men to carry out the plan? We made it for eleven and there are only ten of us left. What if we encounter resistance?"

Eleven. Not twelve. The first mate forgot what's-his-name. The new guy. He was part of the expedition, wasn't he?

"That's why we plan to seize the *Proteus*. It is primarily manned by civilians. The *Yantic* is the naval vessel. Let's set up the camp so that we can be 'rescued.'" With his narrow face, and the wicked gleam in his eye, the first mate really did look a bit like a pirate Sammy thought. He'd heard rumors that in missions to the seventeenth century, he'd rushed into ship boarding operations like a man possessed, waving his weapons. It was a wonder he'd never died. But that kind of boldness and physical knowledge could be handy here, and Sammy was glad to have the larger man by his side.

The *Proteus*, still in good condition despite the blowing snow and whipping winds that made the ice rip across the men's exposed flesh like a thousand tiny razor blades, sailed into the ice-curdled harbor. The captain calculated it true. The ship arrived within about an hour of when he predicted it would. The only question now was whether they could take over the *Proteus* before the *Yantic* and the military men on that ship caught up with them. The *Yantic*, her hull too thin-skinned to challenge any ice, held back from the shore. Captain Damano predicted that the military vessel and the *Proteus* would arrive separately. He was once again right.

Sammy's primary concern was that the plan had been developed for ten men and they were a group of only nine after Ben's disappearance. Captain Damano claimed confidence in the team's ability to overpower the bridge crew and take the *Proteus*.

Sammy wished that the first mate had agreed to come with the group. But he got cold feet shortly before the mission started. They could have used his raw power and skill with downtime weapons when they took over the *Proteus*. Of all of the Time Service employees he was the only one with skill in piracy. It was a mystery why they didn't require him to undertake this mission. The problem with an all-volunteer Time Service, he supposed.

The men had arranged a few tents and several crates on the ice by the shore to lure the *Proteus* and the Yantis. It worked, too. The *Proteus* seeing the encampment sailed directly to them.

From that point on, it had been simple. The story they told was that they were a third ship, one hired by Henrietta Greely herself to rescue her husband and his men. Their ship sank after hitting an iceberg that ripped a hole in the hull. After that it wasn't even a lie to tell how difficult it had been to endure the long hard winter.

Everyone knew that Henrietta Greely was a fierce woman who moved through the world like a battleship with all guns blazing for to rescue her husband. Their story held water, even if their imaginary ship did not.

Captain Garlington of the *Proteus* sent men to help load the crates on board. The men of the Time Rescue Service stowed their gear in the forecastle where the crew slept. It was Sammy's first experience aboard one of these ships. He'd been warned, but nothing prepared him for the stink. Black slime covered the walls of the small space. Thankfully it felt warm, a relief in the Arctic, but he imagined it would be deeply unpleasant in warmer climes. The foul air stank of smoke, old food, farts, and tainted meat.

Once they were on the ship, Captain Damano motioned to the stern. "Ready? It was your idea, after all."

Since the team was down to six people on this mission from the initial complement of eight, Sammy had suggested they try to persuade the captain to take them to Greely. The team could always escalate to force need be, but it would be better if it didn't come to that. As the proponent of the plan, and since Sammy was the first mate, it fell to him to execute it.

Captain Damano and Sammy asked Lieutenant John Colwell to escort them to the poop deck where the captain and the helmsman steered the ship. Sammy stared at the lieutenant, wanting to memorize his face and features. This man would go on to establish the United States' intelligence network in Europe. By all accounts he was a daring man of great cunning, but today he looked like any other young man in his mid-twenties with deep-set brown eyes, a nicely trimmed mustache, and a ready smile.

Captain Damano motioned to Sammy. "Captain, let me introduce First Mate Samuel Westing. He has an idea that may work to get the supplies to Greely's expedition while avoiding the dangers to the *Proteus*."

"I'm listening," Captain Garlington said. Sammy took a look around the poop deck, located at the stern. He'd expected a bridge from the fiction he'd read but apparently these ships just had a raised section protected by a tarp. It was a relief in a way since the air was fresh here. At least compared to below deck. A table with a nautical chart and the compass mounted inside a binnacle stood to the left. To the rear, the large wheel that steered the ship was manned by another neatly dressed young sailor with deep blue eyes. He smiled.

Sammy walked over to the chart and pointed. "Sir, based on our intelligence, we believe that Greely is here. We have explosives in the supplies we brought aboard. We can use those to break the ice ahead of the ship. If we move quickly, we can get in and get out before the ice closes in on us."

Captain Garlington looked at the chart. "We have orders to leave the supplies on the east coast of Grinnell Land. I can't see risking this ship and crew."

"It's a daring plan," Lieutenant Colwell said, stroking his mustache. "If we carry it off, we will ensure Greely's survival. It's been a year since the *Neptune* turned back without provisioning the expedition. How do we know that they aren't in desperate need of our supplies?"

Garlington coughed into his hand. "I am not worried about Lieutenant Greely. He's living in a region stocked with game. Even if he has had to economize on provisions, the rocks and water abound with walrus, reindeer, and the odd bear. They probably eat better than we do."

"I don't believe that is true, sir," Sammy said. "It is critical that we get these supplies to that expedition."

"If they do not receive the provisions, we cannot know that we did our jobs. Our honor depends on it as well as those men's lives," Colwell said. There was an intensity to the man and Sammy found himself re-evaluating him. He seemed to glow with an inner fire.

The discussion continued on for a while. Finally, the captains agreed that they would try to get as close to Greely's encampment as possible, but if the ice closed in, they would turn back.

Icebreaking was a tedious process. The men had to set the explosives just so and then detonate them so that they cleared a path ahead of the ship. Then move the ship and repeat the process. At the same time the men at watch ensured that the ice did not close in behind them.

To Sammy's delight it appeared to be working. July was just past summer solstice. There were still many ice chunks floating through the water looking like peaks of whipped cream in the sea, but there was no better time to do this than now.

He and the others in the Time Rescue Service worked alongside the *Proteus* crew and the soldiers aboard to clear the path. It was a blast to meet these men of the past and work with them. With the exception of Colwell, they didn't seem as heroic as he'd imagined. But it was a singular experience that he would treasure forever. He would never forget this.

He'd argued to the Time Rescue Council, before their mission, that they needed a larger crew. He'd doubted that an initial crew of just six men could take over the *Proteus*, but clearly he'd been wrong. It was going to succeed. It was glorious.

They made it through the worst of the ice before the ship rocked violently.

"We're taking on water."

"What happened?" Garlington asked.

"Looks like we hit something submerged."

A wave of water flooded the ship's deck. Water everywhere. Filling Sammy's lungs like ice.

Sammy glanced around the three grave faces in the Time Rescue Council's meeting. Lila, Mulgrove, and Sanjeev looked tired. Their faces were strained beyond what he'd seen in the past. Lila looked old as if she'd lived a thousand lives in the course of this meeting.

Off to the side Micky, Rascal, and Jason played cards using a standard nineteenth century deck, trying to figure out the old games before they moved back in time. They waited on the decision, just as Sammy did. Their quiet discussion and the thrum of the generator on the floor below comforted him with its soft, rhythmic white noise. He let the sounds wash over him as he thought about what the Council said.

He took a sip of his hot green tea, letting the vegetal bitterness and the light creamy smell of good Japanese sencha distract him. He'd miss it when they travelled back to the past. If they travelled back.

"I don't understand," he said for the eighth time that day. "What is the delay? We agreed on a team of twenty men in two flushes. We can do this."

"It's over. We've tried twenty times. It ends the same way each time."

"But you haven't tried with me, have you? I can do this. Make me the captain of the expedition instead of Damano."

"We tried that, too."

With each sentence Sammy's volume and pitch rose. He pressed his hands together, motioning with them clasped in front of him as he spoke. "You're not going to leave one of our own there? Dead? We're the Time Rescue Service. It's what we do. We find people stuck in time. We don't let them die."

Lila shook her head and her pretty golden curls bounced. Her eyes were bright with tears Sammy remembered that the traveler stuck in the past had been her best friend. "We tried our best. He is unavailable to us. We've made arrangements to place George Von Sprecklson and John Degen on the *Thetis*. If our man survives, we will find him in 1884. If he did not and we cannot find him then, we will have to give up. Sometimes people who drown in the waves of time, cannot be rescued."

How could Sammy have already travelled back to 1882 twenty times. That seemed highly improbable. Shouldn't he remember something? He looked up to argue again for the mission, but they were already heading for the door. Mulgrove gave Lila a hug as they exited.

They'd be back. They couldn't be serious about leaving a man to die, could they?

He wished he could remember it if he had gone twenty times. Twenty different tries. What would that be like? Would it be blurred or like double-exposure art? If he concentrated it did seem like he could see scenes, but they mutated and shifted like dreams. He focused harder but even as he concentrated the dreamy scenes slipped away.

Frustrated Sammy sat down with the book he'd intended to read on their journey to the past, *The Collected Adventures of Sherlock Holmes*. He came across the line that seemed to sum up time travel in general and his situation in particular: "Once you eliminate the impossible, whatever remains, no matter how improbable, must be the truth."

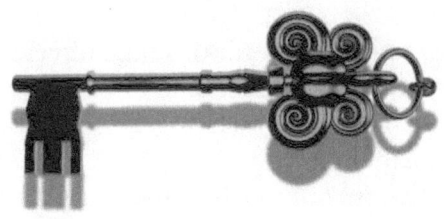

From the Author

For me, this story started with reindeer mittens. And reindeer sleeping bags. And reindeer clothing.

In the race to find the North Pole first, countries sent explorers to confront the brutal icy seascape. Those who went, changed: for better or worse. The Arctic remained the riskiest place to explore until we sent people to space. Many ships never returned. Some ships were found, hulls crushed, their crews missing. Or, even more horribly, barely alive after having eaten their fellow explorers. One horror not anticipated: the deadly ennui of being trapped in a small research cabin, unable to leave, in the unrelieved darkness of Arctic winter. It drove men mad.

One day my husband, an award-winning Naval historian with a sub-specialty in Arctic exploration, sent me a link to Commander Schley's report on the Greely Relief Expedition: one of many attempts to supply and rescue previous Arctic explorers. The supply list, my husband assured me, was fascinating. It might be a good source for details for a game supplement. (Published as "Derelicts on Ice," available from Steve Jackson Games.)

A specification for reindeer clothing, including custom-made mittens, piqued my interest. Why reindeer skin? I read on.

Schley's report is a compendium of contemporaneous documents and photos telling of their heroic mission to resupply and rescue the Greely expedition's members after two previous supply ships failed to reach them. Despite Schley's best efforts, they rescued just seven survivors. One more survivor died on the way home. Had Schley's ships arrived just two days later, there would have been no survivors. A week earlier and they could have saved one additional man.

I saw a perfect pivot point for this time travel story, which went on to win an Honorable Mention in the Writers of the Future contest. Move the date the Greely Relief Expedition arrived by as little as a week in either direction and everything changes.

The story is fiction, but much of the history is real.

As to those reindeer mittens? They were the most suitable for Arctic conditions, something the explorers learned from the Inuit, who are experts on Arctic survival.

About the Author

Carolyn Ivy Stein writes time travel, mystery, fantasy, and romance stories. They appeared in WMG's Winter Holiday Spectacular 2021, JewishFiction.net, and can be found in her collections, Lightning Scarred and Other Stories and Sweet Lifts. She received nine Honorable Mentions from the Writers of the Future Contest. With her husband, Stephen Stein, she writes RPG supplements. Their upcoming book, GURPS: Biremes and Triremes will be out in late-2022 from Steve Jackson Games. When not writing, she plays games, hikes, and conducts dubious experiments trying to replicate historic cuisine.

Find her at www.carolynivystein.com.

The Architects
by
Eve Morton

The Architects

*T*he first time I witnessed a room disappear on campus, I was a proctor for an exam.

When you're in graduate school, you'll take whatever work you can get. All students are desperate, and I was no exception. When all the qualification you need to be a proctor is the necessary gender in order to escort students to the bathroom during the exam, hover outside to make sure they don't cheat, and then take them back to the room, it's an easy gig. Even when it is at seven in the morning, on the first day of winter, and in a part of the school I'd never seen before. Most of the other proctor spots needed men, since they had women profs. This was the only class, for a man named Tom North, who required a woman.

I snapped up the opportunity as soon as I could. I received a confirmation from the admin staff and waited the week until the exam was set. I'd never met Tom North before, but since he was a staple of the old guard on campus, I'd seen his framed face on the wall of the school's teacher's lounge. He was a Big Deal back in the day, but he'd since become a dinosaur. In the age of social media and Rate My Professor, he would have barely received tenure. Then again, they don't do tenure anymore.

I took the bus on the designated morning while it was still dark. Frost dotted the campus lawns as I walked deeper and deeper into the hulking buildings which shifted and changed from one generation of architecture to the next. When the campus first opened, there had only been the brick buildings, the yellow-painted welcome center at the front of the campus, and the expansive library. The brick buildings had now become the designated Arts area, where my office was in a basement. The welcome center stayed roughly the same, save for a few updates to plumbing, and the library was now in the center, rather than the far edge, of the campus itself. The rest of the campus had been added on in the last fifty years, thanks to the school's graduates and reputation becoming more prominent for Math, Sciences, and Engineering. As I walked, the buildings seemed to evolve alongside me. They became sleeker and taller, filled with windows and elongated forms, until it felt as if I had wandered too far from the 1950s brutalism that marked my office and into a sci-fi landscape.

I was amazed. I'd never needed to go beyond the library before. Even when I was on the top floor of that building, and could see the outstretched campus, I never looked too closely at the architecture. Only the foliage and the Canadian geese that stayed here all winter long.

Though I was acting as a proctor for an Arts class—Milton and his Contemporaries, according to the course calendar—exam season demanded bigger rooms, and so, better buildings were used. I had thought I would be ushered into the gym, but the room I needed to go to was in a building called M2. It was for Maths and Sciences. I located it on the edge of the campus, almost a twenty-minute walk from where my own office was, and I arrived with barely ten minutes to spare. I hurried through the glass doors, warming instantly, and walked past large fossils and rock specimens, from the local mines, encased in class. I wanted to stay and linger, examine what seemed to be a hidden museum inside a university campus, but I was more concerned about making a good impression on Tom North.

I located the stairs and headed to the second floor where the exam was. I stepped out and realized I was on the third floor. I doubled back into the stairwell, but there was no other door than the one I'd stepped into. Only two twists of the stairs.

The second floor was gone. Or at least, I had no access to it in the stairwell.

I found the elevator on the ground level. I now only had five minutes until the exam began. In the elevator, I punched the #2 key easily. I stepped out a second later into an area of campus that looked like any other. There were tile floors that scuffed my shoes, thick wooden doors leading into various rooms, and a large foyer.

An empty foyer.

Even though it had been a long time since I'd written an exam myself, there were always early birds outside, hastily cramming until the last minute. Or late stragglers who wandered in from a bus, dazed and disoriented.

But there was no one here. Not even footprints or boot tracks from the limited snow outside. There was no evidence at all that anyone but me had been in the building all morning.

I walked down one of the two corridors that split off from the foyer. I compared the number of the room I'd been given for the exam against the doors around me. I walked in a semi-circle and came out the other side of the large foyer.

There was nothing. No room. And the only way there could have been a room with that number would have been if the exam could take place here, in the foyer. From the way the stairs and the halls curved, it was the only way to make sense of anything.

"Hello?" I called out, thinking of nothing else to do.

No answer.

I started to panic then, believing this to be my error and my error alone. My phone had no signal in the thick walls, so I stepped out of the building—it probably wasn't the right one anyway—and called the front desk in the English Department.

"Hello?" a woman named Margaret answered. "How can I help you?"

I explained the situation to Margaret. "I'm a proctor for Tom North, but I think I'm lost. I can't find the room." I gave her the number. I heard her click the keyboard on the other side. When she was silent a long time, I babbled about receiving a confirmation for the job, and that though I'd never met Professor North before, I didn't want to leave him with a bad impression. "If I'm late, it's one thing. But I don't want to make it so his students suffer, either."

More clicks. Soft breathing from the other side. "This is odd. Says the exam was supposed to be in the Arts department." She listed a number close to my office.

"What? I was never told. I'll head right over."

"Then he cancelled it," Margaret added, her voice thin. "I'm so sorry. I guess no one got around to telling you. It's the end of the year, and—"

"Oh. Oh." I let out a breath. It was a mistake. No one's fault. When Margaret assured me that I'd still be paid for my time, all three hours the exam was supposed to go on, I really had nothing to be mad about.

"Again, we're sorry," Margaret said. "Enjoy your day—and your holidays!"

I spent the rest of the morning in the strange building, looking at the fossils and the rock specimens I'd never seen before. But soon would see, nearly every day, in time.

The second time a room disappeared on campus, I nearly missed it because it wasn't a room at all. It was a hallway that suddenly disappeared, and nearly left me stranded in my office during a winter storm.

A year had passed since the incident with Tom North. I moved on from the preliminary stages of my PhD, passed the classes and the comprehensive exams, and was now in my writing mode. Tom North had retired shortly after the proctor mix-up, and I'd heard through the mailroom gossip circle that he'd died. Not uncommon for professors of his generation. It was one of the main issues—spoken about in hushed, polite tones, of course—that people in the department reminded me of when I selected Maurice Callahan as my own supervisor. He was of Tom North's generation, had started the PhD department when he first began teaching at the university, and was already in his mid-seventies. He'd had no health problems so far, but that seemed to be a strike against him. It would only be a matter of time.

I liked Maury, as he wanted to be called, though. He was funny. He laughed at my jokes. And there was a certain allure to the fact that he was almost as old as the school itself. He'd watched the campus unfold into the strange monolith that it was now.

"It had a completely different reputation ten, twenty years ago," he told me during one of our monthly supervisory meetings. "It was an Arts school, through and through. You know the sculpture that's just outside Hubert Hall?"

I nodded. The sculpture was of a flat man, as if he'd been steamrolled, throwing a ball in the air.

"It's not a ball. It's a shot-put. It was supposed to be a symbol for the sports team—the flames—and a symbol for Prometheus stealing fire."

"Supposed to?"

"Yes, well, I think he sort of loses his context now. The art may stay, but meanings change. And well, it feels like we're strictly in the punishment stage of Prometheus's life, getting our livers plucked out."

I laughed. I could see—and sympathize with—his disdain for the lack of funding the Arts was now receiving. "That's hindsight for you, I guess."

"That's the thing," Maury said. "Prometheus means foresight. We should have seen this coming before, not after, our funding was gutted. Hindsight was Prometheus's brother, Epimetheus."

"I don't know that story," I said, cheeks blushing. I made a note to look it up, but Maury told it to me anyway.

"He was the twin of Prometheus, and together they were tasked with giving animals traits. But since Epimetheus lacks foresight like Prometheus, he didn't give anything to man. He was a fool, in short, which then led his brother to steal fire and stand trial for that crime. Personally, I think we undervalue Epimetheus. He can be the fool, sure, but he's also the kind one. There is no ulterior motive here. He's pure materialism, which is to say, thought comes afterwards. He makes something. Then he tells us about it." Maury laughed. "I think a lot of PhD students can benefit from that attitude. Not you, of course." He gave me a sly smile. "But I see many students tell me what they're going to write, and then never do it. Just write the damn thing, you know? Then you can steal fire somewhere else. Now, let's get back to your project."

It was only three days after that conversation when I became stuck in my office. The hallway that I'd taken to get there had simply disappeared. There were two main stairwells to gain entry to the basement of the building: one was the main entrance, flanked by glass doors and school colors, and then there was the back exit that was barely noticeable, especially in winter, when snow was piled close to the doorway. It was known as the "smoker's exit" since those piles of snow often turned gray in no time with cigarette butts and ash.

I liked using the smoker's doorway. It made coming and going to my office feel clandestine, and since students always seemed to recognize me on campus and want to discuss their grades, being covert was necessary. I'd taken that exit as an entrance like I always did, walked by the bathrooms and the information area, and then settled into my office, next to many other PhD offices. An hour, maybe two, had passed. When I was ready to leave, I wanted to use the bathroom.

But they were gone. The entire information center and its waiting room was gone. There was only a blank wall, nothing hanging on it, where it had once been.

"I don't..." I didn't finish my sentence because I heard it echo. I placed a hand against the wall that I swore had never been there. It was solid. I pressed my ear against it. I swore I could hear something—murmuring, chattering—but it could have been my own heartbeat. I tried to follow the wall, to see if it would lead me somewhere else, but it was truly a dead end. Just a wall where there had once been a way out.

I turned the other direction, in search of the elevator. That was the only other way I knew of getting to the front exit. My heart did not stop pounding in my chest until I stepped out on the first floor, saw the blazing sunlight through the glass doors, and touched them. They were real. They let me leave.

I was too spooked to go around back, where the smokers left their cigarettes, to check if that door was still there. By the time I did, a week and a half later, nothing had changed.

The hallway was back where it had been. There was a smoker's exit again.

But a clear sign had now been posted in red, angry letters NO SMOKING WITHIN 9M OF THE BUILDING. The janitorial staff, and a handful of grad students, were now in obeisance of that law, and stood nine meters back. I wanted to go over and join them, take up smoking simply to ask if they had been there last week, and if so, did they get trapped outside, unable to get back in? When had the hallway come back? What the hell had happened?

But I didn't say a thing to them.

I saw Maurice instead.

"Now that's interesting," he said, after I'd spilled the incident about the hallway and the previous one a year ago with Tom North's non-existent exam room. "You should write a story about that."

"I don't want to," I said. Maurice often worked under the premise that nearly everyone obtaining an English Literature PhD wanted to be a writer in some way. He did when he was young, though, and some of the other grad students also harbored literary ambitions—but I just wanted to understand things. Including the strange campus. "I just want to know that I can trust the campus maps, and trust where I think I'm going."

"You can trust the maps," Maurice said. "Especially the online ones. They update more frequently."

"So, you're telling me that the online map would have reflected that sudden change in my office? Even if it was only for an hour or a week?"

"I don't know. I don't use it myself."

"How do you get around?" I asked him. He'd told me on several occasions that he walked everywhere, including to and from the campus since his house was merely a block away. It kept him young, he joked. But maybe it also kept him with working knowledge of a place that I was starting to realize I could never fully pin down or figure out.

"On foot," he answered obviously.

"But how do you remember where to go?"

"I've been here a long time, remember. I was here when the Dean gave the order to build most of the newer parts of campus. I was even on some committees when they were electing to reshape some of this building, too."

"They've renovated Hubert Hall?" I looked around the thick brick walls of his office, so much like mine in the basement. The architecture itself was so dense cell phones never worked. Even some of the computers that had been installed didn't get Wi-Fi and had to rely on Ethernet cables. "Hard to tell."

"I know, but they did. And it was a serious endeavor and expense, hence the committee. It was in the 1960s," he began, getting somewhat of a dreamy quality to his voice. "I won't bore you with too many details, because I could write a book about this myself."

"Maybe you should."

"Maybe. But I think it's been done. Either way, this meeting was about the foyer. They didn't want a large one for students to congregate inside. In effect, they wanted to avoid protesting. There was a lot of uproar about Kent State, with good reason, and so when I say that the staff didn't want protestors, don't think they were regressive. They merely wanted to save student lives. So, they decided to not have a large foyer, and extend what they needed to do through many hallways instead."

"Really? Like where my office is?"

"Yes. That's why I thought it was interesting that a hallway disappeared. Almost like the school is fighting back, protesting itself."

I didn't want to believe him, yet I could feel it in my bones that he was right. "What about the other building?" I asked a moment later.

"The one where Tom North's exam should have happened, but didn't? M2, Mathematics. That's a newer building, right?"

"It is. But North—oh, he hated that area."

"Hard not to," I said then quickly added, "given the history between arts and sciences and funding. But it was really pretty. There were fossils there. It was nice."

"Yes, I've seen those myself. The architect is a bit better than this brutalism. At least phones work."

"Sometimes," I added. "Not that morning with me."

"Huh." He shrugged, and then ran his hand over his beard. "From what I recall, though, the architect who designed those buildings was related to the first one who did Hubert Hall, version 1.0."

"Including the hallways?"

"I think so. They were brothers?" Maury shook his head. "No, couldn't have been with the generational difference, especially in styles. Must have been father and son, or something like that. I think I remember the surnames being similar. Potter or Pohle or something like that. So yeah, father and son." When he noticed me take a note, he added with a wry smile, "Be sure to double-check my information, of course. I'm not exactly as much of a library as I used to be."

I told him I would. Then I remembered the library. "What about that?"

"What about the library? It's been here as long as I can remember."

"Right. Who built it? Was it the father or the son?"

"That I don't know, but I would assume the father. It hasn't been renovated, though, aside from the tech updates. So maybe it's the only place on campus that will stay still."

"Maybe." I wrote down 'Library' and underlined it several times. Then, as easily and as quickly as we spoke about the campus, we moved onto my PhD research. My dissertation was almost complete, and when it was, my time at this school would be coming to an end.

The third time the campus changed shape for me, I was prepared.

I was teaching a class in the Environmental Sciences building. It was closer to the center of campus, having been one of the first buildings in the expansion of the early 1990s. Everyone on campus back then had welcomed the addition. It was the early days of environmental awareness at a popular cultural level; the legwork in critical Sciences had already been done by Rachel Carson's Silent Spring in the 1960s, and so, having a building on an already liberal and progressive campus devoted to the green movement was easy to understand and push through budgetary approval.

It was also easy to make the building stunning. Filled with high glass windows and large, spacious foyers, there was clearly no fear of protestors here. Entirely one side of the foyer walls was covered in a make-shift trellis, complete with waterfall that allowed whatever greenery on the trellis to bloom and grow and thrive. The staircase into the upper levels was open and allowed for complete viewing of the green wall. I loved looking at it up close—but those stairs gave me vertigo. I often took the elevators to my class on the third floor, or I took the back stairwell when there was a line-up for the elevator.

I was halfway through the spring semester when I noticed the contours of the building change. I took the stairwell to the third floor, but the sign on the doorway out read the second. I continued walking, and added another flight, but came out at the fourth floor.

The third floor had disappeared.

I walked down to the building's ground level and started again. The elevators took me to the third floor, but when I walked out, it was still the second. That was where all the offices, rather than classrooms, were so it was easy to recognize. I doubled back once again and stood in the foyer. Some of my students had already started to arrive, and seeing me, went over to say hello.

"Are you all right?" a girl named Deidre asked me. "You look a little pale, if you don't mind me saying."

I considered lying for a moment, saying I was sick, and cancelling the class. How could I get to the class if the floor didn't seem to exist? But when I saw Shawn, another student of mine, take the free-floating stairs next to the green wall, and make it to the third floor without doubling back, I realized there was only one way to the room.

"I'm fine," I told Deidre. "But will you walk with me? I don't quite like heights."

Deidre was one of those eager to please students, so she took me up on my offer without protest. I made a mental note to give her 100 for participation for the next six weeks, until this class was done, since

I knew I'd be relying on her far more. We found the room together, as easy as pie, except that the nagging feeling of the floor disappearing again bothered me.

We were in the middle of Marilyn Robinson's Gilead this week, a text about an absent father writing to his son who will not remember him, and it felt as if the campus was mocking me in some way. Or aligning in the best way possible. From one of the large glass windows in the room, as I read off the passage, I wanted my students to analyze, I saw the library's ornate edifice and tall, imposing structure.

The library, where nothing seemed to change. The library, where, from its top-most floor, all of the campus could be visible.

I quickly finished my class, with ten minutes to spare, and dismissed them. Deidre stayed behind. "Do you need help getting down the stairs?"

"No thank you," I told her. "Going down is always easier than going up."

She nodded and gave a silent promise to be there the next week. I knew it would not be a problem, though. The campus was going to right itself, even if I had to be the mediator between father and son.

My visits to the library, at first, were uneventful. I went to the top floor, studied the landscape, but still came back with all I'd seen before: a lot of nice greenery, a campus split in two, and those ever-present geese. I wandered through the stacks, trying to find all I could about the architects who built the campus but only came up with names, the thinnest of biographies, and blueprints. Frederick and Philip Pohle. Father and son, much like Maury had said, and with different design schools influencing their work.

When Frederick had died, Philip took over his business but left many clients unhappy with his attempts to become the Canadian Frank Lloyd Wright. He didn't have enough ambition to take on that kind of legacy, however, or the proper work ethic, so most of his designs remained on paper. The only places that came to fruition were ones he inherited from his father: the campus extension, a renovated downtown building that I had never liked, and a hospital a town over that had since been torn down. Philip had no children of his own, and so the family business died with him.

I made photocopies of all the blueprints I could find, giving special attention to the campus extensions. I figured I could take those, at the very least, to Maury who might be able to help me piece the mystery together—but I soon realized the maps fit over one another. Not as a mere expansion of the campus, but as another layer over top. I took the photocopies out of the tray and made sure that what I'd seen in a glimpse could truly fit. Once I found the library on the blueprints, and used it as the centering anchor it was, the campuses aligned. It was perfect. They weren't added on in a spatial way but stacked up in geological time.

"Like those fossils," I said aloud. The library was so quiet my voice, though a whisper, seemed to be a roar. Everyone in the study carrels had on headphones, so no one noticed. But I tip-toed around like a mouse, suddenly afraid that the secret was out.

After asking a librarian for tracing paper, I went into a study area and laid out the maps on top of one another. I traced around them, wondering if I could see the way in which floors and hallways had disappeared on me. I could make the maps work in some instances, but not in others.

Baffled, I logged into some of the online accounts for the school's student body and found a message board. A handful of people described the campus as the most difficult to navigate they'd ever come across. The room I needed seemed to disappear, one person wrote, peaking my attention. It sounds crazy, but that's what happened. I didn't find it until a week later.

I started to link together online reports with my own experiences. Soon enough, when I flipped over the blueprint I'd traced so it was now a mirror image on top of the older campus, the coordinates began to make sense. Father and son had designed the exact same building, but always in opposition.

So how to make them stop feuding, even after death? I wondered about this for a long time. It was only as the semester wore on, and Maury began to get more persistent about my dissertation, that I remembered his words of foresight and hindsight.

Don't be like Prometheus, he wrote to me in an email. You don't want to be repeating this year over and over, even if it seems like fun. You gotta move on and finish that degree.

But what about hindsight? I asked him in return. What if I realize now that I like the campus, and want to stay?

He didn't answer me for a couple days. In the interim, I'd found the sole place of unbalance in my maps of the father and son campus. While the Arts campus had its own figure of Prometheus with a shot-put/fireball, the Science side of campus did not have such a figure. Only a blank area, where someone had put a trash can and where squirrels and geese congregated.

We can talk about alternative plans at your next meeting, Maury wrote back. It's usually better to teach at a different school. Shows depth. But if you really want to stay, we can figure out a way to make it work.

I will be teaching at a different school, I thought. I'd been stuck on the father's side of campus until that proctor exam. Frederick Pohle may have wanted me to, like the olden ways of graduate school, leave and set about on my own—but his son Philip had other plans. He was a bit more dynamic and interesting, if only on paper. He just needed more ambition and work ethic, something I knew I had in droves. If he only had his own monument to hindsight, maybe his father could be proud.

Then, after that, maybe the fighting could stop.

When I met with Maury a week later, I told him of my progress. He didn't seem that surprised that my dissertation, once about the genre known as the campus novel and the subsequent works of Don DeLillo, had now become about the father and son feud that seemed to stretch on for generations in the ever-shifting landscape.

"I told you," he said after I'd explained it all, including the pitch to get another statue to keep the men happy, "you should be a writer."

"Fine. Yes, sure, this is what I'll write my dissertation about, and it will help me get a job here. On Philip's campus, though. It'll be different that way."

Maury didn't say anything for a long time. He picked up the maps I'd given him, and the notes, including my sketch for the matching statue of Epimetheus on the other side. He was a flattened monument like the previous one on the other side, only he held a hammer in his hand rather than a shot-put/flame.

"I wanted the hammer to symbolize materialism," I told Maury in the silence. "The fact that thought here comes after form, after the hammer blow. And I—"

"It'll take a lot of funding to get this to go through," he said, cutting me off. It was not mean, only a fact.

"That's fine. I can help. I don't know how to fund beyond a bake sale, though."

Maury smiled. "You gotta learn grant writing soon. It'll be a great part of your service record. And if you can pull off this statue, especially as a Canadian historical site, while also writing your dissertation, well, then, you'll be a shoo-in as a prof here."

"Really?"

"Yes. Don't expect tenure, though," he added quickly. "No one gets that anymore."

I didn't want tenure. I just wanted to teach in that building with the fossils. I wanted to see a statue of a flattened man, holding a hammer like Epimetheus, and melding the work of father and son into one.

A year, then two, went by. My dissertation passed with few revisions, and I turned it into a book about the father and son team. I applied for a job teaching Writing and Communication to the Science and Math students and was accepted after three rounds of interviews. Not with tenure, of course, but with a three-year contract.

My office is now in the M2 building and overlooks the statue of Epimetheus on the campus.

Though sometimes, when I walk the same stairs that lead to the second floor, it disappears, but I now know how to get it back. I call out for father and son to behave, to develop some hindsight.

Then I take the elevator.

It all sorts itself out in the end.

When the campus is truly temperamental, and foresight or hindsight get us nowhere, then I cancel the class I need to teach entirely. I tell them to go to the library instead, because that's where I'll be. I make sure I am on the top floor, looking down on both time and space, and generations of a family history at once. I look out at all that I've inherited, all that I can claim as my own, with the right map to understand where to go next.

When a student shows up, which sometimes happens and sometimes not, I show them the statues of Prometheus and Epimetheus, and they learn, for at least an hour, how to stay in one place.

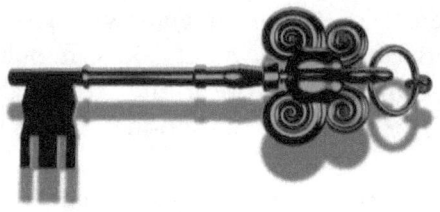

From the Author

"The Architects" was inspired by the event that opens the story: I was a proctor for an exam that didn't exist. While I waited for the prof who didn't show up, I wandered around a nice area of campus I'd never been to before. A mix-up like this gave me the time to think—a luxury!—about how I could be a grad student at a school for years and never see aspects of campus.

The shifting architecture and the family feud at the core of the story came to me as I wrote, and I ended up being very happy with the result. Though the history I made up for the campus is fictional, many of the places I described are real, and I still think of these characters whenever I walk around.

I also wrote another story about my hybrid real/fake school called "The Joke" that was published in *The Vanishing* earlier this year, so if you like this story, I hope you look into that one, too!

About the Author

Eve Morton lives in Waterloo, Ontario, Canada with her partner and two sons. She spends the days running after those boys and the nights brainstorming her next creative project. At some point, she writes things down, usually while drinking copious amounts of coffee. Her latest novel is *The Serenity Nearby* published in 2022 by Sapphire Books.

Find updates at authormorton.wordpress.com

the room, The Door.

by
Gregory J. Glanz

the room, The Door.

I awoke and felt the touch of chilly woodwork on my calves and thighs, my back—except for the small concavity above my butt—and my arms. The back of my head, ignoring the chill for the hardness, ached.

I opened my eyes and there was nothing to see. I was engulfed in darkness. My eyes will adjust, I told myself, and I lay still...

I awoke, and the floor was no less chilly but felt hard under my backbone, and I thought it must have burrowed a hole into the base of my skull.

The darkness was still complete, so I reached out with both hands along the floor and above my head. The floor seemed colder, harder. I sat up, belatedly throwing my hands out to protect myself. But there was nothing to restrict my movements. The lurching sickness of vertigo faded quickly.

I awoke, hands on my lap. I rolled over onto my knees and reached out with both hands along the floorboards. I touched a colder part in the floor and so turned some to my right, reached out again. It felt no less chilly than where I was, so I turned some more.

I reached out and it felt less chilled, but I did not move my knees. The farther I reached the warmer it seemed until at last I was stretched full upon my belly, chest and thighs. I crooked my left arm at the elbow and laid it under my head.

I awoke, shivers showering my back and splashing into my shoulders and arms.

I pulled myself up by my arms and slid my knees forward. Throwing my arms out in front of me, I felt about, and it was warmer. I slowly slid my knees forward.

After reaching out, I began to slide forward again but pulled up short, pain coursing through my knees. I rolled over and sat up.

I ran my hands over the skin below my kneecaps and felt balled up chunks of abraded tissue. There were small spots of wet, stickiness that stung. Ignoring the sensation, I rolled over onto hands and knees. I threw my hands out to feel the temperature of the floor but could no longer discern any difference, nor could I distinguish in which direction I had been heading.

Picking up one hand, I moved it forward and set it down. While balancing the left side of my body on it, I gently lifted my knee and moved it forward. I repeated this process with my right side. In this manner I continued on, feeling for any change in temperature.

I felt no change in the floor and so rolled over to sit down and decide if I should change my direction. I laid back, interlocked fingers behind my head, elbows splayed out on either side.

I awoke and my shoulders ached. I wondered which direction to go but again could not distinguish in which direction I had been heading.

I sat up and rolled over onto my hands and knees, started to crawl forward again, but my hand and head ran into something. I rubbed my forehead and rolled over to put my back against it.

I reached back with both hands to feel it.

"A wall," I said, and my voice rasped across the smooth surface of silence.

"Son," came an answering whisper. "Son." Again.

"Who's there?" I asked, and my voice was harsh, shrill, irritating the silence for a couple of short moments. There was no answer.

I put my hands to my face and there was sweat running down my forehead, over my nose, cheeks and chin. I wiped the moisture away.

With my back firmly planted against the wall, I scrunched my legs up to get my feet under my butt. Placing hands on knees near my chest, I pushed with my arms and legs, straightened my knees. I kept my back planted against the wall and stood still.

I awoke.

I reached out along the wall with my left hand and followed on the floor with my left foot. Then I pulled my right leg up next to my left, sliding my legs, butt, back and head along the wall. As I continued, the floor got warmer until it matched my skin temperature.

I bumped into another wall, running across the path of the First Wall.

"The Second Wall," I said, and reached out along it with my left hand.

"Son." That voice again, but faint and far off, not a whisper as I'd thought.

I sat down, wedged between my two walls. I wrapped arms around legs that were scrunched up to my chest and lay my head on my knees.

I awoke, sweating. "Who addresses me as 'son?'"

"Son." Again, I heard the voice, fading, but urgent.

With one hand on each wall, I stood. I took my right hand from the First Wall and thrust my right leg forward along the path of the Second and set my foot down. I slid my left hand and shoulder forward along the wall as I pulled my left leg even with my right. I continued on but resolved to leave the Second Wall in a path parallel to the First. I stood and started to walk, but after two steps felt a great need to turn back to the wall. In my haste, I took two large steps and rammed my foot into the wall, painfully jamming my toes.

Still resolved, I sat down with the bottoms of my feet against the wall and stretched my full length upon the floor. I reached out to feel the floor as far from the wall as possible, but there was no difference.

I awoke and stood. I began walking along The Second Wall with the fingertips of my left hand gliding along the wall ahead of me. I felt another wall and stopped.

"My Third Wall," I said. "Do you lead back to where I came from?" I asked it. "If I find another wall, I shall have a room."

Again, I considered leaving the wall and angling away from the corner, but if I ran into a wall, I wouldn't know where I was and so might explore the same wall as before.

"Son." The voice again, very close and very quiet! Had I really heard it?

"Who's there?"

"Your mother, Son."

I started walking along the Third Wall. After a few steps I stopped to listen. I stood a long while, not wanting to make a noise.

Breathing. I heard breathing…coming from the floor. I bent down and reached out with my hands.

Something! I pulled back my hands and froze. There was no movement, no sound. I slowly extended one hand again; it was still there.

I felt hair, dry and sparse upon its scalp. I moved closer and felt the face, its scaly, wrinkled skin and cracked lips; a slight exhalation, warm and steady, followed by an inhalation from the nose. My hands continued down to the shoulders and flabby arms, saggy breasts and a soft, fat belly above chubby and shapeless thighs.

This woman called me her son? Was it true?

"Mother?" But no answer came, so I waited.

I awoke and said, "Mother?"

"Son, you're here." And I felt two hands grab hold of my arms and pull feebly. I let their weak tugs guide me down and the arms wrapped around me, and I felt a face against mine and it was wet and small sobs broke from those cracked lips. For some time, she held me like this, and I was satisfied to wait.

She eventually let go of all but my hand and said, "I thought you might not get here before I was dust."

"I didn't know I was supposed to get here."

"No, you didn't. It's just that one gets lonely resting in the place of our ancestors."

I started to ask what she meant, but she shushed me and squeezed my hand. When the hand went limp and I heard her breathing slow, I knew she slept.

I stood to continue on my trek along the Third Wall.

As I walked, my left hand gliding along the wall ahead of me, I felt the floor start to cool. Soon the chill was uncomfortable, though not intolerable.

I heard a scream. "Son!"

And I thought something had happened, so I turned and thrust a leg out while pushing my weight forward from the back leg. Almost before the weight fell on my front foot, I lifted the back one and thrust it quickly forward to take the weight.

I continued along the wall in this manner until the floor warmed. I then slowed to a walk and called to my mother every few steps. On the third call, I was answered by a feeble, "You've returned," and gentle sobbing.

I bent down to hug her, and her face was wet and her body shaking despite the warmth of the floor.

After a while her tears subsided and she caught her breath long enough to say, "Don't leave me, Son, don't ever leave me."

And I calmed her and patted her and assured her that I'd no intention of leaving.

When she slept, so did I, though I woke and slept again before she came to. I had kept hold of her hand while we slept so she wouldn't panic, thinking me absent again. She woke up murmuring thanks, and sighing, hugged my hand to her face.

"Mother, what is away in the direction that your feet point?"

"Oh, you mustn't go that direction, Son."

"Why, Mother? What is up there?"

"Nothing really, just…it's just that the floor gets terribly, unbearably cold, and the soles of your feet can't stand to walk there for long nor your body to sleep. It's nothing up there, really."

"Yes, but is there another wall? I mean, do the three I've been to have a mate and make a room? Do we have a room here mother, or do the walls wander around aimlessly?"

"There's a Fourth Wall alright, and yes, we have a room. But half of it is unlivable."

I started to ask her more, but she shushed me again, saying she was tired, though it was a long time before I felt her grip go limp and heard her breathing slow. And I slept, too.

I awoke and said, "Mother?" There was no answer.

I slid my hand from hers and slowly stood. Balanced on my toes and the balls of my feet so the slap of my soles on the hard floor would not wake her, I snuck away, once again guided by my left hand gliding along the wall.

I knew my mother would be upset, but if I returned before she woke, she wouldn't know, and it wouldn't matter.

After a while I stopped tiptoeing and began to run. When I felt the chill return to the floor, I slowed a bit. And when I was sure it had gotten colder than I had ever felt it, I slowed to a cautious walk.

When my fingertips struck the Fourth Wall, I was drowsy and so lay down to sleep. Sleep came hard on the cold floor, but exhaustion won out.

I awoke. Every part of my body groaned when I stood, and each joint felt as cold as the floor. I began to jog along the Fourth Wall.

I had a brief thought of my mother, alone and no doubt awake by now, wondering, or maybe knowing what had become of her son. Still, the cold was not so bad as she had said, and my body began to warm and loosen with the exertion of my movements.

When my lungs began to burn and my wind gave out, I slowed to a walk. Soon after, as I walked along, still guiding myself with my left hand, I felt a crack in the wall. It was very thin and very tight.

I stood for a while prying at it with my fingers, but it gave nothing. Then I traced it with my fingertips and found that it turned abruptly to my right about a handspan or so above my head. I continued tracing it, and after a several more handspans it turned back down and continued to the floor, breaking twice for metal plates attached to both sides of the crack. Both plates had vertical cylindrical attachments running directly above the crack. At the floor, the slit continued along the base, making a full rectangle of itself.

As I sat there running my fingers this way and that, testing to see if the panel would swing open, but figuring that the attachments were there to prevent this, I bumped my head.

Instinctively my hand went out and I grabbed hold of the hard something that I had struck. It was spherical, with a neck that attached to a metal plate on the panel. I gripped the thing and pulled. Nothing happened. I pushed. Still nothing. I rotated it and heard an audible click.

Frozen in thought, I stood and reflected on what I had found. As I did so, my body must have swayed ever so slightly, because the tiniest of cracks of light appeared near the knob. My eyes stung with it, and I pushed the door shut and released the knob in a sudden panic.

A door! It was a door! But where did it lead? Out of the room?

My mother! Had she known about this door? Did she leave it out of our talk on purpose? Or was it new to the room? Was she so afraid of the cold that she hadn't ventured this way, to the far end of the room? Ever?

No. She knew, I was sure, but chose not to tell me. Why? Was there something beyond the door to fear? Had she been on the other side of the door? Was she trying to protect me from something? Was there some terrible thing beyond the door waiting for me? Or was she afraid because she hadn't seen beyond the door? Was she sheltering me? Or did she really not know what was beyond it? Was there anything beyond it?

I must ask her. And I must get back to her, I knew. She was probably hysterical with worry by now. I had been gone too long.

Before leaving the door, I reached out with my right hand and turned the knob again. It rotated easily under my grip, just as before. When I heard the faint scraping of the mechanism inside it, I let go and stepped back, sweating, wondering if the knob on the other side, if there was one, turned as easily. And if so, what might come through whenever it wished.

I began walking, my right hand guiding me. The sweat on my back, arms and legs began to dry and sent an uncomfortable chill through me that felt like dread.

To warm myself, I jogged back toward the Third Wall, then slowed to a walk when I felt I was nearing it. I stopped for a short rest at the corner and slept. When I awoke, I took off at a run back to my mother.

After a while, my lungs burned and my wind grew short, as did my stride. I continued on though, not wanting to leave my mother alone for longer than I needed.

When I couldn't continue, I sat down and closed my eyes to sleep. But a thin wail followed by harsh sobbing told me I was near home, and so I picked myself up and continued on. The sobbing grew in volume and soon, though she didn't know it, I was standing only a few feet from Mother.

As I stood, wondering what to say to her, the sobbing quieted and her breathing, broken at first, became regular, and I guessed she was asleep. I went to her side and took her hand in mine.

I awoke, refreshed. I sat up and my mother said, "I didn't know if you would come back."

"Why wouldn't I?'

"Well, it's just that… Where did you go?"

"To the door."

"Oh."

"You knew it was there."

"Yes."

"Why didn't you tell me?"

"Because you would want to go see it."

"I did anyway."

"Don't leave me, Son."

"Why would I?"

"I'm dying. I'm aged."

"Mother, why didn't you tell me about the door?"

"It's no good, you know."

"What's not?"

"No good, son. It ages and kills. I've seen what it does. Don't open it, not even a crack. Oh, I know alright, it's done it to me. But not to you, no son, not to you. It won't get you; I'll see to that. I'll warn you. You'll know, and it won't be able to hurt you. You'll know."

I didn't know what she was talking about, but I knew she was upset. So I sat, holding both her hands and soothing her, telling her everything would be fine.

When she calmed, I asked, "Mother, what is it that ages and kills?"

She took a deep breath as if she was about to start a long run across the room and said, "You must promise me not to open the door."

"But why, Mother?"

"If I tell you, will you promise?"

I hesitated, knowing that any promise would be a lie. Not that I had any sure intention of opening the door.

"No promises, Mother. But I must know, and if you don't tell me, I know of only one way to find out."

"You'll break my heart, Son, you'll break my heart." I didn't answer, only waited.

"I didn't go near it for the longest time. Not because I was afraid, I just didn't know it was there. In fact, my father lay on this spot, dying, and I didn't know it until too late.

"I remember finding him and thinking he was dead. I held his hand, not knowing who he was or how he came to be here. Then I heard him say, 'Daughter,' and I pulled away from him. I felt the flush of guilt in my face and so returned my hand to his, which was waving around in the air searching for me. 'Father,' I said.

"He pulled me close and said, 'The door,' and as I sat up, his hand went limp, and I knew he was dead.

"It didn't take long for me to leave him. I wandered around the warm areas, thinking of my father and the only words he'd said to me. Several times I ended up wandering back to this spot.

"The door was all I thought about. I had to find it. But where? I had been throughout the warm part and so knew it must be in the cold area. I began to search the floor, the cold, pitiless floor. I found nothing until once when I leaned against the wall my back was poked by a hard object protruding from the wall. It was a hinge. I had found the door.

"What to do with it? I hadn't any idea. Father had said, 'The door,' that was all. Not 'open the door,' or 'block the door,' or 'stay away from the door,' or 'go through the door,' just 'the door.'

"So I went back to the warm parts, knowing I would return, and thought about what to do. Had father gone through it? No, he mustn't have. Or had he gone through it and returned? Well, I didn't know, and so I had to find out for myself. I went to the door, feeling very tired, limping across the desolate half of the room as the cold gripped my legs, my bones. And when I reached it, I didn't hesitate. I just grabbed hold of the knob and began to turn it. I turned it slowly though, feeling a dread overtake me. When it would turn no longer, I tugged gently to open it a bare crack, and it slid inward. I was suddenly blinded! It seared my eyeballs, and I became disoriented and fell back. I rubbed my eyes and the pain subsided. I covered my eyes with my hands then and peeked through my fingers. And though still painful, its intensity had lessened. I uncovered my eyes and, squinting, reached for the door.

"But then I saw, I saw what it had done to me! My skin sagged. It was dry and gray, lifeless and wrinkled. I closed the door with just a nudge and wandered back to the warm areas. I awoke once and found myself here, so I stayed and waited. Yes, now I knew what it had done to my father and why he had given me that warning. But I hadn't heeded it and so must end as he did."

She sat silent, and I thought her asleep. But after a while she said, "And so I told you, and you are warned. Will you heed me?" And I didn't answer. After a while she fell asleep. She did not ask again.

She woke briefly once and said, "You'll go, I know. But what have you got to fight it with?" And again, I didn't answer but kept silent and she went to sleep. And so did I.

I awoke and she still slept, so I slipped my hand from hers and stood. Once more I tiptoed away down the Third Wall, my left hand guiding me.

When I felt the floor begin to chill, I left the wall and walked into the heart of the room, guiding myself by the discomfort of the soles of my feet. Several times I slept, waking cold and aching.

I thought I must be nearly parallel with the door and so turned myself to the left and walked over what felt like ice until I met the Fourth Wall. Then I sat and slept.

I awoke and stood, fatigued, chilled through my skull, not wanting to continue, not able to stop. I let my left hand guide me and I reached the First Wall again. I propped myself in the corner and slept.

I awoke and was walking, my right hand guiding me. I wondered if I had been awake but not aware. I had no answer, or none I was sure of, so I continued. When I found the door, I didn't stop or slow but kept walking past it, down the Fourth Wall.

I awoke in a corner and guessed I had found the Third Wall. I stood and began walking, using my right hand as guide. I thought of my mother's story, how she was left ignorant, but I was not. She had said of her father, "not knowing who he was or how he came to be here," and I resolved to ask this of mother.

I awoke and my mother's hand lay in mine. It was cold and I said, "Mother." But silence was her answer, as I knew it must be.

I don't know how many times I slept then, nor where I went between and even during those sleeps, but always when I woke, the air was chilled and my body ached, even when the floor was warm.

I visited the door and talked to the walls, and when I returned to my mother's place she was gone and all I found was many layers of dust beneath where she had lain. The dust was undisturbed and its boundaries well defined. I wanted to scatter the dust to the Four Corners, but I only wept and tried to sleep. No sleep came to me, so I left that place and let my left hand guide me down the Third Wall.

After a while I tried to jog, but my legs didn't obey my thoughts; they were listening to my heart and lungs. So I walked and thought of the door.

I slept and walked several times before facing the door. My mind was weary of the thought of it and my shoulders slumped as if I were carrying it. My limbs felt as if they were an extension of the cold under my feet. Each joint was frozen and moved as if they had swelled to twice their normal size. Every muscle was stretched thin, almost unable to move the part of my body each was responsible for. So I sat.

I awoke with my hand on the doorknob. I stood but did not let go. I turned the knob and closed my eyes. But when I pulled on the door, I did not bear my self-imposed blindness for long.

It opened only a crack past the frame, an inch or two. But its intensity blinded me, made my skull scream in agony and I staggered and turned, falling to the ground and writhing, clutching at my eyes and head.

I lay there stunned. When I came to, my hands were over my eyes. I peeked between slightly parted fingers. It shined through the crack and illuminated me. I was ugly, contemptible. My skin was gray and wrinkled and as I ran my hands over myself, I was reminded of my first meeting with mother. I reached out with one foot and pushed The Door shut.

I stood and walked straight away from It, my shoulders hunched, thankful that I didn't need to raise a hand to guide myself.

Each time I woke up, I was less cold. Eventually, I searched and found the bed of dust into which my mother had gone. I lay down and slept. I awoke and felt dead. I felt warm—the warmth of a dead man, the numbness of a dead man.

Only the bottoms of my feet still knew the cold. They hadn't rid themselves of it. They refused to warm, to numb, to die. I ignored them and slept. But when I awoke, they still screamed at me, begged me, ordered me. Their cold chastised me and I told them, "This place, The Place; I was meant to be here, or at least to end here. It's where my daughter must come." But to my mind, the cold in my feet only intensified, as if my feet laughed, humorless and bitter.

I stood and the cold spread to my ankles. I walked and my shins felt it; then my knees, and thighs. My legs gave and I crawled.

I awoke shivering. My hands were numb, dead from the cold. My wrists, forearms and elbows knew the truth though, and set my hands down in front of me. I pulled my legs along with my hips, sometimes lifting my knees and sometimes not; my hips knew but didn't tell me. My arms forgot, and so my shoulders took over.

Each time I awoke, I crawled on, my head hanging between my shoulders, dangling like the fatty tissue around my waist. My knees and the tops of my feet were slick and wet with my own blood. My hands were losing skin on the palms and knuckles. I told myself these things, and my body ignored them as if they didn't matter.

My crawl became endless. I knew it wouldn't end. I slept when I had to, crawled when I could. It was the only thing that had meaning anymore. I didn't want it to end. I would be nothing when it ended. I would be numb with cold, senseless.

I awoke and was slumped against a wall. I reached up and there was a doorknob. I let go when my skinless palms howled to my mind with pain, triggering every other nerve in my body. I screamed my body's agony. It didn't end and I didn't stop.

I awoke, sobbing, knowing what to expect and I bore it, for a little while.

"Daughter!" I yelled, and went to sleep.

Each time I woke, the pain was a little less, my body a little colder and a little weaker. The doorknob might as well be across the room instead of a mere two feet above my head. And each time before sleeping I yelled to my daughter.

I awoke and a hand held mine. She'd made it! She had come! I tried to speak and couldn't. I wanted to cry but was too dry and not a sob came from me. Her hand left mine and I tried to scream at her not to leave me. But she didn't.

She ran her hands over my face and felt my eyes, blind at her touch, and tears rolled out. She moved them down to my cracked lips and the swollen tongue poking out the side of my mouth. She continued moving them over a collarbone that stuck out as if my head were shrunken, and the skin so tight on my ribs that it felt to me as if there were no skin at all. My belly was concave, the muscles in my arms and legs stretched to the point of snapping.

"Father," she said.

"Daughter," I managed, "I am not long for this room."

She shushed me and I slept. When I woke, she was there, her hands clasping mine, gently stroking the backs. But I couldn't feel it, could only sense the motion. I was numb, like a dead man, and I cried. She soothed me, told me she wouldn't leave me, and I knew it was true.

I awoke and said, "Daughter."

"Yes, Father."

"Have you been to the walls?"

"This is my third."

"There are four. You should go to them."

"I will."

And I paused, maybe napped, maybe just became numb for a while.

"Daughter."

"Yes, Father."

"This is our room. It is nothing." And I lifted the hand that held hers and touched it to The Door and said, "This is The Door. It is everything." And I lay my hand back down and the numbness overtook me. And I knew no more.

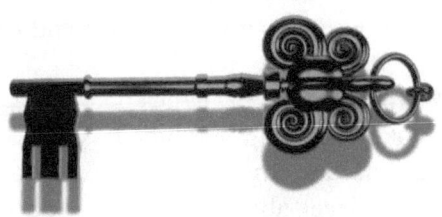

From the Author

This story was born a simple allegory that completely wrote itself before it was ever down on paper. Most stories kick and scream like miscreant children, but this one reached adulthood before the first word was written down. It's such a simple concept but seems prevalent in the way we humans often view ideas, ignore ideas, disbelieve ideas, and ultimately discard ideas we simply refuse to consider, through self-limiting thought and ignorance.

About the Author

Greg has spent a lifetime pursuing creative writing and storytelling. He has a passion for the hidden tale, the ignored subject, the absurd. Whether he is researching the historical, crafting the fantastic or whispering the unnoticed secrets of our time, he believes those rarely noticed subjects are most poignant and lead to undeniable truths. His stories have been published in *Blood & Bourbon*, *MacroMicrocosm*, *WriteHive*, and serialized in *The Dark Sire*.

In his spare time, he loves to travel through the villages of Ireland and document rural, generational Irish pubs in the series, "A Proper Pint," (www.aproperpintfilm.com).

He is a homebrewer and biking enthusiast. Surprisingly, they go exceedingly well together as more and more microbrews pop up near the trails coveting the attention of thirsty bicyclists in ever increasing numbers. He is a giant nerd in both size and scope.

greg@creatureofdreams.com
www.creatureofdreams.com
@gjg_write
www.facebook.com/gglanz

On the Banishment of

Dragons

by
Katie Kent

On the Banishment of Dragons

*A*nother one, Elena?" Andrew peered at me from behind tortoiseshell glasses as a candle flickered next to him. The disappointment was fixed on his face like a mask. I'd come to know that he always scrunched up his nose when he was upset.

"They've reported it already?" I sat down at my desk, picked up a big red stress ball and squeezed it hard. I knew that I couldn't keep my failure from my boss, just like with the other times. But I had hoped that I might have a bit more time to compose myself first, and to try and think up an excuse.

"What's going on with you?" he continued. "You showed so much promise at first. But lately everything seems to be going wrong. Did I make a mistake taking you on?" He closed the book he had open on his desk and put it neatly back on the bookshelf next to him, then blew the candle out.

I felt myself flush. "No! I'll try harder, I promise. I really want this job."

I left his first question unanswered. Even *I* didn't know what was going on with me. I wasn't sure where I would have started trying to explain what was happening in my head.

"Okay then." Andrew seemed relieved, like he had needed evidence of my commitment. He sighed, touching his forehead. I knew he had been overworked lately. "You can go. Maybe try and have an early night. I'll see you tomorrow."

"Later." I took a deep breath as I got up and shut the door behind me, then yawned. I felt wiped out.

He was right, I couldn't keep on like this. But how was I supposed to get over this mental block?

I had been so happy when I'd got this job. *Apprentice magician.* I always knew that there was something magical within me, ever since I was a little girl. I had signed up for magic classes at school and was always top of the class. As soon as I turned 16, I started applying for apprenticeships and was thrilled to have landed the second one I had applied for. My parents had been proudly telling friends that their daughter was a magician.

But that was before I started to struggle.

Arriving at the office the next day, I paused outside the room, one hand on the copper door handle, as I heard raised voices. I strained to make them out. One definitely belonged to Andrew, but I couldn't immediately place the other one. I inched closer to the door and listened in. The wooden doors here didn't easily lend themselves to eavesdropping; luckily both of them were talking loudly.

"She's not ready!" I heard Andrew say.

The other voice replied. "You say you don't have the time. The only alternative is to send the girl."

It was obvious they were talking about me. I was the only *girl* who worked at the small firm; they couldn't really call experienced Maggie a girl, she'd been there for years, and she took care of the books rather than performing spells herself.

"She's not been herself lately. I'm worried she could be sick." Andrew again.

Sick?! I wasn't sick, just a bit confused. I shook my head, as if they could see me hiding behind the door.

"Then let her go! Otherwise, there are dozens of kids out there just waiting for a chance like this."

I gritted my teeth. I didn't want to lose my job! Just as I was about to go in there and plead my case, the other man said something that sent a shiver right down my spine.

"It's a dragon, for Christ's sake! We need someone to eliminate it. If you're too busy and she's not up to the job, then we'll need to find someone else, and quickly!"

"I…" Andrew stopped as I pushed the door handle down and went in to face them.

"I'll do it!" I said. "I'll banish the dragon."

"Good." I recognised the other man now. He was Brian Johnson, the head of the firm. I'd never actually spoken to him in person, but I recognised him from the painting over the reception desk. He was getting old now, and his sight was failing, so he couldn't do much magic himself anymore. "Then get it done as soon as possible." His face was expressionless, his arms folded.

As Mr. Johnson left, the door creaking behind him, Andrew turned to me, his nose scrunched up again. "Elena, are you sure?" he asked me. "What about yesterday, and the other times when you weren't able to complete the jobs?"

"I can do it," I said. It wasn't just that I wanted to do it; I *needed* to. This was a chance to prove myself, to show that I belonged here, and that I could be a great magician.

I would just have to ignore the voices in my head.

I spent the rest of that day hunched over my desk, reading up on the spells by the lamplight; candles might have been traditional, but they weren't for me. I swotted up on the expert text in the field, *On the Banishment of Dragons*. The theory was easy enough—I had always been good at memorising long reams of text and the hand symbols. I knew that the hard part would be putting it into practice.

There was little time to spare; the dragon was causing havoc around town. Reports came in of crops destroyed, people hiding in fear, buildings crumbling. At 5 o'clock, just as I was about to leave for the day and Andrew was coming back from a long assignment, news came in that the dragon had killed a baby boy.

I could tell this had affected Andrew, who was recently a new father himself. He immediately picked up his desk phone and made a call. "Just stay in the house, and don't take your eyes off Courtney," he told his wife.

He was worried for his daughter, and I couldn't blame him. It was time to act.

"I'll go and resolve the situation now," I told him.

He looked aghast. "Elena, I agree that the dragon needs to be stopped as soon as possible. But this is a complicated spell, and you've only had one day to learn it."

I shrugged. "A day is all I need. I'll sort this, I promise."

He rubbed his eyes. "Your determination is admirable, but maybe I should come with you. My latest assignment is finished now."

I shook my head. "You've been working so late recently. You need to go home and look after your family. I've got this." I smiled, probably looking much more confident than I felt. It was a good thing he couldn't see my fingers under the desk squeezing the stress ball once again. The red colouring was starting to peel off.

"Well, alright." He hesitated. "If you're sure."

"I'm sure."

"Okay, well then I guess all I can say is good luck."

"Thanks." I shut the book with a flourish. A cloud of dust rose from the pages and made me cough.

Approaching the town square, where the dragon had last been seen, I wiped my sweaty palms on my black jeans and looked around. It was obvious that a dragon had been here. The place was usually full of people bustling about the market, but instead it was deserted, the stalls empty, some of them pushed to the ground, and the tops of the trees were singed.

People had seen the dragon near the cathedral. As I headed down the path towards it, I tried to psych myself up for the task ahead. The cathedral was bereft of the usual worshippers and tourists, but the doors were open. I peered nervously around the door. "Hello?" I said. It came out as little more than a croak. I wasn't sure why I was even saying it. Announcing my presence was unlikely to set the beast quivering. No, I had to be confident and put an end to this dragon's escapades as soon and as decisively as possible.

I took a deep breath. "I am Elena," I shouted, my voice echoing around the stone walls, "and I am here to banish you!"

A mighty roar came from the back of the cathedral, and heavy footsteps began, getting louder with every step. Next, I saw the dragon's snout, fire emanating from it. I had never seen a dragon in real life before, and I was so captivated that I almost forgot why I was there. But as it came towards me, I came to my senses and raised my arms.

"*Gen mat rar. Hulu tan gesaf,*" I started, bringing the spell I had memorised only hours before easily to mind. I'd always had a photographic memory; that was one of the reasons I was a good magician. You could have a natural ability for magic, for sure—the same way that some people were naturally good at math—but to progress beyond simple spells it had to be learnt.

I was halfway through the spell and growing in confidence. I got to the part where I needed to wave my arms to the left when that little voice whispered in my brain, 'you need to wave your arms to the right now, or your mother will die.'

Not now. I knew that listening to the voice would ruin the spell, and that that would mean bad things. But I didn't want Mum to die. She and I may have had a bit of a strained relationship, but she was my mum, and I couldn't let her die. I felt the tang of blood in my mouth as I realised I had been biting my lip hard, and tried to ignore the voice, but it got more and more persistent, until it seemed that the noise in my head was louder than the dragon's roar. The anxiety was refusing to dissipate, and soon it was like I had almost forgotten why I was there. I was vaguely aware of the dragon out of the corner of my eye, now cowering somewhat as I continued the spell, but it was no longer my main focus. Instead, I was concentrating on the images that were, unprompted, filling my mind—images of Mum dying a horrible death, falling from a building or being trampled by a horse. My stomach was turning somersaults.

I gave in and waved my arms to the right. I couldn't help myself—the urge had been impossible to ignore. The relief I felt straight afterwards was balanced by the moment of dread as I realised that, yet again, I had ruined a spell. But I knew this one had more serious ramifications than the others. I had failed to banish the dragon. It raised its head and snarled, as if mocking me, and took steps towards me. Then I heard a scream, and I looked around. To my horror, a little girl in a blue dress stood to my right, rooted to the spot. She couldn't have been more than six years old. I hadn't even noticed her come in, I had been so wrapped up in my own thoughts.

"Run!" I shouted to the girl, dashing towards her to try and shield her from the dragon. But it was too late. The beast was quicker than I was and reached her before I got there. The girl didn't even move, obviously paralysed with terror, her eyes wide.

"No!" I cried out as the dragon's fiery breath came closer and closer to her. I fell to my knees, sobbing, not caring that the dragon would probably be coming for me next. This was all my fault. I deserved to die.

"*Gen mat rar,*" I suddenly heard behind me. "*Hulu tan gesaf!*"

As I came to my senses, I stood and turned to see Andrew performing the ritual that I had so spectacularly messed up. He looked like a real magician, wearing a red robe, while I felt like a fraud in my everyday clothing. I didn't know why I had thought I could do this. I swallowed and looked back at the dragon, who was slowly getting more and more clumsy. As the spell continued, its head drooped, and it crashed to the ground with an almighty thump. Finally, the air around it started to swirl and after a few minutes the dragon got smaller and smaller, until it eventually vanished completely. As the air stilled, Andrew let out a loud breath.

The girl was lying on her back on the floor, eyes closed. Andrew ran to her and put his ear against her chest. "She's still with us," he said. The relief hit me like a tsunami. I felt out of it, far away. I didn't know how much time had passed, but at some point I was vaguely aware of Andrew picking up the girl and handing her to someone.

Then we were alone again. I kept my eyes focused down at the floor, too scared to look at my boss. I had no idea what he would say to me. My bottom lip trembled and my eyes watered. I had to keep myself from breaking down and crying again.

"Elena?" I tried to ignore Andrew's voice, hoping he would eventually leave me alone to my misery, but then I jumped as I felt an arm around my shoulders. The tears spilt out as he held me. I cried like I had never cried before.

Eventually, I could cry no more. I blew my nose noisily on a tissue from my pocket, trying to stall. I knew I'd have to speak to him sooner or later, to face up to what I had done and what was happening to me, but that thought terrified me.

Andrew prompted me. "Are you ready to talk?"

"No." I wasn't anywhere near ready, but I knew he wouldn't let that go. It was time to face the music. "That poor girl…" I faltered. "It's my fault she's hurt."

He frowned. "Well, ultimately, it's the dragon's fault. She's been taken to hospital and should be fine. But maybe you could have saved her from getting hurt, yes." He was scrunching his nose again.

I winced as the guilt caught up with me again. "I didn't mean for it to happen. Why are you here anyway? I thought you'd gone home."

"I started to go home, but I couldn't relax. I was worried about you."

I stayed silent, chewing on my thumbnail.

"Elena, explain to me what's been going on," he said. "Today, and the other days where the spells went wrong."

"I don't think I can. I…" I struggled for words. Deep down, I knew that my thoughts were ridiculous, and vocalising them would make me sound completely crazy. But they were so persuasive.

"Just tell me the thoughts you get when this happens," Andrew urged. "I'm not here to judge. I only want to help."

I sighed. "You really want me to be honest?"

He nodded.

"I get partway through a spell," I said, looking down at the floor again so that I didn't have to see his expression, "and a voice in my head tells me I need to do certain things or someone I care about will die. I have to move my arms in a certain way, or I have to say a particular phrase. Things that aren't part of the spell. And I'm too afraid of the consequences. I *have* to do what the voice is telling me."

"What if you ignored the voice?" I looked up into Andrew's eyes as a feeling of annoyance surged through me. I'd already told him that I *had* to listen to the voice.

"Someone will die."

"But do you really believe that?" He spoke gently, like he was a teacher reassuring a child.

"Yes." Some part of me believed it, anyway. Otherwise, this wouldn't be so hard.

"Okay, how about we do a little experiment? Perform an easy spell." He pointed to the wooden carved pulpit. "Turn that eagle on the top into a blackbird. And when the voices come, I want you to try and ignore them and carry on with the spell. Do you think you can do that?"

"Probably not." I knew the defeat in my voice was obvious, but I wasn't sure I was strong enough to challenge my thoughts right now. Especially when I hadn't been able to challenge them when it really mattered.

"Go on, give it a try anyway." He smiled encouragingly.

I focused and started the spell. It was a short one, so maybe I would be okay. I got to the last part of the spell before the thoughts came back. I tried to resist, but I knew I was fighting a losing battle. I started to move my arms and Andrew, who had been watching me carefully, knew that it wasn't part of the spell and grabbed them, pinning them to my sides. I tried to push him away, but he was stronger than me.

"Andrew, please." I knew I sounded like a whiny kid, but I *needed* him to let go.

"What are you feeling?" he asked.

I concentrated on the feeling. "Complete panic. My heart is thumping out of my chest."

He let go of my arms, and I waved them about in the pattern my brain was telling me to. The relief was overwhelming. My brain had been telling me that he would die if I didn't do it.

He gave me a sympathetic smile. "I think you should take some time off work. Get yourself sorted."

"What?! No. Please, I need this job." I felt faint all of a sudden.

"The job will still be here for you when you get back." He touched me reassuringly on the arm.

I sat down cross-legged on the floor. I felt tired. I realised I had been fighting this for so long, it had exhausted me emotionally. Andrew sat down next to me.

"What do we tell people?" I put my head in my hands. "That poor girl…"

"Don't worry about that," he said. "I'll handle it. Just look after yourself. Everyone will just be glad that the dragon has been banished. We'll just tell them that we couldn't get there quickly enough to prevent another injury."

"What if you hadn't turned up when you did?" I shuddered. "Other people could have been hurt or even died, and it would all be my fault." My voice cracked again slightly. I wasn't sure how I would be able to forgive myself. Over the past few weeks, I had messed up several other spells, but thankfully none of them had been life or death. This one could have been.

"It is what it is." Andrew let out a breath. "Just be thankful it wasn't worse. Go easy on yourself, you're clearly not well. I have no doubt that you'll be back after your recovery, an even better magician than you were before. You have real talent, Elena. I could tell that from your very first interview. Get yourself well, and I'll see you again soon." He smiled at me as he stood up and walked out.

I lay down on the hard stone, cold on my back. The air still smelt of smoke. I stared up at the remnants of the stained-glass window, the edges sharp where the dragon had broken through it, and reflected how the beauty of the cathedral was so at odds with how I was feeling. I wasn't ready to go home yet, to tell all this to my parents. They had always had such high expectations of me, and I felt like I had let them down. How on earth was I going to tell them that all this stuff was happening in my head?

It was dark by the time I made it home. I paused outside my front door for a few minutes, counting the flowers climbing up over the porch. Anything to delay this conversation for a bit longer.

"Elena!" Mum said as I opened the door, rushing towards me. "Where have you been? We've been worried."

Before I had a chance to say anything, Dad came over and took my coat, peering at me suspiciously. "Have you been crying?"

"I…" I began, and then cut myself off, unsure how to even begin. "I have something I need to tell you."

"Okay." Mum looked to Dad and then back to me, worry etched upon her face. I went in and sat down in the armchair, and they followed my lead, settling next to each other on the sofa. Under other circumstances, I probably would have laughed at their tense expressions.

"What is it?" Dad looked at me impatiently.

I took in a deep breath. "I'm…not well. There's all this weird stuff going on in my head. Andrew suggested I take some time off work to get myself sorted."

"What kind of stuff?" Mum asked, chewing her thumbnail.

I hesitated, not sure how to explain it. "I keep mucking up spells because my head is telling me bad things will happen if I do them."

Dad narrowed his eyebrows. "We all have silly thoughts like that, Elena. We just need to ignore them."

"I can't!" I shouted.

They both looked surprised at my outburst. What did he know? I felt the anger burning up inside me. *He* hadn't been there when I couldn't banish the dragon. When a little girl got hurt because my brain was telling me I had to do those rituals. I clenched my fists. Maybe I shouldn't have said anything, but they would soon have noticed when I stopped leaving the house for work each day.

I tried to calm myself down. "I'm sorry. But it's not that easy. I think Andrew is right, I think the time off will help."

Dad sighed. "I know it's tempting to take time off work when you're not feeling a hundred percent, but how will that look to your employers? They'll think you can't handle it. They might fire you. It might be difficult to get another job. I know how important magic is to you."

"For goodness' sake!" I took a deep breath. "Yes, magic is important to me." I paused. "But my health is more important. It's a shame that it isn't important to you."

"We're not saying that," Mum piped up.

"Well, that's how it sounds to me. It sounds like all you care about is having a successful daughter. Do you know how hard it was for me to come to you and tell you this? I knew how you would react. You haven't even shown any concern about how I'm feeling. Andrew was there when I broke down. Andrew told me it was okay, that it wasn't my fault, that I was clearly ill. He's my boss! It should have been you having that conversation with me."

Neither of them replied, but I could tell from the way they were fidgeting that they were feeling guilty. Mum was tracing a pattern in the carpet with her slipper. I didn't even care. It was about time I was honest with them. But the atmosphere in the room had become so awkward. I got up from the chair and went upstairs, slamming the door behind me as I left.

"So, tell me why you're here." The doctor peered at me over the top of large, bright green glasses the next day. She reminded me of an owl, fixing her gaze upon me.

"I'm a magician," I began, twisting my ring around my finger.

"You are? That's amazing! I've always wanted to meet a magician." She looked at me kindly, and I began to warm to her.

I explained what had happened.

"That must be hard," she said. "Not being able to do your magic."

I nodded my head. "Yeah. It sucks. I want to help people." I had pursued magic to make a difference. "What's wrong with me?" I felt a tear drip down my cheek, and I sniffed.

She passed me a tissue from the box on her desk and I blew my nose.

"Have you ever heard of OCD?" she asked.

I frowned. "Of course. But what's that got to do with anything?"

"I think you might have it."

I laughed. "You should see the state of my desk! My boss is always complaining that I need to be tidier."

"OCD isn't about neatness," she explained gently. "At least not always. It's when you get an obsession about something bad happening, and you have to do compulsions to get rid of the anxiety that the obsession causes. Those compulsions could be virtually anything. You might feel the need to arrange things into straight lines, you might need to wash your hands obsessively. Or you might need to move your arms in a certain way."

I stayed silent, hardly able to process her words.

She gave me a sympathetic smile. "The first step is to refer you for an assessment, which I can arrange. I'm not qualified to diagnose you myself. But it sounds like OCD to me. Why don't you go home and look up some information about it, see what you think?"

"A girl was injured?" Dad seemed shocked when I told him the whole story. I was hit by another pang of guilt and looked away quickly. My gaze settled upon a family photo of us when I was a child. I looked happy, without a care in the world.

"It was an accident." I tried to keep the defensiveness out of my voice. "But don't you see now why I need help?"

"I think it's a good thing that you saw the doctor," Mum said. "Don't you think, Peter?"

"I suppose so. If it really is OCD. But has the doctor seen how untidy your room is?!"

I rubbed my eyes. I wished he was more sympathetic, but I guessed I couldn't really be offended by his comment when I had said the exact same thing to the doctor.

"OCD is all about obsessions," I explained. "I have thoughts that someone will die if I don't do certain things. Then I have to do those compulsions."

"Can't you just do a spell to get rid of this?"

I looked at Dad, my eyebrows raised. "Magic doesn't work like that. I can't use magic to cure my mental health. Magicians still need to see doctors and go to therapy."

"I see." Dad still looked confused, but Mum suddenly swept me up into a hug, taking me by surprise. I swallowed the lump in my throat, trying to stop the tears. I had cried enough lately.

I was diagnosed with OCD at my assessment. As I made my way to my first therapy session, the nerves were threatening to overcome me, but I knew that this was what I needed to make myself well again. In the waiting room, I smiled wryly as I caught sight of a poster advertising our firm pinned to the cork notice board. On the coffee table in front of me, the newspaper reported the full recovery of the little girl who had been hurt by the dragon.

"Elena?" I raised my head to see a friendly-looking troll with red hair smiling up at me. I nodded. "I'm Poppy," she told me, holding out her hand.

I shook her hand and followed her into a room.

"So," she said, as I took a seat. "I have the notes from your referral here. I understand that you are a magician, and that you are suffering from OCD, which is affecting your spells?"

"Yeah." I explained what had happened, from the very first time I began to hear the voice until the most recent episode with the dragon and the little girl.

Poppy took notes as I spoke. Occasionally she nodded, and when I faltered, my voice shaky, she smiled at me encouragingly. When I got to the end, she looked up at me. "Well, the good news is that I think I can help you to get over this. The thing you have to understand about OCD is that everyone gets random thoughts like the ones you have been experiencing. But if you have OCD, your brain gives meaning to those thoughts. That's what leads to the compulsions."

"I don't know how to stop doing them." I sighed.

"Well, that's what I'm here for." Poppy smiled at me again as she crossed her legs. I'd never before seen such a cheerful troll, but then I guess that was probably a pre-requisite for a troll therapist.

"What we will do here is to work through your issues. We will explore why you are putting this extra responsibility on yourself. We will of course also work on stopping your compulsions. That will seem very hard at first because your brain will be screaming at you to do the rituals so someone doesn't die. But we will tackle them bit by bit and you will be able to gradually ignore what your mind is telling you and stop doing those things, and you'll see that nothing bad happens as a result."

As I left at the end of the hour, I felt positive. I'd only had one session, but already I could see a glimmer of hope. I knew that if I put in the hard work, I would be able to recover from this and go back to my magic. The next time a dragon came, I knew I would be ready.

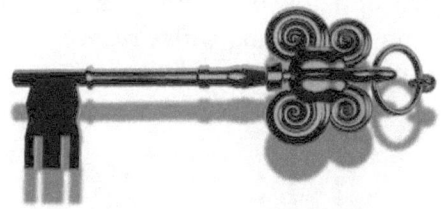

From the Author

On the Banishment of Dragons was one of the first short stories I wrote when I first got back into writing a few years ago. I saw a call for an anthology of mental illness-related fantasy stories, and knew I had to write something for it. This story was the result. Being an OCD sufferer myself, I liked the idea of OCD affecting the life and job of a young magician, and I've always had a fascination with dragons, so I knew I had to feature one in my story.

Considering it was the first short story I had ever submitted for publication, I was pleased when it made the shortlist for the anthology, but when it was eventually rejected, it really knocked my confidence and I considered never writing anything ever again. Luckily I persevered, and now have almost 20 published short stories to my name, but, one shortlisting with *Podcastle* and many rejections later, l had almost given up on this story when I saw the Duotrope entry for *Particular Passages* and decided to give it one last go.

About the Author

Katie Kent wanted to be a writer from an early age. Life and mental illness got in the way but starting a career in Publishing was a way for her to rediscover her love of books, even though she ultimately ended up in journals publishing.

When a colleague started a writing group at her workplace, Katie remembered the joy of writing and hasn't looked back since, even though a year of rejections ate away at her self-esteem. She almost cried when she got her first acceptance from *Youth Imagination,* and here she is now with about 20 published short stories to her name. Her stories are mostly for a YA audience and are particularly about LGTBQ characters, mental illness, time travel and the future—sometimes all in the same story! She's proud to have featured in a number of anthologies including *The Trouble with Time Travel, Summer of Speculation: Catastrophe, Growth* and *My Heart to Yours.* Her non-fiction, mostly mental health-related, has been published in *The Mighty, You & Me Magazine, Ailment, OC87 Recovery Diaries* and *Feels Zine.*

Now working part time, Katie spends her Tuesdays writing on her laptop in bed with her cat Haribo curled up next to her. As well as short stories, she's also working on a few novels. She also lives with her wife Sam and long-haired sausage dog Maverick, who is as naughty as he is cute.

You can visit her website at https:www.katiekentwriter.com and follow her on Twitter @uniKH80.

Swapping Up
by
Arlen Feldman

Swapping Up

*L*arry the janitor wakes with a hand on a woman's breast. Very, very carefully, he moves his hand away and stares. He's never touched a breast before. Never seen one live either. He can't pull his eyes away, as fascinated by the delicate tracery of blue veins as much as by the rosy pink nipple.

Eventually he notices the shape covered by the thin blanket. He thinks that there is almost certainly a second breast under there. His eyes follow the curves of the blanket up and down and he realizes that there might well be a woman underneath. Right there in his bed.

Suddenly terrified, he leaps out of the bed and takes the two steps that should bring him to the bathroom—but don't. He's in the middle of an enormous room, standing on thick-pile carpet, rather than his own dingy rug. The bed he woke up in is huge as well—this explains how two people could have fit into his narrow little bed.

There are doors on several of the distant walls. He tries three before finding a bathroom and locking himself in. Larry splashes some water onto his face, then stares at his reflection in amazement. Rather than his own acne-pocked flesh, the person gawking back is... The only phrase that seems to fit is *godlike*. Ruggedly stubbled. Dazzling teeth. Piercing green eyes. Larry pokes at the chiseled chin and at the muscular chest. The reflection matches him move for move. It is him.

"Hey, Brad." The voice is soft, feminine. It probably belongs to the breast. The woman with the breast, rather. "Your car is here."

"Uh. Oh. Thanks." His own voice is deep. Commanding.

Somehow, he manages to get dressed and bundled into the back of a car so fancy that the doors open backwards. There is a nervous young man in the car, and a woman sitting on a seat facing the wrong way. It might be the woman from inside, and Larry has to concentrate to keep his eyes from trying to compare.

"Uh, Mr. Wiley. Here are the new pages for today."

Larry looks around to see who the young man is talking to. There aren't many options, so it must be him. He is *Brad Wiley, rich guy*. He takes the pages.

"Thank you," he says, which seems to startle the young man. He looks at the top page. It might be in some sort of code:

[INT.OFFICE LOBBY.DAY]

JOEL BLOODSTAR, in his disguise as LARRY THE JANITOR, pushes a cart across the lobby of United Consolidated Bank.

JOEL: Yeah, you can trust me. I'm just a cleaner. Here to *clean out* this bank.

Larry flips through the pages, which are more of the same. This must be a script. Which means that he is *Brad Wiley, Actor.* Nice.

Between the last two pages is a little plastic baggie full of white powder. Larry is a janitor, and has seen everything, including cocaine—although never quite this much. Several of the fights that Larry has had to break up involved drugs. When he finds drugs while working, he generally flushes them down the nearest toilet. But that is probably not an option here.

Not sure what else to do, he hands the baggie back to the young man, who looks horrified.

"But, Mr. Wiley…?"

This catches the attention of the woman, who had been staring at the screen of her phone. She sees what's happening, and smiles. Ships are launched for such a smile.

"He said he doesn't want it, Noah." It is the voice from the bedroom. It is *her.*

Noah gives up and takes the little bag. It disappears into a pocket.

They pull onto the lot of a movie studio, and Larry recognizes it—it is where he works each night, cleaning the long hallways and the trailers. They take him to a trailer with a gold star and the name Brad Wiley in big letters on the door. Larry has cleaned this trailer.

But not today. Today he is visited by makeup people and costume people, and then he is asked to wait to be called. He is all alone, so he cleans up after the makeup people, who left smudges and powder everywhere. And he cleans up bottles. A lot of bottles.

The woman from the apartment comes in and looks at him strangely. He drops a bottle into the trash, and then sits down awkwardly on a built-in sofa.

"I'm a bit of a slob," he says.

She smiles. Larry's heart explodes. She picks up another bottle and an empty pizza box, and hands them to him to throw away.

"Ah, the glamorous life, dating a movie star," she says.

Dating.

There is a knock on the trailer door. The woman answers it.

A man with a clipboard and a really bad combover is standing there. He nods at the woman. "They'll be ready for him in thirty minutes, Amanda."

Amanda. Her name is Amanda.

"Thank you," Larry and Amanda say at the same time, and then both laugh. Combover man has already started to walk away.

"Are you hungry?" he asks Amanda. "There's all sorts of supplies in here. I could make you a sandwich?"

"You?" She looks suspicious now, and he is worried. Perhaps she thinks it is a pickup line. He looks away, embarrassed.

"Sorry. It was just a thought."

"Brad, I would love a sandwich." Her smile melts every plastic surface in the trailer.

"This sandwich is amazing," she says, after he makes it and delivers it to her. He smiles shyly up at her. He is proud of his cooking, and always thought he was good at making sandwiches, but he'd never made one for anyone else before. Thin roast beef, Swiss cheese, mustard, just the very slightest drizzle of horseradish sauce.

"There's, uh, there's a bit of mustard on your chin." He reaches forward with his finger and wipes it away. It is the bravest thing he has ever done.

She leans forward and kisses him lightly on the lips. Her lips are cloud soft and taste slightly of horseradish.

When Larry is next aware of his surroundings, he and Amanda have left the trailer, and are walking between buildings and parking lots. He sees several of the buildings he cleans regularly.

There is one building he sees that nags at him. It is short, maybe two stories, with no windows. He doesn't recognize it, and is sure he never cleaned it, but it seems *really* familiar. They walk past it and several other buildings before entering a cavernous sound stage.

A pretty makeup girl runs up and touches up his makeup. Then he is led to the set. There is a janitor's cart there that is identical to his own, except that it doesn't have the wobble and the squealing wheel. Larry argues briefly with a prop man—the cart is loaded all wrong. *You put the day-to-day things up front, the big bottles at the bottom.* The guy looks bemused, but the director comes over and yells at him.

"If Mr. Wiley says it's wrong, it's wrong. Fix it." Then he turns to Larry and is all smiles.

"So sorry, Brad." Then more quietly, "Amateurs."

Larry says nothing. It was a good first effort, and he hates to see people getting in trouble. He wants to help the poor guy but thinks this might be inappropriate.

Then they film the scenes. If Larry had ever wanted to be an actor, this would have been the role he was born to play. He has a good memory, and so gets the lines right first time. When they are done, the crew applauds, which embarrasses him.

"One more day of being a janitor," says the director, "then you get to be a bank robber."

Larry's heart falls. He doesn't know how to be a bank robber. He used to clean a bank, but that doesn't seem likely to be helpful.

Then he is once more in the car with the backwards doors, along with Amanda and Noah—the man from this morning. Noah is reading aloud from his smartphone screen, a litany of dates and appointments. Larry has no idea what he is talking about, but he tries to at least look interested.

"And, uh, well," Noah pushes himself as far into the corner of the car seat as he can, which it turns out is pretty far. "The Bill Davis show said no." Noah takes a deep breath. "They say that there is no way they'll have you back after what you did."

Larry nods. He feels Amanda's eyes on him. "Well, Noah, I'm sure you did your best. Thank you."

"Oh... I... Oh."

Larry wonders what he did on the Bill Davis show. He also wonders who Bill Davis is. Can he ask? Probably not. But...

"Did I apologize?" he asks. "For what I did."

"Apolo..." Noah splutters. Larry has never seen anyone actually splutter before. "The lawyers wouldn't allow..."

Larry thinks for a moment. An apology should be in person, but that seems unwise—it is hard to apologize for something you have no memory of doing. "Noah, can you please send a note to Bill Davis. Tell him that I am really sorry for what I did, and that I hope he can forgive me some day."

"But...but..."

"And we should send something. I don't know what though."

"Bill loves wine," says Amanda. She isn't smiling, exactly, but there is a crinkle around her eyes.

"Yes," says Larry. "Get a bottle of wine. A really nice one, and send that. Can you do that Noah? I'd really appreciate it."

Noah nods. Larry watches the small man's Adam's apple bob up and down convulsively.

The car leaves them at the front of the building, and Larry waves his thanks to the driver, or to the spot through the mirrored glass that might hold the driver. Then Larry and Amanda go upstairs. Amanda says she is tired, so they both go into the bedroom.

Larry has been dreading this. He doesn't know what is going to happen. There are things he would *like* to happen at a certain rather physical level, but which he is pretty sure would mess with his idea of right and wrong.

In the end, though, it is a non-issue. Amanda disappears into a bathroom—a different one from the one he used that morning. He goes into *his* bathroom and finds a pair of pajamas hanging up, waiting for him. He brushes his teeth, puts on the pajamas, then sits on the edge of the marble bathtub for a really long time.

When he comes out, Amanda is lying on top of the covers, wearing an oversize sweatshirt with the movie studio logo on it. She is asleep, snoring softly and adorably. Larry watches her for a while, then realizes that this is a great example of something that would qualify as *wrong*.

He goes back into the bathroom, puts his clothes back on, then leaves the bedroom and then the apartment as quietly as he can. There is a bus stop close by. He takes a bus back to the studio.

There are guards at the gate and Larry doesn't have his pass. That's okay, though, because a lot of the low-level staff know about the side gate—a scary looking metal thing, with razor wire on the top, that doesn't latch properly. He uses that and makes his way to the building that holds his cleaning supplies. It should also be locked but often isn't.

Larry looks around his office, which is really just a closet, but is large enough to hold a chair and a small table as well as all of his cleaning supplies. It looks very small to him now.

Most of the space is taken up by his cart. He pushes it out of the way and winces at the shriek from the bad wheel. But there is no one else in the building to hear it. He pulls a specific bottle of bleach from the back of one of the shelves and twists the bottom of the container. It comes loose, revealing his emergency supplies; a ten-dollar bill, a photo of his father, and his backup keyring.

He locks up after himself, then goes to the building that he doesn't remember. His master key opens the main door, and several interior ones, too. Then he is standing in front of a big metal door. He doesn't remember being here either, but he remembers the solid *thunk* of that door closing behind him. Larry puts his hand to the door. It is vibrating. He takes a deep breath, then tries his key. It works.

The machine catches his attention first. It looms over the room like something in a Frankenstein movie. There is a big bronze plaque on the machine with its name on it, *The Stanislavski 1000*. From the top of machine runs a rat's nest of cables. He follows them with his eyes to two giant glass pods. One is empty. The other contains a sleeping man—a short man with badly cut hair and acne scars on his face.

Larry stares at himself for a long moment. He is not sure what to think. Is Larry in there, dreaming that he is a movie star? Is Brad Wiley in there dreaming he is a janitor?

A loud noise makes Larry jump out of his skin. Or out of Brad Wiley's skin. Something or someone is pounding against a door that he had not noticed on the far wall. When he looks, he sees that there is a whole row of similar doors.

Larry goes over to the door. There is a sheet of paper taped to it labelled *Shooting Schedule,* with dates starting the day after tomorrow. Right above that is a little hatch. He opens it and looks in. A pair of angry eyes stare back out at him.

"You'd better let me the hell out of here, or there's gonna be hell to pay," says the man.

Larry opens the door.

The man inside freezes. He is an older man, balding, with the face of an angry rabbit. Larry thinks he didn't expect the door to be opened.

"Hey," the man says, "you're that actor..."

"I might be," says Larry. "Are you a bank robber?"

The man blushes so completely that the top of his head starts to glow. "I ain't never been caught robbing nothing," he finally says.

Larry nods. "I think you'd better get out of here."

The man looks around behind him as though not sure he wants to go. Larry understands—the room is *really* nice. It is a prison cell, certainly, but it has a comfortable looking bed, a large screen television, and a table with a vase of flowers and a spread of fruits and breads. But it is still a cell. The man finally nods back at Larry and heads out.

At the big metal door, he turns and looks at Larry. "I liked you in that film. The one with the boat and the woman. And the big snake."

Larry smiles at him.

"There's others," the man says, pointing at the row of doors. Then he is gone.

Larry checks the other cells, and releases a parkour instructor, a chef, and a race car driver. They had all been paid to be there, but had not expected to be held prisoner, and are indignant. Larry just nods and agrees with them until they leave.

Then he goes over to the *Stanislavski 1000* and examines it. He has worked on complicated machines before, but never anything like this. There is a computer console on one side and next to the keyboard he finds a manual. On the cover is a photo of a skydiver, and the words *Be The Role*. Larry sits down and starts to read.

The machine is simple, or at least simple to use—or *misuse*, if someone chooses.

He thinks about this past day, and about how well he was treated. He thinks about the movie set with its lights and props. He thinks about Amanda's smile. He thinks about right and wrong.

Then he turns to the machine and starts pressing buttons.

In the last two weeks, there had been a lot of fuss. People had been fired. People had been arrested. There was even talk about the studio being closed for good. Larry hopes not. He likes his job here— would even miss his little storage closet.

He is moving between buildings. The building to his left is the sound stage where he'd briefly been an actor. He feels a twinge of guilt. Maybe he shouldn't have done it.

But after all, the movie had been cancelled. It won't be missed.

He pushes his brand-new cart. No squeaks and squeals. No wonky wheel trying to take him off course. The props department had really done a nice job, and now it's loaded properly, with all his own supplies. He sighs contentedly. He has learned to take satisfaction where he can.

Then he hears the sound of hurried footsteps behind him. He turns around. It's her—Amanda—standing there. He's just a janitor. They've never met. But she catches his eye, then looks down.

"You're Larry, aren't you."

He nods, unable to speak.

"I read about you in the paper."

"Oh."

Neither says anything for a while.

"How is Brad?" he asks finally.

She shrugs. "He's out on bail. Says he knew nothing about it—that it was all the director and the producer."

"That could be true," says Larry, although he's not quite sure how.

Amanda shakes her head. "He's lying. It's easy to tell—he's a terrible actor. Anyway, I've left him."

Larry thinks this might be the best piece of news he's ever heard.

She looks him in the face, examines his features, then smiles at him.

"I don't suppose…that you could make me a sandwich?" she says.

From the Author

Being simple is not the same as being stupid. Part of my inspiration for this story was to put a simple but good person into a crazy situation and watch the chaos caused by him just continuing to be simple and good—but (hopefully) not as a caricature. I rarely write in present tense (aside from anything else, editors hate it :-), but I think here it helps emphasize Larry's nature. I like to think that Larry will eventually become head of the studio.

It also occurred to me that a lot of directors stuck with movie stars who can't act would jump at the chance of inserting a bit of actual knowledge into their heads!

About the Author

As well as writing fiction, Arlen Feldman is a software engineer, entrepreneur, maker, and computer book author—useful if you are in the market for some industrial-strength door stops. Some recent stories of his appear in the anthologies *The Chorochronos Archives*, *Particular Passages* and Kevin J. Anderson's *Gilded Glass*, and in *Little Blue Marble* and *Nocturne* magazines. He lives in Colorado Springs, Colorado. His website is cowthulu.com. Twitter: @arlenfeldman

From the Editor

It's hard to believe this is the fourth Particular Passages—an idea that I was repeatedly told wouldn't work. Ask authors for stories without giving them a prompt? Ask readers to trust they will like the stories without knowing what kind of stories they are? It won't work!

Often, I think, we get too ingrained in what we expect. We no longer enjoy things that are out of the norm. During the process of putting together these four anthologies, I encountered authors who couldn't write a story without knowing how to make their story fit in with a group of other stories. I encountered others who relished the chance to put out their story that somehow never seemed to fit in. In the end, I think I found a lot of great authors and great stories to fill the four volumes. And I have heard nothing but good things from readers (so far…), which is quite an accomplishment!

The Particular Passages Anthologies are unusual in a few ways. One is that they are curated and edited with a light touch, so if you see a difference in grammar, punctuation, or spelling styles, that may be why. (Not to say typos and mistakes don't get by us, they do.) We are excited to give authors a chance to share a story they like, the way they like it, without trying to make it "fit in," even if that goes against current punctuation conventions.

As an editor and a publisher, I love reading these stories and not having any idea what the next story will be or even what to expect from the story I am reading! As a reader, I hope you found that kind of excitement in the stories of these anthologies as well.

If you liked an author's story, reach out and let them know. The *best* way to make sure your favorite authors write more stories is to tell them you loved one of their stories. (Not to mention it will make their day!)

If you liked this kind of anthology, comments to us, or to our authors, on our social media, websites, or in an email are the best ways to make sure we do another one. The next best is to tell people about the anthology so they buy the book. The third best way is to leave reviews.

I hope to see you again when the next Particular Passage opens up.

Sam Knight
9/2/2022

Additional Copyright Information

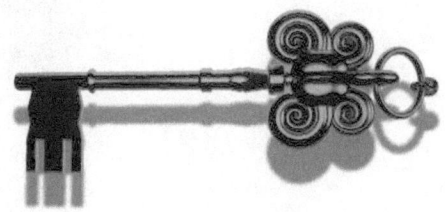